WARLIGHT

"A rare and beautiful thing—a deeply retrospective novel about war secrets that feels neither overstated nor overly ethereal. . . . One of the most absorbing books I've read all year."
—Esi Edugyan,
The Times Literary Supplement (London)

"Lyrical. . . . Ondaatje illuminates the rubble-strewn landscape [of postwar London] from angled sidelights. . . . His prose matches a mood of mystery and suspicion that tantalizes."
—*The Economist*

"Wonderfully atmospheric, beautifully paced, subtle storytelling. . . . Tells the hidden, barely spoken, tale of war, especially its impact on children. Ondaatje skillfully moves back and forth through time, finally offering an extraordinary narrative twist that feels as earned as it is unexpected."
—2018 Man Booker Prize jury citation

"[Ondaatje] casts a magical spell, as he takes you into his half-lit world of war and love, death and loss, and the dark waterways of the past."
—*The New York Review of Books*

"A novel of shadowy brilliance."
—*The Times* (London)

"An intricate ballet of longing and deception. . . . If writers are cartographers of the heart, Michael Ondaatje's oeuvre could fill an atlas."
—*O, The Oprah Magazine*

"A meditation on the lingering effects of war on family."
—Barack Obama (personal pick for recommended summer reading)

"Mr. Ondaatje has stepped into John le Carré's world of spies and criminals. . . . His novel views history as a child would, in ignorance but also in innocence and wonder."
—*The Wall Street Journal*

"Our book of the year—and maybe of Ondaatje's career. . . . A terrifically tense spy thriller and a delicate coming-of-age tale."
—*The Daily Telegraph* (London)

"Wonderful. . . . This elegiac novel combines the stealth of an espionage thriller with the irresolute shifts of a memory play, purposefully full of fragments, loss and unfinished stories."
—*Daily Mail* (London)

"With the force of something familiar, intimate, truthful. . . . *Warlight* sucked me in deeper than any novel that I can remember; when I looked up from it, I was surprised to find the twenty-first century still going on about me. . . . A work of fiction as rich, as beautiful, as melancholy as life itself, written in the visionary language of memory."
—Alex Preston, *The Guardian*

"Majestic. . . . Show-stoppingly magnificent. . . . Golden? Adamantine."
—*New Statesman*

"A haunting mystery. . . . By turns lyrical and wrenching. . . . A rich, satisfying read."
—*People*

"Irresistible. . . . An exceptionally entertaining literary journey."
—*The Irish Times*

"Compulsively and grippingly readable. . . . Michael Ondaatje is a marvelous writer, and *Warlight* is a novel which will continue to play in the reader's imagination."
—*The Scotsman*

"A superb wartime mystery. . . . Ondaatje's is an aesthetic of the fragment. His novels are constructed, with intricate beauty, from images and scenes that don't so much flow together as cling together in vibrating, tensile fashion."
—*The Boston Globe*

"A masterpiece of shifting memory."
—*Los Angeles Times*

"An entrancing and masterfully crafted story."
—*The New Republic*

"The author's prose is as bright and startling as we've seen it since *The English Patient*."
—*Condé Nast Traveler*

"[A] quiet, lushly shaded and haunting novel. . . . Immensely rich and rewarding."
—*Pittsburgh Post-Gazette*

MICHAEL ONDAATJE

WARLIGHT

Michael Ondaatje is the author of six previous novels, a memoir, a nonfiction book on film, and several books of poetry. *The English Patient* won the Booker Prize in 1992 and the Golden Man Booker Prize in 2018; *Anil's Ghost* won the Irish Times International Fiction Prize, the Giller Prize, and the Prix Médicis. Born in Sri Lanka, Michael Ondaatje now lives in Toronto.

INTERNATIONAL

WARLIGHT

WARLIGHT

MICHAEL ONDAATJE

VINTAGE INTERNATIONAL

VINTAGE BOOKS

A Division of Penguin Random House LLC

New York

FIRST VINTAGE INTERNATIONAL
OPEN-MARKET EDITION, APRIL 2019

Copyright © 2018 by Michael Ondaatje

All rights reserved. Published in the United States by Vintage Books, a division of Penguin Random House LLC, New York. Originally published in hardcover in the United States by Alfred A. Knopf, a division of Penguin Random House LLC, New York, in 2018.

Vintage is a registered trademark and Vintage International and colophon are trademarks of Penguin Random House LLC.

This is a work of fiction. Names, characters, places, and incidents either are the product of the author's imagination or are used fictitiously. Any resemblance to actual persons, living or dead, events, or locales is entirely coincidental.

The Library of Congress has cataloged the Knopf edition as follows:
Name: Ondaatje, Michael, 1943– author.
Title: Warlight / Michael Ondaatje.
Description: New York : Alfred A. Knopf, 2018.
Identifiers: LCCN 2018934580
Classification: PR9199.3.O5 W37 2018 | DDC 813/.54—dc23
LC record available at https://lccn.loc.gov/2018934580

Vintage International Open-Market ISBN: 978-0-525-56686-1
eBook ISBN: 978-0-525-52120-4

Book design by Pei Loi Koay

www.vintagebooks.com

Printed in the United States of America
10 9 8 7 6 5 4 3 2

For Ellen Seligman, Sonny Mehta, and Liz Calder

over the years

"Most of the great battles are fought in the creases of topographical maps."

PART ONE

A TABLE FULL OF

STRANGERS

In 1945 our parents went away and left us in the care of two men who may have been criminals. We were living on a street in London called Ruvigny Gardens, and one morning either our mother or our father suggested that after breakfast the family have a talk, and they told us that they would be leaving us and going to Singapore for a year. Not too long, they said, but it would not be a brief trip either. We would of course be well cared for in their absence. I remember our father was sitting on one of those uncomfortable iron garden chairs as he broke the news, while our mother, in a summer dress just behind his shoulder, watched how we responded. After a while she took my sister Rachel's hand and held it against her waist, as if she could give it warmth.

Neither Rachel nor I said a word. We stared at our father, who was expanding on the details of their flight on the new Avro Tudor I, a descendant of the Lancaster bomber, which could cruise at more than three hundred miles an hour. They would have to land and change planes at least twice before arriving at their destination. He explained he had been promoted to take over the Unilever office in Asia, a step up in his career. It would be good for us all. He spoke seriously and our mother turned away at some point to look at her August garden. After my father had finished talking, seeing that I was confused, she came over to me and ran her fingers like a comb through my hair.

I was fourteen at the time, and Rachel nearly sixteen, and they told us we would be looked after in the holidays by a guardian, as our mother called him. They referred to him as a colleague. We had already met him—we used to call him "The Moth," a name we had invented. Ours was a family with a habit for nicknames, which meant it was also a family of disguises. Rachel had already told me she suspected he worked as a criminal.

The arrangement appeared strange, but life still was haphazard and confusing during that period after the war; so what had been suggested did not feel unusual. We accepted the decision, as children do, and The Moth, who had recently become our third-floor lodger, a humble man, large but moth-like in his shy movements, was to be the solution. Our parents must have assumed he was reliable. As to whether The Moth's criminality was evident to them, we were not sure.

I suppose there had once been an attempt to make us a tightly knit family. Now and then my father let me accompany him to the Unilever offices, which were deserted during weekends and bank holidays, and while he was busy I'd wander through what seemed an abandoned world on the twelfth floor of the building. I discovered all the office drawers were locked. There was nothing in the wastepaper baskets, no pictures on the walls, although one wall in his office held a large relief map depicting the company's foreign locations: Mombasa, the Cocos Islands, Indonesia. And nearer to home, Trieste, Heliopolis, Benghazi, Alexandria, cities that cordoned off the Mediterranean, locations I assumed were under my father's authority. Here was where they booked holds on the hundreds of ships that travelled back and forth to the East. The lights on the map that identified those cities and ports were unlit during the weekends, in darkness much like those far outposts.

At the last moment it was decided our mother would remain behind for the final weeks of the summer to oversee the arrangements for the lodger's care over us, and ready us for our new boarding schools. On the Saturday before he flew alone towards that distant world, I accompanied my father once more to the office near Curzon Street. He had suggested a long walk, since, he said, for the next few days his body would be humbled on a plane. So we caught a bus to the Natural History Museum, then walked up through Hyde Park into Mayfair. He was unusually eager and cheerful, singing the lines *Homespun collars, homespun hearts, Wear to rags in foreign parts,* repeating them again and again, almost jauntily, as if this was an essential rule. What did it mean? I wondered. I remember we needed several keys to get into the building where the office he worked in took up that whole top floor. I stood in front of the large map, still unlit, memorizing the cities that he would fly over during the next few nights. Even then I loved maps. He came up behind me and switched on the lights so the mountains on the relief map cast shadows, though now it was not the lights I noticed so much as the harbours lit up in pale blue, as well as the great stretches of unlit earth. It was no longer a fully revealed perspective, and I suspect that Rachel and I must have watched our parents' marriage with a similar flawed awareness. They had rarely spoken to us about their lives. We were used to partial stories. Our father had been involved in the last stages of the earlier war, and I don't think he felt he really belonged to us.

As for their departure, it was accepted that she had to go with him: there was no way, we thought, that she could exist apart from him—she was his wife. There would be less calamity, less collapse of the family if we were left behind as opposed to her remaining in Ruvigny Gardens to look after us. And as they explained, we could not suddenly leave the schools into which we had been admitted with so much difficulty. Before his departure we all embraced our father in a huddle, The Moth having tactfully disappeared for the weekend.

So we began a new life. I did not quite believe it then. And I am still uncertain whether the period that followed disfigured or energized my life. I was to lose the pattern and restraint of family habits during that time, and as a result, later on, there would be a hesitancy in me, as if I had too quickly exhausted my freedoms. In any case, I am now at an age where I can talk about it, of how we grew up protected by the arms of strangers. And it is like clarifying a fable, about our parents, about Rachel and myself, and The Moth, as well as the others who joined us later. I suppose there are traditions and tropes in stories like this. Someone is given a test to carry out. No one knows who the truth bearer is. People are not who or where we think they are. And there is someone who watches from an unknown location. I remember how my mother loved to speak of those ambivalent tasks given to loyal knights in Arthurian legends, and how she told those stories to us, sometimes setting them in a specific small village in the Balkans or in Italy, which she claimed she had been to and found for us on a map.

With the departure of our father, our mother's presence grew larger. The conversations we used to overhear between our parents had always been about adult matters. But now she began telling us stories about herself, about growing up in the Suffolk countryside. We especially loved the tale about "the family on the roof." Our grandparents had lived in an area of Suffolk called The Saints, where there was little to disturb them, just the sound of the river, or now and then a church bell from a nearby village. But one month a family lived on their roof, throwing things around and yelling to one another, so loudly that the noises percolated down through the ceiling and into her family's life. There was a bearded man and his three sons. The youngest was the quiet one, mostly he carried the pails of water up the ladder to the ones on the roof. But whenever my mother walked from the house to collect eggs from the henhouse or get into the car, she saw him watching them. They were thatchers, fixing the roof, busy all day. At dinnertime they pulled down their ladders and left. But then one day a powerful wind lifted the youngest son so he was tilted off balance, and fell from the roof, crashing down through the lime bower to land on paving stones by the kitchen. His brothers carried him into the house. The boy, named Marsh, had broken his hip, and the doctor who came sealed his leg in plaster and told them he could not be moved. He would need to stay on a day-bed in the back kitchen until the roof work was completed. Our mother's job—she was eight years old at the time—was to bring him his meals. Now and then she brought him a book, but he was so shy he barely spoke. Those two weeks must have felt like a lifetime to him, she told us. Eventually, their work done, the family gathered up the boy and were gone.

Whenever my sister and I recalled this story, it felt like part of a fairy tale we did not quite understand. Our mother told us about it without drama, the horror of the boy's fall removed, the way things happen in twice-told tales. We must have asked for more stories about the falling boy, but this was the only incident we were given—that storm-filled afternoon when she heard the thick, wet thud of him on the paving stones, having torn through the twigs and leaves of the lime bower. Just one episode from the obscure rigging of our mother's life.

The Moth, our third-floor lodger, was absent from the house most of the time, though sometimes he arrived early enough to be there for dinner. He was encouraged now to join us, and only after much waving of his arms in unconvincing protest would he sit down and eat at our table. Most evenings, however, The Moth strolled over to Bigg's Row to buy a meal. Much of the area had been destroyed during the Blitz, and a few street barrows were temporarily installed there. We were always conscious of his tentative presence, of his alighting here and there. We were never sure if this manner of his was shyness or listlessness. That would change, of course. Sometimes from my bedroom window I'd notice him talking quietly with our mother in the dark garden, or I would find him having tea with her. Before school started she spent quite a bit of time persuading him to tutor me in mathematics, a subject I had consistently failed at school, and would in fact continue to fail again long after The Moth stopped trying to teach me. During those early days the only complexity I saw in our guardian was in the almost three-dimensional drawings he created in order to allow me to go below the surface of a geometry theorem.

If the subject of the war arose, my sister and I attempted to coax a few stories from him about what he had done and where. It was a time of true and false recollections, and Rachel and I were curious. The Moth and my mother referred to people they both were familiar with from those days. It was clear she knew him before he had come to live with us, but his involvement with the war was a surprise, for The Moth was never "war-like" in demeanour. His presence in our house was usually signalled by quiet piano music coming from his radio, and his current profession appeared linked to an organization involving ledgers and salaries. Still, after a few promptings we learned that both of them had worked as "fire watchers" in what they called the Bird's Nest, located on the roof of the Grosvenor House Hotel. We sat in our pyjamas drinking Horlicks as they reminisced. An anecdote would break the surface, then disappear. One evening, soon before we had to leave for our new schools, my mother was ironing our shirts in a corner of the living room, and The Moth was standing hesitant at the foot of the stairs, about to leave, as if only partially in our company. But then, instead of leaving, he spoke of our mother's skill during a night drive, when she had delivered men down to the coast through the darkness of the curfew to something called "the Berkshire Unit," when all that kept her awake "were a few squares of chocolate and cold air from the open windows." As he continued speaking, my mother listened so carefully to what he described that she held the iron with her right hand in midair so it wouldn't rest on and burn a collar, giving herself fully to his shadowed story.

I should have known then.

Their talk slipped time intentionally. Once we learned that our mother had intercepted German messages and transmitted data across the English Channel from a place in Bedfordshire called Chicksands Priory, her ears pressed against the intricate frequencies of a radio's headset, and again from the Bird's Nest on top of the Grosvenor House Hotel, which by now Rachel and I were beginning to suspect had little to do with the effort of "fire watching." We were becoming aware that our mother had more skills than we thought. Had her beautiful white arms and delicate fingers shot a man dead with clear intent? I saw an athleticism as she ran gracefully up the stairs. It was not something we had noticed in her before. During the month after our father departed, and until she left at the beginning of our school term, we were discovering a more surprising and then more intimate side to her. And that brief moment with the hot iron poised in her hand in midair as she watched The Moth remembering their earlier days left an indelible perception.

With our father's absence our house began to feel freer and more spacious, and we spent as much time with her as we could. We listened to thrillers on the radio, the lights left on because we wanted to watch one another's faces. No doubt she was bored by them, but we insisted she be with us while we heard foghorns and wolf-like winds across the moors and slow criminal footsteps or a window splintering, and during those dramas I carried in my mind the half-told story of her driving without lights to the coast. But as far as radio programmes went, she was more at ease lying on the chaise on Saturday afternoons, listening to *The Naturalist's Hour* on the BBC and ignoring the book she was holding in her hands. The programme reminded her of Suffolk, she said. And we would overhear the man on the radio going on endlessly about river insects, and chalk streams he had fished in; it sounded like a microscopic and distant world, while Rachel and I crouched on the carpet working on a jigsaw puzzle, piecing together sections of a blue sky.

Once the three of us took a train from Liverpool Street to what had been her childhood home in Suffolk. Earlier that year our grandparents had died in a car crash, so now we watched our mother roaming their house silently. I remember we always had to walk carefully along the edge of the hall, otherwise the hundred-year-old wood floor squawked and squealed. "It's a nightingale floor," our grandmother told us. "It warns us of thieves in the night." Rachel and I always leapt onto it whenever we could.

But we were happiest with our mother on our own in London. We wanted her casual and sleepy affection, more than what we had been given before. It was as if she had returned to an earlier version of herself. She had been, even before my father's departure, a quick-moving and efficient mother, leaving for work when we left for school and returning usually in time for supper with us. Was this new version caused by a release from her husband? Or in a more complex way was it a preparation for withdrawal from us, with clues of how she wished to be remembered? She helped me with my French and my *Caesar's Gallic War*—she was a wonder at Latin and French—preparing me for boarding school. Most surprisingly, she encouraged various homemade theatrical performances in the solitude of our house where we would dress up as priests or walk like sailors and villains on the balls of our feet.

Did other mothers do this? Did they fall gasping over the sofa with a flung dagger in their backs? None of this would she do if The Moth was about. But why did she do it at all? Was she bored with looking after us on a daily basis? Did dressing up or dressing down make her another, not just our mother? Best of all, when first light slipped into our rooms, we'd enter her bedroom like tentative dogs and gaze at her undressed face, the closed eyes, the white shoulders and arms already stretched out to gather us in. For, whatever the hour, she was always awake, ready for us. We never surprised her. "Come here, Stitch. Come here, Wren," she would murmur, her personal nicknames for us. I suspect that was the time Rachel and I felt we had a real mother.

In early September the steamer trunk was brought out of the basement and we watched as she filled it with frocks, shoes, necklaces, English fiction, maps, along with objects and equipment she said she did not expect to find in the East, even what looked like some unnecessary woollens, for she told us the evenings were often "brisk" in Singapore. She made Rachel read out loud from a Baedeker about the terrain and the bus services, as well as the local terminology for "Enough!" or "More," and "How far is it?" We recited the phrases out loud with our clichéd accents of the East.

Maybe she believed that the specifics and calmness of packing a large trunk would assure us of the sanity of her journey rather than make us feel even more bereft. It was almost as if we expected her to climb into that black wooden trunk, so much like a coffin with those brass corner edges, and be deported away from us. It took several days, this act of packing, and felt slow and fateful in its activity, like an endless ghost story. Our mother was about to be altered. She would evolve into something invisible to us. Perhaps for Rachel it felt different. She was more than a year older. It may have looked theatrical to her. But for me the act of continual reconsidering and repacking suggested a permanent disappearance. Prior to our mother's leaving, the house had been our cave. Only a few times did we walk along the embankment of the river. She said that travel was something she would be doing too much of in the coming weeks.

Then suddenly she had to leave, for some reason sooner than expected. My sister went into the bathroom and painted her face a blank white, then knelt with that emotionless face at the top of the stairs and circled her arms through the railings and would not let go. By the front door I joined our mother in an argument against Rachel, attempting to persuade her to come downstairs. It was as if our mother had arranged things so there would be no tearful goodbyes.

There's a photograph I have of my mother in which her features are barely revealed. I recognize her from just her stance, some gesture in her limbs, even though it was taken before I was born. She is seventeen or eighteen, and snapped by her parents along the banks of their Suffolk river. She has been swimming, has climbed into her dress, and now stands on one foot, the other leg bent sideways in order to put on a shoe, her head tilted down so that her blond hair covers her face. I found it years later in the spare bedroom among the few remnants she had decided not to throw away. I have it with me still. This almost anonymous person, balanced awkwardly, holding on to her own safety. Already incognito.

*

In mid-September we arrived at our respective schools. Having been day students so far, we were unaccustomed to boarding-school life, whereas everyone there already knew they had been essentially abandoned. We could not stand it and within a day of our arrival wrote to our parents care of a mailbox address in Singapore, pleading to be released. I worked out that our letter would travel in a van to the Southampton docks, then make its way by ship, reaching and then leaving distant ports without any sense of urgency. At that distance and after six weeks I already knew our list of complaints would appear meaningless. For instance, the fact that I had to walk down three flights of stairs in darkness in order to find a bathroom at night. Most of the regular boarders usually pissed into one selected sink on our floor, beside the one where you brushed your teeth. This had been the custom at the school for generations—and decades of urine had worn a clear path in the one enamel basin used for this activity. But one night while I was drowsily relieving myself into the sink, the Housemaster strolled past and witnessed what I was doing. At assembly the next morning he made an outraged speech about the despicable act he had stumbled upon, going on to claim that even during the four years he had fought in the war he had never witnessed anything so obscene. The shocked silence among the boys in the hall was in fact disbelief that the Housemaster was unaware of a tradition that had been in existence when Shackleton and P. G. Wodehouse had been great men at the school (although one of them was rumoured to have been expelled, and the other knighted only after much disagreement). I too hoped to be expelled but was simply beaten by a prefect, who could not stop laughing. In any case, I did not expect a considered reply from my parents, even after including the postscript of my crime in a quickly written second letter. I clung to the hope that becoming a boarder at school had been our father's idea more than our mother's, so she might be our chance of release.

Our schools were half a mile away from each other and the only communication possible between us was to borrow a bicycle and meet on the Common. Rachel and I decided that whatever we did we would do together. So in the midst of the second week, before our pleading letters had even reached Europe, we slipped away with the day students after the last class, hung around Victoria Station till evening, when we were sure The Moth would be home to let us in, and returned to Ruvigny Gardens. We both knew The Moth was the one adult who seemed to have our mother's ear.

"Ah, you could not wait for the weekend, is that it?" was all he said. There was a thin man sitting in the armchair my father always sat in.

"This is Mr. Norman Marshall. He used to be the best welterweight north of the river, known as 'The Pimlico Darter.' You may have heard of him?"

We shook our heads. We were more concerned that The Moth had invited someone we did not know into our parents' home. We'd never considered such a possibility. We were also nervous about our escape from the school and how it would be taken by our untested guardian. But for some reason our midweek escape did not concern The Moth.

"You must be hungry. I'll warm up some baked beans. How did you get here?"

"The train. Then the bus."

"Good." And with that he walked into the kitchen, leaving us with The Pimlico Darter.

"Are you his friend?" Rachel asked.

"Not at all."

"Then why are you here?"

"That's my father's chair," I said.

He ignored me and turned towards Rachel. "He wished me to come here, sweetheart. He's considering a dog at White-chapel this weekend. Ever been there?"

Rachel was silent, as if she had not been spoken to. He was not even a friend of our lodger. "Cat got your tongue?" he inquired of her, then turned his pale blue eyes towards me. "Been to a dog race?" I shook my head, and then The Moth returned.

"Here you are. Two plates of beans."

"They've never been to a dog race, Walter."

Walter?

"I should bring them this Saturday. What time's your race?"

"The O'Meara Cup is always three p.m."

"These kids sometimes can get out on weekends, if I write a note."

"Actually . . ." Rachel said. The Moth turned towards her and waited for her to continue.

"We don't want to go back."

"Walter, I'm off. Looks like you've got a complication."

"Oh, no complication," said The Moth breezily. "We can

sort it out. Don't forget the signal. I don't want my coins put on a useless dog."

"Right. Right . . ." The Darter rose, put a reassuring hand rather strangely on my sister's shoulder and left the three of us alone.

We ate the beans and our guardian watched us without any sense of judgement.

"I'll ring the school and tell them not to worry. They're no doubt shitting a brick or two right now."

"I'm supposed to have a maths test first thing tomorrow," I said, coming clean.

"He was nearly expelled for urinating in a sink!" Rachel said.

Whatever authority The Moth had he used with quick diplomacy, accompanying us back to school early the next morning and speaking for thirty minutes to the Master, a short, terrifying man who always moved silently down the halls in crepe-soled shoes. It shocked me that the man who usually ate street meals on Bigg's Row had this authority. In any case, I went back into my class that morning as a day boy, and The Moth took Rachel down the road to her school to negotiate the other half of the problem. So in our second week we became day students again. We did not even consider how our parents were going to feel about this radical resettlement of our lives.

Under The Moth's care, we began eating most of our dinners from the local street barrows. Bigg's Row, since the Blitz, remained an untravelled road. A few years earlier, some time after Rachel and I had been evacuated to live with our grandparents in Suffolk, a bomb probably intended for Putney

Bridge had landed and exploded on the High Street, a quarter of a mile from Ruvigny Gardens. The Black & White Milk Bar and the Cinderella Dance Club were destroyed. Nearly a hundred had been killed. It was a night with what our grandmother called "a bomber's moon"—the city, towns, and villages in blackout but the land below clear in the moonlight. Even after we returned to Ruvigny Gardens at war's end, many of the streets in our area were still partly rubble, and along Bigg's Row three or four barrows carried food cycled out from the centre of the city—whatever had not been used by West End hotels. It was rumoured The Moth was involved with steering some of that leftover produce into neighbourhoods south of the river.

Neither of us had eaten from a barrow before, but it became our regular fare—our guardian had no interest in cooking or even being cooked for. He preferred, he said, "a hasty life." So we would stand with him almost every evening alongside a female opera singer or local tailors and upholsterers with tools still attached to their belts, as they discussed and argued over the day's news. The Moth was more animated on the street, the eyes behind his spectacles taking in everything. Bigg's Row appeared to be his real home, his theatre, where he seemed most at ease, whereas my sister and I felt we were trespassers.

In spite of his gregarious manner during those outdoor meals, The Moth kept to himself. His feelings were rarely offered to us. Apart from some curious questions—he kept asking me casually about the art gallery that was a part of my school and whether I could draw its floor plan for him—as with his war experiences he kept silent about his interests. He was not really at ease speaking to the young. "Listen to this. . . ." His eyes looked up momentarily from the newspaper spread out on our dining room table. 'Mr. Rattigan was overheard saying that *le vice anglais* is not pederasty or flagellation, but the inability of the English to express emotion.'" He stopped and waited for some response from us.

We thought, during our confidently opinionated teens, that women were not likely to be attracted to The Moth. My sister made a list of his attributes. Thick black horizontal eyebrows. A large though friendly stomach. His big honker. For a private man who loved classical music, and who drifted through the house mostly in silence, he had the loudest sneezes. Bursts of air were expelled not just from his face but seemed to originate from the depths of that large and friendly stomach. Then three or four more sneezes would immediately follow, crashing loudly. Late at night, they could be heard, fully articulate, travelling down from his attic rooms as if he were some trained actor whose stage whispers could reach the furthest row.

Most evenings he sat and grazed through *Country Life,* peering at the pictures of stately homes, all the while sipping what seemed to be milk from a blue thimble-like glass. For a person who spoke so disapprovingly of the advance of capitalism, The Moth had an inflamed curiosity about aristocracy. The place he was most curious about was the Albany, which one entered through a secluded courtyard off Piccadilly, and he once murmured, "I'd love to wander around there." It was a rare admission of criminal desire in him.

He usually disappeared from us at sunrise and was gone till

dusk. On Boxing Day, knowing I had nothing to do, The Moth took me along with him to Piccadilly Circus. By seven a.m. I was walking beside him in the thick-carpeted lobby of the Criterion's Banquet Halls, where he oversaw the daily work of the mostly immigrant staff. With the war over, there seemed to be a surge of celebrations. And within half an hour The Moth had set up their various duties—the vacuuming of hallways, the soaping and drying of stair carpets, varnishing of bannisters, the transporting of a hundred used tablecloths down to the basement laundry. And depending on the size of the banquet that was to occur that evening—a reception for a new member of the House of Lords, a bar mitzvah, a debutante ball, or some dowager's last pre-death birthday party—he choreographed the staff into transforming the immense empty banquet rooms in an evolving time-lapse, until they eventually contained a hundred tables and six hundred chairs for the night's festivities.

Sometimes The Moth had to be present at those evening events, moth-like in the shadows of the half-lit periphery of the gilded room. But it was clear he preferred the early-morning hours, when the staff who would never be seen by the evening's guests worked mural-like in the thirty-yard-long crowded Great Hall that raged with giant vacuum cleaners, with men on ladders holding thirty-foot whisks to pluck cobwebs off chandeliers, and wood polishers who disguised the odours from the previous night. Nothing could be more unlike my father's deserted offices. This was more like a train station where every passenger had a purpose. I climbed a narrow metal staircase to where the arc lights hung, waiting to be turned on for the hours of dancing, and looked down seeing them all; and in the midst of this great human sea, the large figure of The Moth sat alone at one of the hundred round dinner tables, with that pleasure of chaos around him as he filled out worksheets, knowing somehow where everyone was or should be in the five-storey building. All morning he organized the silver polishers and cake decorators, the oilers of trolley wheels and lift gates, the lint and vomit removers, the replacers of soap at each sink, the replacers of chlorine medallions in the urinals, and the men hosing the pavement outside the entrance, as well as immigrants who squeezed out English names they had never spelled before onto birthday cakes, diced up onions, slashed open pigs with terrible knives, or prepared whatever else would be desired twelve hours later in the Ivor Novello Room or the Miguel Invernio Room.

We slipped out of the building promptly at three that afternoon, and The Moth disappeared and I went home alone. Sometimes he returned to the Criterion in the evenings to deal with emergencies, but whatever my guardian did from three p.m. until he returned to Ruvigny Gardens was not to be known. He was a man of many doors. Were there other professions he nestled into, even briefly for an hour or two? An honourable charity or some upheaval of order? A person we met hinted that for two afternoons of the week he worked with the Semitic and radical International Tailors, Machinists and Pressers Union. But that was perhaps a fabrication, such as his activities as a fire watcher with the Home Guard during the war. The roof of the Grosvenor House Hotel, I've since discovered, had simply been the best location for clear transmission of radio broadcasts to Allied troops behind enemy lines in Europe. It was where The Moth had first worked with our mother. We had once hung on to these wisps of stories of them in the war, yet after she left, The Moth retreated and kept such anecdotes at a distance from us.

Hell-Fire

At the end of that first winter, while we were living with The Moth, Rachel made me follow her down to the basement, and there, under a tarpaulin and several boxes that she had pulled away, was our mother's steamer trunk. Not in Singapore at all, but here. It seemed an act of magic, as if the trunk had returned to the house after its journey. I said nothing. I climbed the stairs out of the cellar. I feared, I suppose, we would find her body there, pressed against all those clothes so carefully folded and packed. The door slammed as Rachel left the house.

I was in my room when The Moth returned late at night. He said it had been a crisis evening at the Criterion. Usually he left us alone if we were in our rooms. This time there was a knock on my door and he came in.

"You didn't eat."

"I did," I said.

"You didn't. There's no evidence of that. I'll cook you something."

"No, thank you."

"Let me . . ."

"No, thank you."

I would not look at him. He stayed where he was and didn't say anything. Finally, "Nathaniel," he said quietly. That was all. Then, "Where is Rachel?"

"I don't know. We found her trunk."

"Yes," he said quietly. "It's here, isn't it, Nathaniel." I remember his precise wording, the repetition of my name. There was more silence; my ears may have been deaf to any sound, even if it existed. I remained hunched over. I don't know how much later it was but he got me downstairs and we went into the basement and The Moth began to open the trunk.

Inside, pressed, as if permanently and forever, were all the clothes and objects we had watched her pack so theatrically, each justified with an explanation of why she would need this specific calf-length dress or that shawl. She had to take the shawl, she had remarked, since we had given it to her for her birthday. And that cannister, she would need it there. And those casual shoes. Everything had a purpose and a usefulness. And everything had been left behind.

"If she's not there, is he not there too?"

"He is there."

"Why is he there if she isn't?"

Silence.

"Where is she?"

"I don't know."

"You must know. You worked out the thing with the school."

"I did that on my own."

"You are in touch with her. You said."

"Yes. I said that. But I don't know where she is right now."

He held on to my hand in that cold basement until I got

free of him and returned upstairs to sit by the gas fire in the unlit living room. I heard his steps come up, ignore the room where I was, then go up to his attic rooms. When I think of my youth, if you asked me to quickly remember just one thing, it would be the dark house that night during the hours after Rachel disappeared. And whenever I come across that strange phrase, "hell-fire," it is as if I have found a label to attach to that moment, when I remained in the house with The Moth, and barely moved away from that gas fire.

He tried persuading me to eat with him. When I refused he opened up two cans of sardines. Two plates—one for him, one for me. We sat by the fire. He joined me in the darkness, in the small fall of red gaslight. I remember now what we spoke of with confusion, with no chronology. It was as if he were attempting to explain or break open something that I did not know about yet.

"Where is my father?"

"I've had no communication with him."

"But my mother was joining him."

"No." He paused a moment, thinking how to proceed. "You must believe me, she isn't there with him."

"But she is his wife."

"I'm aware of that, Nathaniel."

"Is she dead?"

"No."

"Is she in danger? Where's Rachel gone?"

"I'll find Rachel. Let her be for a moment."

"I don't feel safe."

"I am staying here with you."

"Till our mother comes back?"

"Yes."

A silence. I wanted to get up and walk away.

"Do you remember the cat?"

"No."

"You had a cat once."

"No, I didn't."

"Yes."

I was silent, out of politeness. I never had a cat. I don't like cats.

"I avoid them," I said.

"I know," The Moth said. "Why is that, do you think? That you avoid them?"

The gas fire sputtered and The Moth got on his knees and put a coin in the meter to revive it. The flames lit the left side of his face. He stayed as he was, as if he knew when he leaned back he would be in darkness again, as if he wanted me to see him, keep the contact intimate.

"You had a cat," he said again. "You loved it. It was the only pet you had when you were a child. It was small. It would wait for you to come home. One doesn't remember everything. Do you remember your very first school? Before you moved to Ruvigny Gardens?" I shook my head, watching his eyes. "You loved the cat. At night, when you fell asleep, it seemed to sing to itself. But it was really a howl, not a beautiful sound, but it liked to do this. It irritated your father. He was a light sleeper. In the last war he took on a fear of sudden noises. Your cat's howling drove him mad. You were all living in the outskirts of London then. Tulse Hill, I think. Around there."

"How do you know this?"

He seemed not to hear me.

"Yes, Tulse Hill. What does that mean? *Tulse?* Your father used to warn you. Do you remember? He would come into your room that was next to his and your mother's and take the cat and put it outside for the rest of the night. But this made it worse. It would only sing louder. Your father did not think it was singing, of course. Only you did. That is what you told him. The thing was, the cat would not start its howling until you were asleep, as if it did not want to disturb you while you were beginning to fall asleep. So your father killed it one night."

I did not avert my eyes from the fire. The Moth leaned even closer into the light so I had to see his face, that it was human, even though it looked as though it was burning.

"In the morning you couldn't find your cat, and so he told you. He said he was sorry but he could not stand the noise."

"What did I do?"

"You ran away from home."

"Where? Where did I go?"

"You went to a friend of your parents'. You told that friend that you wanted to live there instead."

A silence.

"He was brilliant, your father, but he was not stable. You must understand that the war damaged him badly. And it was not only his fear of sudden noise. There was a secrecy about him, and he needed to be alone. Your mother was aware of that. Perhaps she should have told you. Wars are not glorious."

"How do you know all this? How do you know?"

"I was told," he said.

"Who told you? Who . . ." And then I stopped.

"It was me you came to stay with. You told me."

We were both quiet then. The Moth stood up and moved back from the fire until I could barely see his face in the darkness. So it felt easier to talk.

"How long did I stay with you?"

"Not very long. Eventually I had to take you home. Remember?"

"I don't know."

"You did not speak for some time. You felt safer that way."

My sister didn't return until late that night, long past midnight. She appeared unconcerned, barely spoke to us. The Moth did not argue with her about her absence, only asked if she had been drinking. She shrugged. She looked exhausted, her arms and her legs were filthy. After this night The Moth would intentionally grow close to her. But it felt to me that she had crossed a river and was now further from me, elsewhere. She had after all been the one to discover the trunk, which our mother had simply "forgotten" when she'd boarded the plane for the two-and-a-half-day journey to Singapore. No shawl, no cannister, no calf-length dress she could swirl in on some dance floor during a tea dance with our father, or whoever she was with, wherever she was. But Rachel refused to talk about it.

Mahler put the word *schwer* beside certain passages in his musical scores. Meaning "difficult." "Heavy." We were told this at some point by The Moth, as if it was a warning. He said we needed to prepare for such moments in order to deal with them efficiently, in case we suddenly had to take control of our wits. Those times exist for all of us, he kept saying. Just as no score relies on only one pitch or level of effort from musicians in the orchestra. Sometimes it relies on silence. It was a strange warning to be given, to accept that nothing was safe anymore. " '*Schwer*,'" he'd say, with his fingers gesturing the inverted commas, and we'd mouth the word and then the translation, or simply nod in weary recognition. My sister and I got used to parroting the word back to each other—"*schwer*."

*

There are times these years later, as I write all this down, when I feel as if I do so by candlelight. As if I cannot see what is taking place in the dark beyond the movement of this pencil. These feel like moments without context. Picasso as a youth, I'm told, painted only in candlelight, to admit the altering movement of shadows. But as a boy, I sat at my desk and drew detailed maps radiating out to the rest of the world. All children do this. But I did this as precisely as I could: our U-shaped street, the shops on Lower Richmond Road, the footpaths beside the Thames, the exact length of Putney Bridge (seven hundred feet), the height of the brick wall at the Brompton Cemetery (twenty feet), ending with the Gaumont cinema at a corner of Fulham Road. I did this each week, making sure of any new alteration as if what was not recorded might be in danger. I needed a safe zone. I knew if I put two of those homemade maps beside each other they would look like a newspaper quiz where you had to find ten things that were different between two seemingly identical panels—the time on a clock, a jacket unbuttoned, this time a cat, this time no cat.

Some evenings, in the darkness of my walled garden during an October gale, I sense the walls shudder as they steer the east coast wind into the air above me, and I feel nothing can invade or break a solitude I've found in this warmer darkness. As if I am protected from the past, where there's still a fear of recalling The Moth's face lit by a gas fire while I asked question after question, trying to force an unknown door ajar. Or where I rustle awake a lover from my teenage years. Even if that time is a seldom visited place.

There was a period when architects were responsible not just for buildings but for rivers as well. Christopher Wren constructed St. Paul's Cathedral but also converted the lower reaches of the Fleet, broadening its borders so it could be used for transporting coal. Yet with time the Fleet ended its life as a path for sewage. And when even those underground sewers dried up, their grand Wren-like vaulted ceilings and arcades became illegal meeting places beneath the city where people would gather during the night, in the no-longer-damp path of its stream. Nothing lasts. Not even literary or artistic fame protects worldly things around us. The pond that Constable painted dried up and was buried by Hampstead Heath. A thin tributary of the River Effra near Herne Hill, described by Ruskin as a "tadpole-haunted ditch," whose waters he sketched beautifully, exists now possibly only in an archive drawing. The ancient Tyburn disappeared and was lost, even to geographers and historians. In much the same way I believed my carefully recorded buildings along Lower Richmond Road were dangerously temporary, in the way great buildings had been lost during the war, in the way we lose mothers and fathers.

What was it that allowed us to be so seemingly unconcerned about the absence of our parents? My father, whom we had seen board the Avro Tudor for Singapore, I'd barely known. But where was my mother? I used to sit on the top level of a slow-moving bus and peer down at the empty streets. There were parts of the city where you saw no one, only a few children, walking solitary, listless as small ghosts. It was a time of war ghosts, the grey buildings unlit, even at night, their shattered windows still covered over with black material where glass had been. The city still felt wounded, uncertain of itself. It allowed one to be rule-less. Everything had already happened. Hadn't it?

Let me admit there were times I thought The Moth was dangerous. There was an unevenness to him. It was not that he was unkind to us, but he did not know, as a single man, how to speak the truth to children—and that is what it often felt like, The Moth breaking apart an order that should have existed safely in our house. You witness it when a child hears a joke that should be told only to an adult. This man we had thought of as being quiet and shy now seemed dangerous with secrets. So even if I did not wish to believe what he spoke of that evening beside the gas fire, I saved that information in my pocket.

During our first weeks alone with The Moth after our mother left, the house had only two visitors, The Pimlico

Darter and the opera singer from Bigg's Row. Coming home
from school, I would notice her at times sitting at our dining
table with The Moth, leafing through pages of sheet music and
tracing the central musical path with a pencil. But that was
before our home became crowded. Over the Christmas holidays the house had filled up with The Moth's acquaintances,
most of them staying late into the night, the conversations
entering our bedrooms as we slept. At midnight I'd see the
stairwell and living room brightly lit. Even at that hour the
talk was never casual. There was always tension and inquiry
over urgently needed advice. *"What's the most undetectable drug to
give a racing dog?"* was a question I heard once. For some reason
my sister and I thought such conversations were not unusual.
They felt similar to how The Moth and our mother had once
talked about their war activities.

But who were they all? Were they people who had worked
with The Moth during the war? The verbose beekeeper, Mr.
Florence, apparently under a cloud for some unspoken misdemeanour in the past, could be overheard discussing how
he'd learned his questionable talents for anaesthetics during
the Italian campaign. The Darter claimed there was now so
much illegal sonar activity on the Thames that the Greenwich
Town Council suspected a whale had entered the estuary. It
was clear The Moth's friends stood a little to the left of the
new Labour Party—about three miles or so. And our house, so
orderly and spare when inhabited by my parents, now pulsed
like a hive with these busy, argumentative souls who, having at
one time legally crossed some boundary during the war, were
now suddenly told they could no longer cross it during peace.

There was a "couturier," for instance, whose name was never voiced, except with the nickname "Citronella," who had swerved from a successful career as a haberdasher into working as a spy for the government during the war and now had eased himself back into being a couturier for minor members of the royal family. We had no idea what such people were doing in The Moth's company, while we sat there toasting our crumpets at the gas fire after returning from school. The house seemed to have collided with the world outside.

The evenings ended with the sudden and simultaneous departure of everyone, and there would be silence. If Rachel and I were still awake, we knew by now what The Moth was preparing to do. We'd seen him a few times holding a record delicately in his fingers, blowing dust off it, wiping it gently with his sleeve. A crescendo began filling the downstairs. It was no longer the peaceful music we used to hear coming from his room when our mother was there. This felt violent and chaotic, without courtesy. What he chose to play at night on our parents' gramophone felt more like a storm, something tumbling loudly from a great height. It was only after that ominous music was over that The Moth would play another record—a quiet voice singing alone—and after a minute or so I almost imagined a woman had joined in, someone I believed was my mother. It was what I waited for, and somewhere during that I fell asleep.

Before half-term, The Moth proposed that if I wished to earn a little money he probably could arrange a job during the coming holiday. I nodded cautiously.

"The Sinister Benevolence of the Lift Boy"

There were nine giant laundry tubs revolving endlessly in the basement of the Criterion. It was a grey universe, windowless, separate from any daylight. I was with Tim Cornford and a man named Tolroy, heaving in tablecloths, and when the machines stopped we dragged them across the room onto other machines that pounded them flat with steam. Whatever we wore was heavy with dampness, and before loading the ironed tablecloths onto trolleys to roll them down the hall, we stripped and ran our clothes through the wringers.

On my first day I thought that when I got home I would tell Rachel everything about what it had been like. But in the end I kept it all to myself—at first it was just the way I was embarrassed by the pains in my shoulders and legs, or the rush of pleasure I had had eating a stolen trifle I'd lifted off the coming evening's dessert trolley. All I did when I got home was crawl into bed, leaving my still-wet clothes drying on the bannister. I'd been thrown into an exhausting pond life and now rarely saw my guardian, who was kept busy at the hub of a thousand spokes. At home he refused to listen to even an approach of a complaint by me. How I behaved or was treated at work did not concern him.

I was offered the chance of night work at pay and a half and leapt for it. I became a lift jockey, bored, invisible in my velvet-lined carriage, and another evening wore a white jacket and worked in the bathrooms, pretending to be essential to guests who really had no need of me at all. Tips were welcomed, but those evenings were tipless and I would not be home before midnight, then up again at six. No, I preferred the laundry. Once, past midnight, after some party had ended, I was told I was needed to help with the transportation of artworks out from the cellar. Significant sculptures and paintings had apparently been transported out of London during the war and hidden in Welsh slate mines. Lesser works were housed in the basements of large hotels and temporarily forgotten, but now they were being gradually lifted back into the light.

None of us really knew how far the tunnels under the Criterion stretched, they may even have travelled under Piccadilly Circus, but down there was unbearable heat and the night staff worked almost naked as they wrestled those similarly naked statues out from the dark. My job was to work the manual lift in order to deliver these men and women, some with missing limbs, some lying in state with dogs at their feet or wrestling a stag, from our labyrinth of tunnels up to the foyer, and for a while the main lobby would appear as it did during the busiest hours of guest arrivals, a queue of dust-covered saints, some with arrows in their armpits, courteously lined up, as if waiting to register. I stroked the midriff of a goddess as I reached past her to pivot the brass handle so we could travel up one floor, barely able to move in the limited space of that service lift. Then I pulled open the grille and they all drifted away on skids into the Great Hall. So many saints and heroes I never knew. By dawn they were travelling towards various museums and private collections in the city.

At the end of that short break I carefully studied my reflection in the school bathroom mirror to see if I had changed or learned anything, then returned to mathematics and the geography of Brazil.

Rachel and I often competed over who could best imitate The Darter. He had for instance a furtive walk, as if he were saving energy for a later moment. (Maybe he's waiting for the "*schwer*," Rachel said.) My sister, always the better performer, could make it look as if she were scurrying to evade a searchlight. Unlike The Moth, The Darter was dedicated to quickness. He appeared most at ease in a limited space. After all, he had found early success as The Pimlico Darter, crouching in the modest square of a boxing ring, and we believed, unfairly, that at some point he may have spent a few months of his life in the similarly restricted nine by six feet of a prison cell.

We were curious about prisons. A week or two before our mother's departure, Rachel and I, imitating trackers in *The Last of the Mohicans,* had decided to follow her across London. We changed buses twice and then were appalled to see our mother talking to a very tall man who, holding her by the elbow, led her inside the prison walls of Wormwood Scrubs. The two of us retreated home, never expecting to see her again, and sat in our empty living room uncertain about what to do, then were even more confused when she returned in time to cook dinner. I would in fact half believe, after the discovery of the trunk, that my mother had never gone to the Far East at all but had dutifully returned to those prison gates to carry out her postponed sentence for some criminal act or other. In any case, if our mother could be incarcerated, then surely the more obviously anarchic Darter must at one time have ended up in such a place. We thought him the kind of man who would be most at ease escaping through a claustrophobic tunnel.

During the following holiday I caught another job at the Criterion, washing dishes. This time I was surrounded with company and most of all could listen to the numerous stories being told or invented. How one had entered the country smuggled among chickens in the hold of a Polish ship and then leapt covered in feathers into the sea at Southampton; how another was the illegitimate son of an English cricket player who had bedded his mother beyond a boundary in Antigua or Port of Spain—all these confessions were dramatically shouted out while surrounded by the 360-degree din of plates, forks, water rushing out from taps like time itself. I was fifteen years old now and I loved it.

During the silence of the staggered meal breaks, there was a different atmosphere. One or two sat on a hard chair for the thirty-minute lunch, with the rest of us on the floor. Then the anecdotes about sex began, where words like "quim" were used—and which involved sisters or brothers or mothers of best friends who seduced and educated youthful boys and youthful girls with a generosity and lack of ownership most of them would never witness in real life. The drawn-out, careful lessons of intercourse in all its varieties, described by Mr. Nkoma, a remarkable man who had a scar on his cheek, took the whole lunch break, and I would end up washing dishes and pots for the rest of the afternoon, barely recovering from what I had heard. And if, with luck, Mr. Nkoma was working beside me at Sink One the next day or the day after, the plot— like a long, intricate serial of my new friend's youth—would continue with a further sexual episode. He was describing a universe of charms, with all the time in the world and with seemingly absent husbands as well as the absence of children. The young Mr. Nkoma had enjoyed piano lessons with a Mrs. Rafferty and, as if to climax the whole of his apparently fictional storytelling, late one afternoon when some twelve of us were decorating the stage in a banquet room for the night's upcoming event, Mr. Nkoma rolled a stool over to the piano and sat down to play a luxurious melody while we worked. It lasted ten minutes and everyone became still. There was no singing, just his educated hands riffling the keys in a sultry and wise way, so it was impossible not to be thereby amazed at the truth of what we had thought were his earlier fictions. And when he finished he sat there for half a minute and eventually closed the piano quietly as if that in itself was the end of the story, the truth or proof of it, of what Mrs. Rafferty in the town of Ti Rocher, four thousand miles from Piccadilly Circus, had taught him.

What did that glimpse of storytelling do to the boy I was? When I think of those episodes it is not the forty-six-year-old

Mr. Nkoma with his scar I see, but Harry Nkoma, a boy, as I was then, when Mrs. Rafferty made him a tall glass of soursop, told him to sit down, and asked a series of quiet questions about what he wished to do with his life. For I believe that if anything was invented, it was just the graphic paragraphs of sex that he described so freely to his small lunchtime audience, the older man's knowledge from his later life most likely layered on top of a more innocent youth. The truth was in the boy, scarred or perhaps still unscarred, who came with two other delivery boys to Mrs. Rafferty's house, where she had said to him on that first meeting, "You go to the same school as my son, don't you?" and Harry Nkoma had said, "Yes, ma'am."

"And what do you wish to do with your life?" He was looking out of the window, not really paying attention to her. "I would like to be in a band. Play the drums."

"Oh," she said, "anyone can play the drums. No, you should learn the piano."

"She was so beautiful," I still recall Harry Nkoma saying, describing to us all, with a novel-like skill, her coloured dress, her thin bare feet, the slim dark toes, and the pale paint on those nails. All those years later he remembered that clear line of muscle in her arm. So without any disbelief I fell in love, as Harry Nkoma had, with this woman who simply knew how to speak to a youth, taking her time to listen and think about what he had said, or what she was going to say, pausing, bringing something from the fridge, all of that leading, according to Harry's grown-up tale, to a preparation for those sexual stories none of us could have imagined or was prepared for as we sat on the floor by the sinks at the Criterion, while Mr. Nkoma sat above us, on one of the two available chairs.

He said her hands felt like leaves on him. After he had come in her—this curious and startling act of magic—her palms had brushed his hair back from his face until his heart stopped speeding. It felt like every nerve was finally stilled. He became aware she had most of her clothes on. In the end it had all been hurried, there had been no uncertainty or torment. Then she slowly undressed, then bent sideways so she could lick the last drop from him. They bathed by an outdoor tap. She poured three or four buckets of water onto his skull and it coursed down, his body suddenly aimless. She raised the bucket and the water fell along her body and she slipped her hand down within the run of it to clean herself. "You can play concerts in other parts of the world," she said, later, during another afternoon. "Would you like to do that?"

"Yes."

"Then I shall teach you."

I sat silent on the floor, listening to this fairness of sharing I already knew existed nowhere else in the world, which could occur only in dreams.

In the trolley hall, between the kitchen and the service lifts that rose to Banquet Level, a game of Scratch Ball took place. Whatever stage an anecdote had reached, whatever tiredness existed among the staff, the last ten minutes of our lunch were given over to two teams of five, who charged each other in the rectangle of uncarpeted concrete that was six feet across. Scratch Ball was not so much the skill of passing or running as it was of balance and brute force, where you heaved the scrum of your team forward, all your fury seeming more furious because it had to be done in silence. No verbal damnation, grunts, or yells of pain to betray the anarchy of what was happening in the trolley hall, like old silent footage of a riot. The squeak of shoes, the sound of falling bodies, was all that gave away our lawlessness. Then we lay there, breathing heavily, got up and went back to work. Mr. Nkoma and I returned to the large sinks, thrust fragile glasses into the rotating bristles, and tossed them a half-second later into boiling water so the person drying would pluck them free as they bounced back up and stack them. We could do over a hundred glasses in fifteen minutes. Plates and cutlery took longer but for now someone else was doing that, and it was just Harry Nkoma and I with our recent lunchtime anecdotes subsiding into what felt like needed sleep, where they belonged naturally. There was only the great noise of the kitchen in our ears, the taps gushing out water, the huge wet brushes humming in front of us.

Why do I still remember those days and nights at the Criterion—that springtime fragment of a boy's youth, a seemingly unimportant time? The men and women I would meet at Ruvigny Gardens were more incendiary, became more significant in the path of my life. Perhaps because it was the only time that boy was alone, a stranger among strangers, when he could choose his allies and opponents for himself from those who worked beside him at the sinks or played on the Scratch Ball teams. When I broke Tim Cornford's nose by accident, he needed to disguise it in order to continue working the rest of the afternoon so he wouldn't lose his pay. He sat there in a daze, got up, scrubbed the blood off his shirt under a tap, and returned to work repainting a chipped floorboard so it could dry by the time guests arrived. For by six p.m. most of the ground-floor staff would have left the building, like little shoe-makers needing to disappear before the real owners returned.

I was pleased by now that The Moth took no interest in how I was surviving the job or what trouble I was getting into. I hid what I was learning, not just from him but from my sister, with whom I had once shared everything. The sexual fables of Harry Nkoma went no further, but the afternoons with Mrs. Rafferty would stay, and there was to be a brief, ten-tative bond with Harry. I remember us raucous at a couple of football matches we went to, or comparing at the end of an exhausting day our boiled hands and the pucker of flesh on each finger—even on those deft ones that had played the piano so surprisingly, stilling a room of Criterion workers. Where did he go eventually with that skill? He was already middle-aged. For all I knew, Harry would continue to corner others with his stories. But where was the future that Mrs. Rafferty had promised him? I would never know. I lost him. The two of us used to walk to the bus stop if we finished at the same hour. It took me less than thirty minutes to get home. It took him two buses and an hour and a half. It never occurred to either of us to visit where the other lived.

*

Now and then someone would refer to The Moth as "Walter," but Rachel and I felt the vagueness of our chosen name for him was more apt. We did not have a stable perception of him yet. Was he really protecting us? I must have longed for some truth and security, much like the six-year-old boy who had once gone to him to escape a dangerous father.

For instance, what was the sieve in The Moth that made him choose these specific individuals who filled our house? Rachel and I gloated with excitement over their presence, even if it felt wrong. If our mother had ever thought to phone us from wherever she was, we would no doubt have lied cautiously and said everything was fine, not mentioning the strangers who happened to be crowding into the house at that moment. They did not in any way resemble a normal family, not even a beached Swiss Family Robinson. The house felt more like a night zoo, with moles and jackdaws and shambling beasts who happened to be chess players, a gardener, a possible greyhound thief, a slow-moving opera singer. If I attempt now to recall the activities of one or two of them, what emerges are surreal non-chronological moments. Mr. Florence, for instance, pumping his "smoker," which he normally used to calm and stultify his bees, into the face of a guard at the Dulwich Picture Gallery, forcing him to inhale fumes of burning wood combined with a sleep-inducing coal. The uniformed man had his hands held behind his chair as this was happening, and it took a while before his head fell forward, calm as a sleeping bee, so we could walk out of the gallery with two or three watercolours, while Mr. Florence pumped a last gasp of smoke at the unconscious face. "Right!" he barked quietly, pleased, as if he had painted an immaculate straight line, and handed me the hot smoker to put away safely. There are many such incomplete and guilty moments I have packed away, meaningless as those unused objects in my mother's suitcase. And the chronology of events has fallen apart, for whatever defensive reason.

Each day Rachel and I took a bus and then the train from Victoria Station to our respective schools, and for about fifteen minutes before the bell I would mill around with the other boys, talking excitedly about radio shows they'd heard the night before, a *Mystery Hour* or one of those half-hour comedies where the humour depended almost totally on the repetition of stock phrases. But now I rarely heard those programmes, as our radio listening was constantly interrupted by visitors dropping by to see The Moth, or he would take us around the city and I returned too tired to be curious about another *Mystery Hour.* I am sure that Rachel, like me, never revealed what our home life had really become—the existence of The Darter, the bee man still under a cloud for his past misdemeanour, and most of all that our parents had "gone away." I suspect she pretended, like me, to have heard all those shows and so nodded and laughed and claimed to being scared by a thriller neither of us had heard.

The Moth was sometimes gone for two or three days, often without warning. We ate our dinners alone and trudged off to school the next morning. He would mention later that The

Darter had cruised by in his car to make sure the place was "not in the midst of a conflagration," so we had been utterly safe, though the idea of The Darter's nearby presence on those nights did not give us a sense of security. We'd heard him on other evenings, churning the engine of his Morris—both accelerator and brake pressed down simultaneously—while dropping off our guardian at midnight, and recognized his drunken laughter filling the street as he drove away.

The music-loving Moth appeared blind to the evident anarchy in The Darter. Everything the ex-boxer did was at a precarious tilt, about to come loose. Worst were the crowded car rides when the two of them sat in the front, while Rachel and I and sometimes three greyhounds squabbled in the back on the way to Whitechapel. We were not even certain that the dogs belonged to him. The Darter rarely recalled their names, as they sat tense, shivering, their bony knees digging into our laps. There was one that preferred to lounge round my neck like a scarf, its warm belly against me, and once, somewhere around Clapham, it proceeded to urinate, through either fear or need, onto my shirt. I was supposedly going to a school friend's house after the dog races, and when I complained, The Darter laughed so excessively he had to avoid hitting a Belisha beacon. No, we did not feel safe around him. It was clear he was just putting up with us and would have preferred we had remained at "Walter's house," which was how he referred to our parents' home. Was this even his car? I wondered, for I noticed the number plates on the blue Morris were frequently changed. But The Moth was content to move in The Darter's slipstream. Shy people are drawn to such types for camouflage. In any case, the tensions we felt whenever The Moth left home were the result not of our guardian's absence but of the knowledge that The Darter had permission to oversee us with that grudging, uninterested concern.

One day I was fighting with Rachel over a book I had lost. She had denied taking it, and I then discovered it in her room. Her arms flailed against my face. I grabbed her neck and she froze, fell out of my grip and began shuddering and banging her head and her heels against the wood floor. Then a cat-like noise, the pupils slid away, replaced by the whites of her eyes, her arms still flailing. The door opened, letting in noise from the crowd downstairs, and The Darter walked in. He must have been passing her room. *"Go away!"* I yelled. He closed the door behind him, knelt down, took my book, the stolen *Swallows and Amazons,* and jammed it into Rachel's mouth at the moment she gasped for air. He pulled a blanket that was on the bed over her, then lay down beside her and enclosed her in his arms. Until there was only the noise of her breath.

"She stole my book," I whispered nervously.

"Bring some cold water. Rub it on her face, cool her down." I did that. Twenty minutes later the three of us were still together on the floor. We could hear The Moth's acquaintances downstairs.

"Has this happened before?"

"No."

"I had a dog once"—he said it casually—"who was epileptic. Now and then he'd go off like a firecracker." The Darter leaned against the bed, winked at me, and lit himself a cigarette. He knew Rachel hated him smoking around her. Now she just watched him silently. "That's a crap book," he announced, rubbing his fingers over Rachel's bite marks on the cover. "You need to take care of your sister, Nathaniel. I'll show you what to do."

How surprising The Pimlico Darter could be whenever that other side of him emerged. How good he was that evening, while The Moth's party continued downstairs.

In those days there was more fear about the effects of epilepsy, along with the assumption that frequent fits impaired a person's memory. Rachel mentioned these limits after reading about them in the library. I suppose we choose whatever life we feel safest in; for me it is a distant village, a walled garden. But Rachel tossed away such concerns. "It's just '*schwer*,'" she would say to me, using her fingers to emphasize the quotation marks.

*

A woman who was going out with The Darter had begun strolling into my parents' house, accompanying him, or arriving at whatever hour she was to meet him there. On her first visit, The Darter arrived too late to explain who she was, so my sister and I, just home from school, were left to introduce ourselves in the vacuum created by his absence. It meant we got a good look at her. We were careful not to mention other females The Darter had already escorted into the house, so we answered her inquiries about him somewhat stupidly, as if we could not remember much about his associates or even what he did, or where he might be. We knew he liked to breast his cards.

Still, Olive Lawrence was a surprise. For someone like The Darter, who was so one-sided in his opinions as to the role women ought to have in the world, he appeared to have an almost suicidal tendency to select highly independent women to go out with. They were tested right away by being taken to crowded and noise-filled sports events at Whitechapel or Wembley Stadium, where there was no possibility of private conversation. The triple-forecast bets were supposed to provide enough excitement for them. Besides, for The Darter there were no other interesting public locations to visit. He'd never stepped inside a theatre in his life. The idea of watching someone pretend to be real, or of someone saying lines on stage that came from previously written dialogue, felt untrustworthy to him, and as a man on the edge of the law he needed to feel secure about how reliable the truth was that he was hearing. Only cinemas appealed to him; for some reason he believed truth had been caught there. Yet the women he was attracted to seemed to be in no way humble or easily persuaded maidens who would happily exist under his rules. One was a painter of murals. Another, after Olive Lawrence departed, was an argumentative Russian.

Olive Lawrence, who appeared alone that first afternoon so that the three of us had to introduce ourselves, was a geographer and ethnographer. She was, she told us, often in the Hebrides recording wind currents, at other times in the Far East being a solitary traveller. There was something in these professional women that suggested it was not a case of The Darter's selecting them but of the women's choosing him; as if Olive Lawrence, a specialist in distant cultures, had stumbled suddenly on a man who reminded her of an almost extinct medieval species, a person still unaware of any of the principal courtesies introduced in the past hundred years. Here was someone who had never heard of people eating only vegetables or opening a door for a woman so she might enter a building ahead of him. Who else would have fascinated a person like Olive Lawrence but this man who seemed to be frozen in time, or perhaps released from a recently discovered sect now miraculously in evidence in her own home town. Yet there appeared to be little choice in how women participated with The Darter. The only rules played by were his.

The hour Olive Lawrence spent with us, as she waited for her new beau, was given over to telling us in a somewhat amazed voice about the first dinner they had shared. He had found her among The Moth's friends and then steered her to a

Greek restaurant, a narrow rectangle of a place with five tables and submarine lighting, then proposed they seal a newly found intimacy (that had not in fact occurred but would shortly) with the sharing of a meal of goat and a bottle of red wine. Did something cross her mind then, some gale warning or other? But she acquiesced.

"And bring us the cooked head," he requested of the waiter. The dark, horrific sentence was said so casually that he could have been asking for a sprig of fennel. She paled at the mention of the goat head, and the nearby customers proceeded to slow their own meals in order to witness the oncoming domestic contest. The Darter may not have liked theatre, but what followed was a Strindberg-like performance that lasted an hour and a half with five or six couples watching. We knew The Darter was a "quick scoffer," because whenever we travelled with him during the dog-racing season he'd crack open and consume a couple of raw eggs while driving his Morris, then toss the shells into the back seat. But at the Star of Argiropulos he took his time. Olive Lawrence sat on a stiff-backed kitchen chair in front of us and reenacted the moment, describing every insistence and refusal when she had to be convinced or persuaded or bullied, as well as maybe charmed—she was not sure which, she no longer knew, it was all confusing as a nightmare—into eating the carcass of a goat slaughtered, she was sure, in someone's basement near Paddington.

Then the head.

The Darter had won, it appeared. And the intimacy he was expecting did occur a few hours later in his flat. The two bottles of wine had helped, she told us, still downcast. Or perhaps it was because he had believed so securely that he was right, that he was not arguing about consuming the goat's head and the one eye she had to swallow in a vindictive way. The eye had the texture of snot. She actually used that word. And the head had a texture of . . . of . . . *what,* she did not know. She ate it because she could tell he believed in it. It was something she would never forget.

By the time The Darter arrived at our house, full of not very convincing excuses for being late, we had decided we liked her.

She had spoken to us of Asia and the ends of the earth as if they were distant boroughs of London, easily reachable. She spoke about these places in a voice unlike the beleaguered one she had used to describe her Greek meal. When we asked her what she did in her job, she told us exactly what she did. "*Eth-nog-ra-phy,*" she said, slowing the syllables as if we should write the word down fragment by fragment. She spoke of her pleasures as a traveller, told us that in the river deltas of southern India she had drifted on a boat with just a minimal two-stroke motor somewhere in its bowels. She described the speed of monsoons—you were sopping wet and five minutes later your clothes were dried by the sun. She spoke of a pink-lit tent that housed a small statue of a minor god at ease in its shade while the world outside was devastated by heat. She was providing us with descriptions our distant mother might have sent in letters. She had been along the Chiloango River regions in Angola, where there was ancestor worship so that ghosts had supplanted gods. Her talk sparkled.

Like The Darter she was tall and slim, with a dazzle of unkempt hair, shaped and reshaped I am sure by whatever weather she was in. An independent creature. I suspect she would have eaten a goat if she had slain it herself in some Turkish meadow. The indoor world of London must have made her restless. In retrospect it was probably the extreme difference between her and The Darter that allowed their attachment to last longer than we expected it would. Yet whatever his fascination for her, she also seemed itching to be on her way. Perhaps she was on a break and needed to remain in London writing her reports, after which she would be off again. That small god in its pink tent had to be revisited. It meant leaving every attachment and domestic utensil behind.

But it was The Moth's relationship with her that we found most curious. Caught between The Darter's and Olive Lawrence's differing opinions about practically everything whenever they clashed in our living room, or worse, in the reverberating confines of The Darter's car, The Moth refused to take sides. He obviously had need of The Darter professionally, for whatever reason, and yet we saw that though she was most likely just a temporary presence, The Moth was intrigued by her. We loved being around the three of them, witnessing their fights. The Darter appeared more complex and shaded now, with this generous flaw in him that preferred the company of a woman who contradicted his opinions. Not that his opinions would change. And we loved the dilemma The Moth was in, his awkwardness when The Darter and Olive Lawrence broke into flames. Suddenly he seemed like the headwaiter who could only brush away the broken glass.

Olive was the one person who came into our house who appeared capable of clear judgement. She was consistent in her views of The Darter. She admitted his tiresomeness alongside his quick and peculiar charm, was appalled as well as fascinated, she told us, by the consummately male taste evident in his disorganized flat at The Pelican Stairs. And I had also seen her regard The Moth as if never quite certain if he were a positive or negative force. What was his hold on The Darter, her present temporary lover? And was he a benign guardian to the orphan-like boy and girl she had come to know? She always focused on the possibility of character. She weighed character, could discover it in a few grains of a person, even in one's noncommittal silence.

"Half the life of cities occurs at night," Olive Lawrence warned us. "There's a more uncertain morality then. At night there are those who eat flesh by necessity—they might eat a bird, a small dog." When Olive Lawrence spoke it was more like a private shuffling of her thoughts, a soliloquy from somewhere in the shadows of her knowledge, an idea she was still unsure about. One evening she insisted we catch a bus with her to Streatham Common and walk its slow rise of land to the Rookery. Rachel felt uncertain in that open darkness, wished to go home, said it was cold. But the three of us kept moving forward, until we were eventually in the trees and the city had evaporated behind us.

Around us were untranslatable sounds, something in flight, a series of footfalls. I could hear Rachel's breath but there was no sound from Olive Lawrence. Then in the dark she began to talk, to distinguish the barely heard noises for us. "It's a warm evening . . . and the pitch of those crickets is in D. . . . They have that sweet quiet whistle, but it's made with the rub of their wings, not by breath, and this much conversation means there will be rain. That's why it's so dark now, the clouds are between us and the moon. Listen." We saw her pale hand point near us, to the left. "That scrape is a badger. Not digging, just his paws moving. Really, it's something tender. Perhaps the end of a fearful dream. Just the remains of a small uneven nightmare in his head. We all have nightmares. For you, dear Rachel, it might be imagining the fear of a seizure. But there need not be fear in a dream, just as there's no danger from the rain while we are under the trees. Lightning rarely comes during this month, we are safe. Let's walk on. The crickets might move with us, the branches and underbrush appear to be full of them, full of high C's and D's. They can reach as high as an F at the end of summer when they are laying eggs. Their cries seem to fall on you from above, don't they? It feels like an important night for them. Remember that. Your own story is just one, and perhaps not the important one. The self is not the principal thing."

Hers was the calmest voice I knew when I was a boy. There was never argument in it. She had just this tactile curiosity about what interested her, and that calmness allowed you to be within her intimate space. In daylight she always caught your eye as she talked or as she listened, she was completely with you. As she was with the two of us that night. A night she wanted us to remember, as I have. Rachel and I would not have walked through the darkness of that forest alone. But we were confident that Olive Lawrence had some tracing in her head from a faint light in the distance or a shift of wind that told her exactly where she was and what she was going towards.

There were other times, however, when a different ease took over and she'd fall asleep unconcerned in my father's leather chair at Ruvigny Gardens, her feet tucked under her, even if the room was full of The Moth's friends, the look on her face still intent, focused, as if continuing to receive information. She was the first woman, in fact the first person, I ever saw do that, sleep so casually in the presence of others without guilt. Then wake refreshed half an hour later when others were beginning to tire, and stride off into the night, refusing The Darter's not-too-convincing offer to drive her home—as if she now wished to walk through the city alone, with a new thought. I would go upstairs and watch her from my bedroom window as she entered and passed each pool of streetlight. I could hear her whistling faintly as if recalling a tune, something unknown to me.

In spite of our night journeys, I knew Olive's profession usually meant daylight work, measuring the effects of nature on coastlines. She had worked apparently within the Admiralty on sea currents and tides, barely out of her teens, during the first stages of the war. (She admitted to this modestly only after it had been almost revealed by someone in The Moth's group.) There were all these landscapes within her. She could read the noise of forests, she had timed the rhythm of the tidal slop along the embankment at Battersea Bridge. I am always curious why Rachel and I never ventured into a life like hers and her vivid example of independence as well as empathy for everything around her. But you must remember we did not know Olive Lawrence for that long. Though the night walks— accompanying her along the bombed-out docklands or into the echoing Greenwich Foot Tunnel, our three voices singing a lyric she was teaching us, "*Under stars chilled by the winter, under an August moon . . .*"—I will not forget.

She was tall. Lithe. She must have been lithe, I suppose, with The Darter when she was his lover for the brief period of that unlikely relationship. I don't know. I don't know. What does a boy know? I always saw her during that time as self-sufficient, for instance when she slept in our semi-crowded living room in a state of separateness from all the others. Is this the censorship or tact of the young? I can more easily see her embracing a dog, lying on the floor beside it, the weight of its head on her throat, so she is scarcely able to breathe but content to let the animal remain there, that way. But a man dancing close to her? I imagine a response of claustrophobia in her. She thrilled to open space and weather nights, as if she could never be contained or fully revealed there. And yet of all those acquaintances and strangers who walked into and out of the house at Ruvigny Gardens, she was the most distinct. She appeared to be the accident, the outsider at our table, whom The Darter had discovered at my parents' house, and more surprisingly taken up with so she would soon be known as "The Darter's Girl."

"I'll send you two a postcard," Olive Lawrence said when she eventually left London. And then was gone from our lives.

But somewhere on the borders of the Black Sea or at some small village post office near Alexandria, she would indeed mail us a platonic *billet-doux* about a cloud system in the mountains that suggested an alternative world, her other life. The postcards became our treasures, especially as we knew there was now no communication between her and The Darter. She'd journeyed out of his life without a backward glance. The idea of a woman mailing a postcard as part of a promise to two children far away indicated an expansiveness as well as aloneness, a hidden need in her. It signalled two very different states. Though perhaps not. What did that boy know. . . .

There are moments after I've put down such thoughts about Olive Lawrence when I almost believe I am composing a possible version of my mother, while she was away, doing something I knew nothing about. Both these women were in unknown locations, though of course it was only Olive Lawrence who courteously and beyond the call of duty mailed postcards to us from wherever she was.

And there is the third corner of the triangle these two women made up, which I also consider now. It is Rachel, who needed a close relationship with a mother during that time, to protect her in the way a mother could. She had walked between Olive and me that night up the slow incline of hill into Streatham woods, being told that when she was in the darkness with us there would be no danger, that there was no danger even in dreams or during the unstable tumult of her seizures. There were only crickets in song above us, only the scratch of a badger as it turned in comfort, only the hush and then a sudden whisper of the oncoming rain.

What had our mother assumed would happen to us in her absence? Did she think our lives would be like that popular play of the day, *The Admirable Crichton*—which she had taken us to see in the West End, our first play—where a butler (in our case, I suppose, the equivalent of The Moth) kept an aristocratic family well disciplined and therefore secure in a sort of upside-down world on a castaway island? Did she really assume that the shell of our world would not crack?

Sometimes, under the influence of whatever he was drinking, The Moth became cheerfully incomprehensible to us, in spite of the fact that he appeared assured about what he thought he was saying—even if what he said involved a few clauses falling away from the path of the previous sentence. One night when Rachel had been unable to sleep, he pulled a book called *The Golden Bowl* from my mother's shelf and began reading to us. The manner of the paragraphs, as the sentences strolled a maze-like path towards evaporation, was, to the two of us, similar to The Moth's when he was being drunkenly magisterial. It was as if language had been separated from his body in a courteous way. There were other evenings when he behaved strangely. One night the radio described the manic act of a man who had pulled passengers out of a Hillman Minx in front of the Savoy and then set fire to the car. The Moth had returned only an hour earlier and listening intently to the report groaned, "Oh God, I hope that was not me!" He glanced down at his hands as if he might find traces of paraffin on them, then seeing our concern dismissed the possibility with a wink. It was clear we now did not even understand his jokes. In contrast to him, The Darter, while more excessive in his inventions, had no sense of humour, like any person who is not fully legal.

Still, The Moth had this almost reliable stolidness. And

perhaps he was our Admirable Crichton after all, even when measuring that cloudy liquid into his small blue glass cup that had once been attached to a bottle of eyewash, and drinking it down as if it were sherry. We did not mind the habit. It was the one time he was serenely open to our wishes, and Rachel could always persuade him at these moments to take us into parts of the city he appeared to know well. The Moth had an interest in abandoned structures, such as a nineteenth-century hospital in Southwark, which had been active long before the days of anaesthetic. Somehow he got us into the place and lit the sodium lamps so they shivered against the walls of the dark operating room. So many unused locations in the city that he knew of, lit by nineteenth-century light, shadowed and ominous to us. I wonder whether Rachel's later theatrical life was formed by those half-lit evenings. She must have perceived how one could darken and make invisible or at least distant what is unhappy or dangerous in a life; I think her eventual skill with limelight and fictional thunder allowed her to clarify for herself what was true and what was false, safe and unsafe.

By now The Darter was stepping out with the Russian, who owned such a flaring temper that he was to bail out from that relationship before she could discover his address. This of course meant she too would turn up at Ruvigny Gardens looking for him at odd hours, sniffing the air for a scent of him. He became careful and never parked his car on our street.

The presence of The Darter's various partners meant I was suddenly closer to women than I had ever been, apart from my mother or sister. The school I went to took only boys. It was a time when my thoughts and friendships should have been with them. But Olive Lawrence's ease of intimate conversation, the way she spoke so directly about her wishes, even her desires, brought me into a universe that was distinct from anywhere I had previously been. I became intrigued by women who were outside my realm, with no blood or sexual motive. Such friendships were not controlled by me, and they would be passing and brief. They replaced family life yet I could remain at a distance, which is my flaw. But I loved the truth I learned from strangers. Even during those dramatic weeks with the spurned Russian girlfriend, I hung around the house more than I needed to and hurried home from school in order to simply watch her pace our living room with that unsatisfied look on her face. I would walk past her and brush her arm so I could collect that moment. I once offered to accompany her to the dog track at Whitechapel, supposedly to help her find The Darter, but she waved my offer away, perhaps guessing I might have another motive to get her out of the house. She was unaware, in fact, how close she was to The Darter, who was hiding in my room, reading *The Beano.* In any case, the curious pleasure of female company was in me now.

Agnes Street

That summer I found a job in a fast-paced restaurant in World's End. I was back to washing dishes and filling in as a waiter whenever someone was ill. I was hoping to meet up with Mr. Nkoma, the piano player and fabulist, but there was no one I knew. The staff were mostly quick-witted waitresses—North Londoners and girls from the country—and I could not take my eyes off them, because of how they talked back to bosses, how they laughed, how they insisted they were enjoying themselves even though the work was hard. They had a higher status than those of us in the kitchen, so we were barely worth talking to. That did not matter. I could watch and learn about them from a distance. I worked there, shy at the centre of the busy pauseless restaurant, and their speed of argument and laughter kept me entertained. They'd walk past carrying three trays, proposition you, and walk off during your stammer. They rolled up their sleeves to show you their stringy muscles. They were forward then suddenly distant. A girl, a green ribbon holding back her hair, came across me in a corner during my lunch break and asked if she could "borrow" the small piece of ham out of my sandwich. I did not know what to say. I must have handed it to her silently. I asked what her name was and she looked shocked at my forwardness, ran back and organized a group of three or four waitresses to circle me and sing about the dangers of desire. I was about to enter a borderless terrain between adolescence and adulthood.

When a few weeks later I had my clothes off in the company of that girl on a worn carpet of an empty house, I found the pathway towards her invisible. What I knew of passion was still an abstract thing, layered with hurdles and rules I did not yet know. What was just and what was unjustified? She lay beside me and there was no submission. Was she as nervous as I was? Besides, the real drama of the episode was not about us but the situation, which had involved illegally entering a house on Agnes Street with keys she had borrowed from her brother, who worked for an estate agency. There was a "For Sale" sign outside; inside there was no furniture, just carpeting. It was nightfall and I could interpret her responses only with the help of a streetlight or from a series of single matches held above a section of carpet that we checked later for bloodstains, as if there might have been a murder there. It did not feel like romance. Romance was the energy and sparkle of Olive Lawrence, it was the incandescent sexual fury of The Darter's spurned Russian whose beauty was increased by her heightened suspicion of him.

Another evening in midsummer. We have a cold bath in the house on Agnes Street. There's no towel to dry ourselves, not even a curtain we can rub ourselves against. She pulls back her dark blond hair, then shakes her head, and her hair loosens into an aura.

"Everyone else, they're probably having cocktails now," she says.

We dry ourselves by walking through the empty rooms. This is the most intimate we have been since entering the house around six o'clock. There's no longer the plot of sex or focused desire, just ourselves naked as well as invisible to each other in the dark. I catch, because of the swerve of a car light, a smile from her in recognition of this. A small awareness between us.

"Watch," she says, and does a handstand into the dark.

"Didn't see it. Do it again." And this once seemingly unfriendly girl somersaults towards me, saying, "Catch my feet this time." Then, "Thank you," as I slowly lower her down.

She sits on the floor. "I wish we could open a window. Run in the street."

"I don't even know what street we're on anymore."

"It's Agnes Street. The garden! Come—"

In the hall downstairs she pushes me to move faster, and I turn, grab her hand. We are wrestling against the staircase, each unable to see the other. She leans forward, bites my neck, and pulls away from an embrace. "Come on!" she says. "Here!" Banging into a wall. It's as if neither of us thinks of anything except to escape this closeness, and it is only closeness that will help us escape. We are on the floor kissing whatever we reach. Her hands beating my shoulders as we fuck. It isn't lovemaking.

"Don't. Don't let go."

"No!"

Escaping her tightening arm I hit my head on something, a wall, bannister, then come down hard onto her chest, suddenly aware of her smallness. Somewhere here we lose consciousness of each other, simply discovering the joy in the sport of it. Some people never find it, or don't find it again. Then we are asleep in the dark.

"Hello. Where are we?" she says.

I roll onto my back, taking her with me, so she's on top. She opens my lips with her tiny hands.

"Og Hagness Steef," I say.

"What's your name again?" She laughs.

"Nathaniel."

"Oh, posh! Love you, Nathaniel."

We can barely dress ourselves. We hold hands as if we might lose each other as we go slowly through the darkness to the front door.

The Moth was often away, but his absence, like his presence, rarely mattered. My sister and I were by now foraging for ourselves, becoming self-sufficient, Rachel disappearing into the evenings. She said nothing about where she went, just as I was silent about my life on Agnes Street. For both of us school now felt like an irrelevancy. In my conversations with other boys, who should have been the friends I'd have normally attached myself to, I never admitted to what was occurring at home. That existed in one pocket while my school life remained in the other. In youth we are not so much embarrassed by the reality of our situation as fearful others might discover and judge it.

One evening Rachel and I took off to a seven o'clock screening of a film, and sat in the front row of the Gaumont. At some point the hero's plane plunged towards the earth, with his foot caught among the controls so he couldn't get free. Tense music filled the theatre, along with the scream of the plane's engine. Caught up in the moment, I was unaware of what was happening around me.

"*What's wrong?*"

I looked over to my right. Between the voice that had said "What's wrong?" and me sat Rachel, shuddering, a moan, a cow-like noise coming out of her that I knew was going to get louder. She was shaking from side to side. I opened her shoulder bag, got out the wooden ruler to put between her teeth, but it was too late. I needed to use my fingers to pry her mouth open, and she was biting down with her thin little teeth. I slapped her and in the midst of her gasp jammed in the wooden ruler and pulled her down to the floor. Above us the plane crashed into the earth.

Rachel's unmoored eyes were looking at me to gain security, for the safe way out of where she was. The man was bending over her too.

"Who is she?"

"My sister. It's a seizure. She needs food."

He had his ice cream in his hand and gave it to me. I took it and pressed it onto her lips. Her head pulled back, then realizing what it was took it in greedily. The two of us crouched in the dark on that filthy carpet of the Gaumont. I tried lifting her to get her out of there, but she had taken on dead weight, so I lay down on the floor and hugged her to me the way The Darter had done. She looked, in the light that fell from the screen, as if she were still witnessing something terrible. As of course she was, for whenever such episodes occurred, she would later describe to me calmly what she had seen. The voices on the screen filled the theatre, continued the plot, and we stayed there on that floor for ten minutes with my coat over her to make her feel secure. There are medications now to swerve a body away from this sort of collision, but there weren't any then. None that we knew of, anyway.

We slipped out through a side exit and walked beyond the dark curtain towards the lit world. I got her into a Lyons Corner House. She had barely any energy. I made her eat something. She drank milk. Then we walked home. She did not speak about what had happened, as if by now it was immaterial, some deadly shore she had recently passed. It would always be the next day when she needed to discuss it—not about the embarrassment or chaos in her, but with a wish to try to define the thrill building towards what was going to happen before everything dismantled. Then she could not remember any further, the brain by then unconcerned with remembering. But I knew there had been a brief time at the Gaumont when, seeing the pilot struggling to escape, she herself, half thrilled, had moved alongside him.

If I do not speak of my sister in this story so much, it is because we have separate memories. Each of us witnessed clues about the other we did not pursue. Her secret lipstick, a boy on a motorcycle once, her crawling home late giddy with laughter, or how she'd become surprisingly fond of talking with The Moth. I suppose she must have found a confessor in him, but I held on to my secrets, kept my distance. In any case, Rachel's version of our time at Ruvigny Gardens, though it might nestle with mine in certain ways, would be spoken of in a different tone, with an emphasis on different things. It turned out we would be close only during that early period when we shared a double life. But now, these years later, there is a separateness towards the other, and we fend for ourselves.

On the carpet there is food wrapped in brown butcher paper—cheese and bread, slices of ham, a bottle of cider—all stolen from the restaurant we work in. We are in another room, another house without furniture, the walls blank. Thunder fills this unlived-in building. According to her brother's schedule this one will take a while to sell, so we have become used to camping here at the end of a day when his customers are unlikely to turn up.

"Can we open a window?"

"No, we'll forget it."

She is strict about her brother's rules. He even needed to check me out, looking me up and down, saying I looked a bit too young. A strange audition. Max was his name.

We fuck where the dining room must have been. My fingers touch the dent of impressions where table legs once rested on the carpet. We would have been under the table, there would normally have been a meal over us. I say this as I look up, seeing nothing in the dark.

"You're a strange one, aren't you? Only you'd ever think that right now."

The storm abandons itself over us, shattering the soup tureens, throwing spoons onto the floor. A back wall damaged by a bomb has still not been rebuilt, and the dry thunder enters loudly, searching out our nakedness. We lie defenceless, without furniture, without even an alibi for what we are doing there, where all we have is butcher paper for a plate, and an old dog bowl for water. "I had a dream I was fucking you on the weekend," she says, "and there was something in the room, near us." I am not used to talking about sex. But Agnès—she calls herself that now—does, charmingly. It's natural to her. What is the best way to give her an orgasm, where specifically to touch her, how soft, how hard. "Here, let me show you. Give me your hand. . . ." My mute response half mocked by her, her smiling at my shyness. "Boy, you have many, many more years to get used to this, to keep becoming. There's abundance here." A pause, then, "You know . . . you could teach me about you."

By now we like each other as much as we desire each other. She talks about her sexual past. "I had this cocktail dress I borrowed for a date. I got drunk—it was the first time. I woke up in a room and no one was there. And no dress. I walked to the Tube and got home in just a raincoat." A pause as she waits for me to say something. "Anything like that happen to you? You can tell me in French if you want. Would that be easier?"

"I failed French," I lie.

"Bet ya didn't."

Along with the wildness of her talk I loved her voice, the thickets and rhymes of it, a sea change after the way the boys at my school talked. But something else made Agnes different from others. The Agnes I knew during that summer was not the Agnes she would be later. Even then I knew it. Was that future woman I imagined aligned with her wishfulness for herself? Just as she may have believed in something further in me? It was different with everyone else I knew at that time in my life. During that era teenagers were locked into what we thought we already were and therefore would always be. It was an English habit, the disease of the time.

The night of that first storm of summer—both of us holding each other frantically within it—I found a gift in my trouser pocket when I eventually got home. Unfolding a section of the crumpled brown butcher paper that had been our plate, I came on a charcoal drawing of the two of us on our backs, hand in hand, and above us the great unseen storm—black clouds, lightning bolts, a dangerous heaven. She loved to draw. Somewhere in the paths of my life I lost that drawing, though I had meant to save it. I still remember what it looked like, and now and then I have searched for a version, hoping to find an echo of that early sketch in some gallery. But I have never found such a thing. For so long I knew nothing more of her than "Agnes Street," where the first house we entered together had been. During our illegal days and nights in various skeletal homes she insisted with a defensive humour on taking that as a nom de plume for herself. "Nom de Plume," she pronounced it grandly. "You know what that means, right?"

We slipped out of the house. We had to be at work early. There was a man pacing up and down by the bus stop, watching us as we approached him, who then turned to look at the house, as if curious about why we had come out of it. He boarded the bus as well, and sat behind us. Was this just co-incidence? Was he a wartime ghost from the building we had invaded? We felt guilt, not fear. Agnes was worried about her brother's job. But as we got up to leave, he got up too and followed us. The bus stopped. We stood at the exit. As the bus started and began moving faster, Agnes leapt off, staggered, then waved at me. I waved and turned back past the man, and later, at some point in central London, I jumped off and he couldn't catch me.

The Mussel Boat

Our first day on the Thames, Rachel and I and The Darter travelled west until we were almost free of the city. I'd need a good river map now to show you the places we passed or paused at, whose names I learned by heart during those weeks, along with the charts of tidal information, the intricate causeways, old tollhouses, draw-docks we entered and left, building sites and gathering places we learned to recognize from the boat—Ship Lane, Bulls Alley, Mortlake, the Harrods Depository, several power stations, along with the twenty or so named and unnamed canals that had been cut a century or two earlier like spokes fingering north from the Thames. I used to lie in bed repeating all the declensions of the river in order to memorize and so remember them. I still do. They sounded like the names of kings of England, and they became more thrilling to me than football teams or mathematics tables. Sometimes we travelled east beyond Woolwich and Barking, and even in the darkness knew our location by just the sound of the river or the pull of the tide. Beyond Barking there was Caspian Wharf, Erith Reach, the Tilbury Cut, Lower Hope Reach, Blyth Sands, the Isle of Grain, the estuary, and then the sea.

There were further hidden locations along the Thames where we paused to meet seagoing vessels that unloaded their surprising cargo, then walked the several animals that had hesitatingly disembarked, all of them attached to one long rope. In this way they defecated and relieved themselves after their four- or five-hour journey from Calais, before we coaxed them onto our mussel boat for another brief journey, to be collected later by people we saw only briefly, whose names we never knew.

Our involvement with these river activities had begun the afternoon The Darter overheard us talking about the approaching weekend. Casually, speaking as if Rachel and I were not in the room, he asked The Moth if we might happen to be free to help him out with something or other.

"Day work or night work?"

"Probably both."

"And is it safe?"

This was said sotto voce by The Moth as if we should not be hearing it.

"Absolutely safe," The Darter answered loudly, looking towards the two of us, offering a false smile and suggesting complete security with an offhand wave. The question of legality never surfaced.

The Moth murmured, "You can swim, can't you?" And we nodded. The Darter threw in, "They like dogs, don't they?" And this time it was The Moth who nodded, having no idea whether we did.

*

"It's resplendent," The Darter claimed that first weekend, one hand on the wheel, the other attempting to remove a sandwich from his pocket. He did not appear fully focused on the steering of the barge. A cold wind scalloped the water, gusting and shuddering against us from all sides. I supposed we were safe with him. I knew nothing about boats, but I immediately loved the landless smells, the oil on the water, brine, fumes sputtering out of the stern, and I came to love the thousand and one sounds of the river around us, that let us be silent as if in a suddenly thoughtful universe within this rushing world. It *was* resplendent. We almost grazed the arch of a bridge, The Darter leaning his body away at the last minute as if that would make the boat follow him. Then a near collision with a quartet of rowers who were left buffeting in our wash. We heard their yells and witnessed The Darter's wave towards them as if it were fate, not anyone's fault. That afternoon we would pick up twenty greyhounds from a silent barge near the Church Ferry Stairs and deliver them in silence to another location downriver. We had not been aware of the existence of such moveable cargo, did not know of the strict laws countering the illegal importing of animals into Britain. But The Darter appeared to know everything.

Our theories about The Darter's style of walking in a crouch completely changed when he took us onto that mussel boat. Rachel and I moved cautiously down the slippery ramp, while The Darter barely watched what he was doing, half turning to make sure Rachel did not miss her footing while simultaneously tossing his cigarette into the four-inch gap between the embankment and the lilting boat. Steps that felt hazardous to us were an easy dance floor for him, and that wary crouch was now replaced by casualness as he moved along the foot-wide gunwales covered in rain and grease. He later claimed he had been conceived during a twenty-four-hour storm on the river. His ancestors were generations of lightermen and thus he had a river body that showed an accent only on land. He knew every tideway between Twickenham and Lower Hope Point and could identify docks by their smell or the sound of loading cargo. His father had been "a freeman of the river," he boasted; this in spite of the fact that he also spoke of him as a cruel man who'd forced him into the boxing profession in his teens.

The Darter also had a mouthful of whistles, for every barge, he told us, had its own signal. You learned it when starting work on a new boat. It was the only signal you were allowed to use over the water as a recognition or a warning, and each whistle was based on a bird call. He'd met river people, he said, who walking in a landlocked forest had suddenly heard their own barge whistle though there was no river in sight. It turned out to be a kestrel protecting its nest, a breed of bird that must have once lived by a river a hundred years before, whose sound had been borrowed and learned by generations of bargemen.

After that weekend, I wanted to keep helping The Darter with the dogs, but Rachel began spending more time with The Moth. I suspected she wanted to be more of an adult. But I'd be waiting for The Darter in my waterproof coat when he swung by in his car. He had barely concerned himself with me the first times we met at Ruvigny Gardens, when I was just some boy in a house he happened to be visiting. But I now discovered The Darter was an easy man to learn from. He cared less about you than The Moth did, but told you precisely what he needed you to do, as well as what about him was to be kept from others. "Breast your cards, Nathaniel," he'd say, "always breast your cards." What he needed, it turned out, was someone like me, a semi-reliable person to help him gather greyhounds two or three times a week from one of those silent European vessels, and so he persuaded me to leave my job at the restaurant and instead help him transport them in darkness on the mussel boat to various locations where a van would then spirit his living cargo further away.

We managed about twenty of those shy travellers on each boat ride. They sat shivering on deck during our journeys, which sometimes lasted as late as midnight, and were spooked easily by a loud noise or the searchlight of a launch suddenly alongside us. The Darter worried about what he called "preventative men," and it meant I had to nuzzle my way into their midst under the blankets and calm them in the fetid dog air as the river police slid by. "They're after more serious things," The Darter announced, justifying his low-level criminality.

It became clear that what we were delivering had in fact no guarantee of financial success. There was no assurance about these animals as racing dogs, no knowledge whether they were fast or slow. All that was valuable about them was that they provided "the unknown element" and, as the public was uncertain about their worth, it guaranteed reckless betting— bets made by strangers relying on looks as opposed to authentic bloodlines that could recommend them or reveal them as worthless. A reckless bet meant active money. You put pound notes on a dog with no past because of a seemingly knowing glance from the leashed creature or the line of its thigh, or the overheard whisperings of others you hoped might know but in truth did not. The dogs we had were wastrels with no recorded past, either kidnapped from a château or saved from a meat factory to be given a second chance. They were as anonymous as roosters.

On the moonless night river I calmed them by simply raising my teenage head in a gesture of strictness whenever they attempted to bark. I felt I was quieting an orchestra, and it had the charm and pleasure of first power. The Darter stood at the wheelhouse guiding us through the night, humming "But Not for Me." It always sounded like a sigh the way he sang it to himself, his mind elsewhere, barely conscious of the lyrics in his mouth. Besides, I knew the sadness of that song in no way reflected his intricately dovetailed relationships with women. I knew this from having to provide alibis for him or deliver false messages from a public phone box that would excuse his absence some evenings. Women could never be certain of his exact hours of work, let alone what the work actually was.

Those days and nights, as I began to enter the shadowy timetable of The Darter's life, I found myself within a confabulist pattern that drew together barge smugglers, veterinarians, forgers, and dog tracks in the Home Counties. Bribed veterinarians provided distemper shots to these aliens. Sometimes we needed temporary boarding kennels. Forgers typed up canine birth certificates to provide evidence of owners in Gloucestershire and Dorset, where the dogs had supposedly been whelped—dogs that had never heard a word of English till now.

That first magical summer of my life we smuggled more than forty-five dogs a week at the height of the racing season, collecting the gun-shy creatures from a dock near Limehouse onto the mussel boat, and riding the river in darkness into the heart of London towards Lower Thames Street. Then we travelled back downriver the way we had come, and those late-night river returns, the boat now empty of dogs, were the only moments The Darter was free of his complicated schedules and there would be no interruptions. I was curious now about The Darter's universe. And during those nights he talked openly about himself and the complexities of dog racing, and he occasionally questioned me. "You met Walter when you were very young? Isn't that so?" he asked me once. And when I looked at him, startled, he withdrew the sentence like a too-forward hand on a thigh. "Ahh, I see," he said.

When I asked him how he had met Olive Lawrence, I prefaced it by admitting to him that I liked her. "Oh, I noted that," he said. This was a surprise, for The Darter had always appeared unaware of and unconcerned with my responses.

"So, how did you meet her?"

He pointed to the cloudless sky. "I needed advice, and she is this specialist . . . a geographer, an *eth-nog-ra-pher*." He dragged the word out as she had done. "Who knew there were people like that? Who still read weather by the kind of moon it might be, or by the form of a cloud? Anyway, she was useful for something I was involved with, and I like women smarter than me.

Mind you, she is . . . well, she surprises you. Those ankles! I didn't think she'd walk out with me. She's Mayfair, you know what I mean? She likes the lipstick, the silk. She's a barrister's daughter, but I don't think the dad's going to help me out if I'm in trouble. Anyway, she was going on about lenticular clouds and anvil clouds and how to read a blue sky. Though it was the ankles I was leaning towards. She's got that greyhound line I appreciate, but you can never win, not with her. You can get hold of only a corner of her life. I mean, where is she now? Not a word from her. But still, that night with the goat, you know, I think she liked it. She wouldn't admit it, of course, but it was like signing a peace treaty during our dinner. Quite a dame . . . but not for me." I loved it when The Darter spoke this way, as if I were an equal who might understand those unstable subtleties in women. Besides, hearing another version of the goat incident was a further layering in the world that I was entering. I felt I was a caterpillar changing colour, precariously balanced, moving from one species of leaf to another.

We continued through the dark, quiet waters of the river, feeling we owned it, as far as the estuary. We passed industrial buildings, their lights muted, faint as stars, as if we were in a time capsule of the war years when blackouts and curfews had been in effect, when there was just warlight and only blind barges were allowed to move along this stretch of river. I watched the welterweight boxer whom I once had perceived as harsh and antagonistic turn and look towards me, talking gently as he searched for the precise words about the ankles of Olive Lawrence, and about her knowledge of cyan charts and wind systems. I realized he had probably stored away that information for some aspect of his work, even as it also diverted him from that slow blue pulse at her neck.

He grabbed my arm, placed it on the wheel, and walked over to the edge to relieve himself into the Thames. He exhaled a groan. He always had some soundtrack alongside his actions, and I suspect it was there during amorous moments when the pulse at Olive Lawrence's neck beat beneath a thin film of sweat. I recalled the first time I witnessed The Darter urinating, at the Dulwich Picture Gallery during a reconnaissance, whistling, the fingers of his right hand holding a cigarette as well as his penis, which was aimed towards the edge of the urinal. "Pointing Percy at the Porcelain," as he called it. Now, as I steered the barge, I could hear that dutiful soliloquy. *I've found more clouds of grey—than any Russian play—could guarantee.* He murmured it within the privacy of himself, womanless at this late hour.

The barge slowed. We moored up tight against the fenders of the dock and climbed out. It was one in the morning. We walked to his Morris and sat there for a moment, paused, as if we were attaching ourselves now to another element. Then his foot pressed the clutch, the key turned, and the noise of the car broke the silence. He always drove quickly, almost dangerously, through the crosshatching of narrow, unlit streets. These were parts of the city that since the war were only partially lived in. We passed streets of rubble, now and then a bonfire. He lit a cigarette and kept the windows open. It was never a straight route home, he weaved left, right, certain when to slow, suddenly turning into an unseen lane as if testing a getaway route.

Or did he need this risk taking to keep him awake at this hour? *Is it safe?* I mouthed The Moth's question silently into the air outside my window. Once or twice, if he thought I was not tired, The Darter climbed out with false weariness and took my place in the passenger seat to let me drive. He'd give a sidelong glance as I dealt with the clutch and cluttered over Cobbins Brook Bridge. Then we drifted into the inner suburbs, our conversations ended by now.

I was often exhausted by these far-flung duties I was given. Bone and blood tests needed to be fictionalized. False seals from the Greater London Greyhound Association had to be forged so our immigrants could enter any of the one hundred and fifty dog tracks in the country, as if they all were preparing to gather at the Count of Monte Cristo's ball with false identities. A vast mongrelization of pedigree dogs was taking place, and the greyhound industry would never recover from it. Before she departed, Olive Lawrence, upon discovering The Darter's scheme, had rolled her eyes and remarked, "What next? Imported foxhounds? An imported child stolen from the Bordeaux region?"

"Of course it would be Bordeaux," The Darter retaliated.

Still, it was our nights on the mussel boat I loved. The boat, originally a sailing kotter, had now been equipped with a modern diesel. The Darter was borrowing it from "a respected dockland merchant," who needed it only three days a week; unless, he warned us, a royal wedding was suddenly announced, which would mean the hurried importation of cheap crockery with a royal image fired up and shipped from some satanic mill in Le Havre. In that event the transportation of dogs would have to be postponed. It was a long grey boat, built in Holland, he said, which used to coast low over mussel fields. It was distinct from other barges, and a rare object on the Thames. The ballast tank in the hold could open and fill with salt water, so that the gathered mussels could be stored and kept fresh until arriving at port. But the main virtue of the kotter for us was its shallow draught, which allowed us to travel the length of the Thames, from the estuary to as far west as Richmond, even Teddington where the river was too shallow for most tugs and barges. The Darter could also use it for other dealings, when he travelled into the channels and canals that led north and east out of the Thames towards Newton's Pool and Waltham Abbey.

I still hold on to those names... Erith Reach, Caspian Wharf, as well as the streets I drove with The Darter, long past midnight into the city. We would have just completed one of our turbulent barge journeys and he would be trying to keep me awake by telling me plots of some of his favourite films. His voice took on an aristocratic pitch as he reenacted lines of dialogue from *Trouble in Paradise*: "Do you remember the man who walked into the Bank of Constantinople and walked out with the Bank of Constantinople? I am that man!" The car barrelled along the unlit roads, and he would turn towards me to regale me about Olive Lawrence's habits during an argument, or rattle off the names of the key streets we were driving through—Crooked Mile, Sewardstone Street, or a cemetery we were passing—saying, "Learn these by heart, Nathaniel, in case I have to send you off one night on your own." We moved at speeds so high we often reached the city in less than half an hour. Now and then there'd be lyrics The Darter would sing out loud, about *"the bride—with the guy on the side"* or *"the dame—who was known as the flame."* He did this jauntily, suddenly gesturing with his arm as if he had to interrupt himself to remember one more example of deceitful passion that had just occurred to him.

Greyhound racing was already a jubilantly illegal profession. Millions of pounds changed hands. Huge crowds came to White City Stadium or the Bridge at Fulham, or visited the temporary tracks that had sprung up all over the country. The Darter had not leapt quickly into the business. First of all he investigated the territory. The sport had a pariah-like status and he knew there would eventually be government controls. Stern editorials in the *Daily Herald* were warning the public that there existed in greyhound racing "a moral decline that derived from passive leisure." But The Darter did not feel the public's leisure was passive. He'd been at Harringay when, after a three-to-one favourite was disqualified, the crowd burned the starting traps to the ground, he being one of many who was knocked flat by a water hose manned by the police. He guessed there would soon be dog licences, recorded bloodlines, stopwatches, even rules for the official speed of the mechanical hare. The possibilities of chance would grow small, betting would be based on reason. He needed to locate or invent a quick, slender entrance into the business, something up to now hidden from view, and squeeze himself into that margin between what had been thought about and what had not yet been considered. And what The Darter saw at the dog tracks was unjudgeable talent among indistinguishable creatures.

By the time we ran into him at Ruvigny Gardens he was importing a dubious population of unregistered foreign dogs. He had already spent a few years in the shifting tents of spivery. He had finessed the art of doping, not so much to give dogs strength and endurance, but to cause a hypnotic slowness in them, by feeding them Luminal, a tranquilliser used for epileptic seizures. The procedure involved careful timing. If they were given it too close to the beginning of a race, the animals would tumble into sleep in their starting gates and have to be carried away by one of the bowler-hatted stewards. But with a two-hour interval between consumption and the race they would run convincingly, then become dizzy when cornering the bends. Luminal-flavoured liver was administered to a particular group of dogs—for instance brindle dogs, or male dogs—so you could avoid betting on them.

Other concoctions invented on someone's home chemistry set were tried. Dogs fed liquids gathered from human genitalia infected with a social disease suddenly became distracted by itching or were overpowered by unwanted erections and slowed down during the last hundred yards. The Darter then started using chloretone tablets, bought in bulk from a dentist and dissolved in hot water. Once again a hypnotic trance ensued. North American park rangers, he said, had been using it to anaesthetize trout during their tagging process.

Where and when in his past had The Darter learned about such chemical and medicinal information? I knew he was a curious man and could extract information from anyone, even an innocent chemist sitting next to him on a bus. Much the way he had picked up details about weather systems from Olive Lawrence. Yet he did not reveal himself easily. A trait perhaps left over from his days as the boxer from Pimlico, when he was light on his feet while verbally solemn, enigmatic but curious about another's body language—a counterpuncher, a close observer, and then a mocker of another man's style. It was much later that I would make the connection between his familiarity with such drugs and his awareness of my sister's epilepsy.

By the time I began working with him the golden years of doping were almost over. Thirty-four million people were attending greyhound races a year. But now the racing clubs were setting up saliva and urine tests, so The Darter needed to find another solution where betting on dogs would once again not rely only on logic and talent. What followed was The Darter's use of imposters or ringers in order to bring confusion and chance back to the tracks, and I became fully caught up in his plans, accompanying him as often as I could on his barge, the flood tides carrying us into or out of London on those night journeys I sometimes still yearn for.

It had been a torrid summer. We were not always confined to the mussel boat. Sometimes we picked up four or five dogs from a well-hidden Anderson shelter in Ealing Park Gardens and drove out of London with them in the back seat, peering out from the Morris expressionless as royalty. At a small-town gymkhana we raced them against the local dogs, watched them dart like cabbage whites across the marked fields, then drove back to London with more money in The Darter's pocket, the dogs sprawled exhausted behind us. They were always eager to run, often in any direction.

Whether our imported ringers would be natural racers or collapse from distemper we never knew. But no one else did either, which was its financial charm. All we knew of the dogs lounging behind us as we drove towards Somerset or Cheshire was that they were fresh off the boat. The Darter never bet on them. They were simply there like useless cards in a deck to camouflage a favourite. Amateur tracks were sprouting up everywhere and we followed every rumour of them. I'd be struggling with a large unfolding local map, searching for a village or a refugee camp that had an unofficial third-rate track. In some of them dogs chased a bunch of pigeon feathers tied to a branch dragged by a car in an open field. One track we visited used a mechanical rat.

I remember on those drives how The Darter, whenever he stopped at a traffic light, would lean back to stroke the scared animals gently. I do not believe it was because he loved dogs. But he knew they had stepped on English soil only a day or so earlier. Perhaps he thought it would calm them, make them feel they owed him something when they raced for him on those distant tracks a few hours later. They would be with him only a short time, and by the end of the day there would be fewer dogs returning to London. Some would simply not have stopped racing and would have disappeared into the woods, never to be seen again. One or two he'd sell to a vicar in Yeovil or maybe to someone at the Polish refugee camp in Dodding-ton Park. There was never sentimentality in The Darter about heritage or ownership. He scorned bloodlines among dogs as well as humans. "It's never your family that's the problem," he announced, as if quoting some surprisingly overlooked line from the Book of Job, "it's your damn relatives! Ignore them! Find out who can be a valuable father. It's important to disturb rare bloodlines with changelings." The Darter had never kept in touch with his own family. After all, they had practically sold him into the Pimlico boxing rings at sixteen.

One evening he entered 13 Ruvigny Gardens carrying a heavy book he had removed with difficulty from a local post office, where it had been chained to the counter. It was a ledger published by the Greyhound Association eager to warn the public of "track spivery," listing all persons suspected of criminal offences. Besides mug shots—some of them blurry and some of them vain—there was a list of incidents that ranged from forgery to the printing of tote tickets, as well as doping, race fixing, pickpocketing, and even warning of those who "coursed" through crowds with an intent to seduce. The Darter asked Rachel and me to leaf through the three-hundred-page list of criminals and find him there. But of course we could not. "They have absolutely no idea who I am!" he exclaimed proudly.

He was by now sophisticated in his methods of tunnelling under the rules of dog racing. And he once confessed to us somewhat shyly about his first upsetting of the rules. He had thrown a live cat onto the track during a race. The dog he had put his money on—it was his first and last bet—had accidentally bounced off a fence at the first bend. Now a cat had been flung in front of the other dogs, who became so distracted that the only object still continuing the race was the mechanical hare, aided by a two-horsepower motor that ran at 1,500 revs per minute. The race was declared void, the cat disappeared, as did The Darter after getting his original stake back.

None of The Darter's lady friends ever wished to accompany him on these out-of-town journeys, but never having had a dog in my life I chose to sit in the back with their heat-seeking muzzles reaching over to rest on my shoulder. They were quick, mischievous company for a boy who was a solitary.

We reentered the city around dusk, the dogs asleep against one another. Not even the blaze of city lights woke them, not even a crust from one of The Darter's sandwiches tossed back over his shoulder a half-hour earlier. It turned out The Darter had a dinner engagement he wished to keep, and he persuaded me to take his Morris and return the dogs to the Anderson shelter in Ealing Park Gardens. He would be forever in my debt. I dropped him off at a Tube station to meet a new paramour, the scent of greyhounds still on his clothes. I had no licence, but I had a car. I kept the dogs with me and drove out of the depths of the city towards Mill Hill.

I was to meet Agnes in another of those empty houses, and I rolled the windows down as I arrived to give the dogs air. I walked towards the house, turned and saw them watching me tragically, spectres of disappointment. Agnes opened the door. "One minute," I said. I ran back and ushered the dogs into the small front garden so they could relieve themselves. I was herding them back into the Morris when she suggested we all come in. Without a pause they rushed past me and leapt into the darkness of the house.

We left the keys at the foot of the front door and followed the excited barking. Once again there was no possibility of turning lights on in the three-storey building. This was the largest house either of us had been in, and it was undamaged. Her brother was moving up in the post-war property world. We heated two cans of soup on the blue circle of gas, then settled in on the second floor so we could watch each other and talk in the spill of a streetlight. We were more at ease now, there was less tension as to what would, could, and should not happen between us. We drank the soup. The dogs rushed into the room and out again. We had not seen each other for a while, and if we hoped our night would be passionate, it would be, but not in the way we expected. I didn't know enough about Agnes's past, but as I said, no dog had ever entered the rooms of my childhood, and now in the large semi-dark rooms of this borrowed house, we wrestled them to the ground, their long mouths warm against our bare hearts. We raced from one room to another, avoiding street-lit windows, signalling each other with whistles. One dog was caught simultaneously in both her and my arms. She turned her face up to the ceiling and howled through it to the moon. The dogs like pale ant-eaters in the half-light. We followed them into distant rooms. We met them coming down the strict narrow darkness of the stairs.

"Where are you?"

"Behind you."

Car lights filled a window and I saw Agnes naked to the waist with a hound hanging off her hip as she lifted it down to a lower landing, the one we had discovered was nervous of stairs: a sacred moment in my life I carry secure within whatever few memories I hold from that time, filed and labelled in that half-completed way. Agnes, with dog. Unlike other memories it has a location and a date—it was during the last days of that torrid summer—and there is a wish in me to know if that long-ago teenage friend of mine still remembers and thinks of that series of borrowed houses in East London and North London and the three-storey house in Mill Hill where we crashed our bodies into dogs that were in chaotic delight after being restrained for hours in the back seat of a car, now scattering their racing claws like high heels up and down the carpetless stairs. It was as if Agnes and I had given up every desire except to run alongside their high-pitched barking and pointless virility.

We were reduced to being servants, butlers, providing fresh bowls of water that they slurped without grace, or throwing remnants of our stolen sandwiches into the air, so they were leaping high as our heads. They ignored thunder when it came, but when it began to rain they paused and veered towards the large windows and with tilted heads listened to its suggestive clicks. "Let's stay the night," she said. And when they curled up to sleep we slept on the floor beside them as if all around us these animals were our longed-for life, our wished-for company, a wild unnecessary essential unforgotten human moment in London during those years. When I woke, a dog's thin sleeping face was beside me, breathing calmly into mine, busy with its dreams. It heard the change in my waking breath and opened its eyes. Then shifted position and placed its paw on my forehead gently, either as a gesture of careful compassion or superiority. It felt like wisdom. "Where are you from?" I asked it. "What country? Will you tell me?" I turned and saw Agnes standing, already dressed, her hands in her pockets, watching and listening to me.

Agnes of World's End. Of Agnes Street, of Mill Hill, and Limeburner's Yard where she had lost that cocktail dress. I knew even then I needed to keep this part of my life away from The Darter and The Moth. Theirs was the world I was living in after my parents disappeared. And the world of Agnes was where I now escaped to alone.

*

It was now autumn. The race tracks and gymkhanas were closing down. But I was still so much a participant and essential go-between in The Darter's world that he would find it easy to persuade me to skip school when term started. It began with missing just two days a week but I would soon be claiming a host of illnesses, from mumps, which I had just read about, to whatever disease was going around, and with my new contacts I could provide forged letters about my health. Rachel knew about some of this, especially when it had progressed to three days a week, but The Darter cautioned me not to tell The Moth, giving one of those complex waves of his hand that I knew how to interpret by then. In any case, this was more intriguing work than the time I was supposed to be spending preparing for my School Certificate exams.

The Darter's mussel boat began drifting with a new purpose. These days he was transporting European china for "the respected dockland merchant." Boxed cargo was more manageable than greyhounds, but he claimed to have a bad back, and so needed help—"too much sex standing up in a dark mews or cul-de-sac. . . ." He tossed the line out like a spectacular morsel. So he persuaded Rachel back onto our boat on the weekends for an extra shilling or two, and we now found ourselves travelling up narrow canals that ran north from the Thames, which we had been unaware of till then. Our starting points and destinations always varied. It might be the rear entrance of the Custom House at Canning Town, or we might find ourselves floating along the shallow streams by Rotherhithe Mill. There was no longer a need to silence twenty dogs, and it was daylight work and autumn silence. The days grew colder.

Being so much in The Darter's company, I was now at ease with him. Sunday mornings as the barge travelled under the trees, he sat on a crate and searched through newspapers for any upper-class scandals, reading choice ones out loud. "Nathaniel—the Earl of Wiltshire has accidentally asphyxiated himself by tying a rope round his neck then tying the other end to a large lawn roller while half naked. . . ." He refused to explain why a person in the nobility might do this. In any case, the lawn's gentle slope meant the roller had serenely continued downhill pulling the Earl's undressed body along with it and strangling him. The lawn roller, the *News of the World* concluded, had been in the Earl's family for three generations. My more serious sister ignored such stories and concentrated on learning her lines in *Julius Caesar,* for she was to play Marc Antony in the school play that term. By this point I was simply expecting to fail my School Certificate exams and ignored rereading *Swallows and Amazons,* that "crap book" as The Darter had called it.

Now and then he would lean his head back and attempt a conversation with me, showing concern as to how I was doing at school. "Fine," I would say.

"And your mathematics—do you know what an isosceles triangle is?"

"Yes, of course."

"Splendid."

Not that we are touched by such things as concern, even if false, when we are young. But now, in retrospect, I am touched.

We steered our way up a narrowing cut. It was a different atmosphere now, with sunlight falling through yellowing leaves, the smell of wet earth rising from the riverbanks. We had loaded the barge with boxes at Limehouse Reach, where The Darter said they made quicklime centuries earlier. Immigrants disembarked there from the East India ships and walked into the new country without a common language. I told The Darter I had heard a Sherlock Holmes mystery on the radio called "The Man with the Twisted Lip" that took place where we'd loaded the china that morning, but he shook his head doubtfully, as if literature had nothing to do with the world he belonged in. The only books I'd seen him read were westerns and bodice rippers, specifically one that merged the two genres called *Kicking Whores Pass*.

One afternoon we needed to urge the barge between the narrowing banks of the Romford Canal, my sister and I stationed on opposite sides of the deck yelling directions to The Darter at the wheel. The last hundred yards of the cut were almost fully overgrown. At its end there was a lorry waiting, and two men approached the boat and unloaded the boxes wordlessly, The Darter barely acknowledging them. Then we reversed the barge like a cornered dog for a quarter of a mile until the channel became wider.

Romford Canal was just one of our destinations. Another journey took us along Gunpowder Mills Canal. At one time only shallow-draught powder boats and ballast barges had travelled along it, transporting munitions. The innocent-looking canal had been used for this purpose for almost two hundred years because at the end of it was Waltham Abbey, a gentle edifice lived in by monks as far back as the twelfth century. During the recent war, thousands had worked on the grounds of the abbey, and its explosives were transported along those same cuts and tributaries down to the Thames. It was always less dangerous to transport munitions on quiet waterways than on public roads. Sometimes the roped barges were pulled along by horses, sometimes by teams of men on either side of the canal.

But now the munitions factories had been dismantled and the unused canals were silting up, becoming narrower between their overgrown banks. And on weekends this was where

Rachel and I, the sidekicks of The Darter, now floated in the silence of those waterways, listening to a new generation of birdsong. What we carried was probably not dangerous, but we were never sure. And after our constantly changing routes and destinations, Rachel and I no longer fully believed The Darter's stories about the delivery of European china to pay back the merchant who had let him borrow his barge during dog-racing seasons.

In any case, until the weather turned harsh, we travelled those barely used waterways, guiding the boat along the narrowing rivers. The Darter with his shirt off, his white-ribbed chest bare to the October sun, and my sister memorizing her exits and entrances for *Julius Caesar*. Until the brown stones of Waltham Abbey rose into view.

We sidled towards the bank and once again heard whistles and once again men appeared and loaded our boxes onto a nearby lorry. Again no words were passed between us. The Darter stood there half dressed and watched them with not even an acknowledgement or nod of his head. His hand was on my shoulder, which committed me to him, or him to me, and it made me feel safe. The men departed, the lorry bouncing away under the overhanging branches up a dirt road. The sight of two teenagers in a boat, one bent over her schoolwork, one with a rakish school cap on his head, must have seemed innocent enough.

What kind of family were we a part of now? In retrospect Rachel and I were not too different in our anonymity from the dogs with their fictional papers. Like them we had broken free, adapting to fewer rules, less order. But what had we become? When you are uncertain about which way to go as a youth, you end up sometimes not so much repressed, as might be expected, but illegal, you find yourself easily invisible, unrecognized in the world. Who was *Stitch* now? Who was *Wren*? Did my assignations with Agnes insert a thief's guile into my nature? Or my escapes from school to spend time with The Darter? Not because of the pleasure or gall of it, but because of the tension and risk? When my report card arrived I boiled a kettle and steamed open the official envelope to discover my marks. The comments by teachers were so dismissive I was embarrassed to hand it over to The Moth, who was to hold it for my parents' return. I burned its pages on the gas stove. There was just too much information. The days I missed school were legion. And words such as "mediocre" appeared on almost every entry like a chant. I tucked the ashes under the carpet on one of the stair steps, as if back into an envelope, and for the rest of the week complained that while Rachel's report had arrived, mine had not.

Most of the laws I broke during that period of my life were small. Agnes stole food from the restaurants she worked in, until one evening, before leaving work, she tucked a thick slice of frozen ham under her armpit. Held up with last-minute errands, hypothermia got to her and she fainted at the entrance, the ham sliding out from under her blouse onto the linoleum. Somehow the concern for her—she was popular—made her employers ignore the crime.

The Moth kept reminding us still of *schwer* and to prepare for serious times. But I skated over and ignored what might be heavy or indigestible. The illegal world felt more magical than dangerous to me. Even being introduced by The Darter to someone like the great Forger of Letchworth thrilled me, just as Agnes's shifting rules did.

Our parents had been gone beyond the promised year—and the spirit level or whatever it was tilted in Rachel. She was now a night person, The Moth recommending her to his friend the opera singer to get her a part-time job in the evenings at Covent Garden. Anything to do with stage work fascinated Rachel—the floppy sheet of metal that produced the sound of thunder, trapdoors, stage smoke, blue reflections of limelight. Just as I had been altered by The Darter, Rachel now evolved into the world of theatre, becoming a stage prompter, not to nudge the tenors on their Italian or French arias, but for the props department who needed a cue to hurry on stage with cloth rivers, or to dismantle a city wall in sixty seconds of darkness. So our days and nights did not feel like the time of the *schwer* that The Moth had warned us about. They were to us wondrous doorways into the world.

One night, after spending a long evening with Agnes, I was travelling home on the Underground. I needed to make numerous changes to return to central London and I was sleepy. I got off the Piccadilly Line at Aldwych and walked into a lift that I knew always shook and rattled up three levels from the depths of the Tube station. The deserted space in that slow-moving lift could have held fifty commuters during rush hour, but now there was only me. A dim globe light hung in the centre of it. A man came in after me carrying a walking stick. Another man came up behind him. The scissored gate closed and the lift began to move up slowly in the dark. Every ten seconds, as we passed each floor, I could see them watching me. One was the man who had followed Agnes and me onto the bus weeks earlier. He swung his stick, shattering the bulb while the other pulled the emergency lever. An alarm went off. The brakes jammed. Suddenly we were hanging in midair, bouncing on the balls of our feet, trying to keep our balance within that dark hanging cage.

My bored evenings at the Criterion saved me. I knew most lifts had a switch at shoulder or ankle level to free the brake. One or the other. I backed into a corner of the cage as the two men moved towards me. I felt it at my ankle, kicked the locked brake free, and it released. Red lights pulsed in our cage. The lift began moving again and then the doors scissored open onto street level. The two men stepped back, and the one with the stick flung it into the middle of the floor. I was running into the night.

I got home scared, half laughing. The Moth was there and I told him of my clever escape—that lift at the Criterion had taught me something. They must have thought I had money, I said.

*

A man named Arthur McCash slipped into our house the next day, The Moth announcing he was a friend he had invited for dinner. He was tall and skeletal. Spectacles. A shock of brown hair. One could tell he would always have the presence of a boy in his last year at college. A bit too frail for group sports. Squash perhaps. But this first image of him was inaccurate. I remember he was the only person at the table that first night able to unscrew the cap off an old bottle of mustard. He torqued it open casually and left it on the table. With his sleeves rolled up, I saw the powerful string of muscles along his arms.

What did we ever really know or discover about Arthur McCash? He spoke French, as well as other languages, though he never referred to this ability. Perhaps he assumed he would be mocked. There was even a rumour, or was it a joke, that he knew Esperanto, the supposed universal language, which no one spoke. Olive Lawrence, who spoke Aramaic, might have appreciated such knowledge, but she had left us by then. McCash claimed he'd recently been stationed abroad doing crop studies in the Levant. Later I would be told that the character of Simon Boulderstone in Olivia Manning's *Fortunes of War* may have been based on him. In retrospect it feels almost believable—he did seem part of another era, one of those Englishmen who are happier in desert climates.

Unlike other guests, McCash was quiet and modest. He somehow always positioned himself alongside whoever was arguing loudly—it meant he was not expected to intercede at all. He nodded over a questionable joke, though he never told any—save for a surprising night when, possibly intoxicated, he recited a limerick that involved Alfred Lunt and Noël Coward, which startled the room. It was never quite remembered properly even the next day by those who had been near him.

Arthur McCash would confuse my understanding of The Moth's activities. What was he doing in this company? He seemed unlike the rest of that opinionated group, behaving as if powerless and without self-worth, or perhaps with so much that he did not wish to expose it. He kept to himself. It is only now I recognize that there may have been in him a shyness, possibly disguising another self. Rachel and I were not the only ones who were young.

I am still unable to give precise ages to the individuals who had taken over our parents' home. There's no trustworthy recording of ages when seen through the eyes of youth, and I suppose the war had further confused the way we read age or the hierarchies of class. The Moth felt the same age as my parents. The Darter a few years younger, but only because he appeared less controllable. Olive Lawrence younger still. She appeared that way, I think, because she was always glancing to see what she could go towards, what might capture her and change her life. She was open to alteration. Give her ten years and she could have a different sense of humour, whereas The Darter, though full of shadowed surprises, was clearly on a path he had beaten down and travelled along for years. He was incorrigible, that was his charm. That was the safety in him for us.

I got off the train at Victoria Station the next afternoon and felt a hand on my shoulder. "Come with me, Nathaniel. Let us have a tea together. Here, let me take your satchel. It looks heavy." Arthur McCash took hold of my school bag and walked towards one of the railway cafeterias. "What are you reading?" he said over his shoulder, but kept walking. He bought two scones and some tea. We sat down. He wiped the oilcloth on the table with a paper napkin before leaning his elbows on it. I kept thinking of him coming up behind me and touching my shoulder, taking my satchel. They were not usual gestures for someone who was essentially a stranger. The train announcements, loud and incomprehensible, continued above us.

"My favourite writers are French," he said. "Can you speak French?"

I shook my head. "My mother can speak French," I said. "But I don't know where she is." I surprised myself at mentioning this so easily.

He looked at the side of his cup. After a moment he lifted it and slowly drank the hot tea, watching me over the brim. I stared back. He was an acquaintance of The Moth, he had been in our house.

"I must give you some Sherlock Holmes," he said. "I think you will like him."

"I've heard him on the radio."

"But read him as well." Then he began quoting something as if in a trance, intoning in a high, clipped voice.

"I was certainly surprised to find you there, Holmes."

"But not more so than I to find you."

"I came to find a friend."

"And I to find an enemy."

The quiet McCash seemed energized by his own performances, which made the lines funny.

"I hear you had a close call in one of the Underground

lifts. . . . Walter told me about it." And he proceeded to ask me about it in detail, exactly where it had happened, and what the men looked like. Then, after a pause, he said, "Your mother is probably concerned, don't you think? Being out that late at night?"

I stared at him. "Where is she?"

"Your mother is away. Doing something important."

"Where is she? Is it dangerous for her?"

He made a gesture as if sealing his lips and stood up.

I was unnerved. "Shall I tell my sister?"

"I have spoken with Rachel," he said. "Your mother's all right. Just be careful."

I watched him disappear into the crowd at the station.

It had felt like an unravelling dream. But the next day, arriving at Ruvigny Gardens again, he slipped me a paperback of Conan Doyle stories, and I began to read them. Yet although I was full of curiosity for answers to what was happening in our lives, there were for me no fog-filled streets or back alleys where I might find clues as to my mother's whereabouts, or what Arthur McCash was doing in our house.

*

"'I used often to lie awake through the whole night, and wish for a large pearl.'"

I was almost asleep. "What?" I said.

"Something I read in a book. Some old man's wish. I still remember it. I say it to myself every night." Agnes's head on my shoulder, her eyes looking at me through the dark. "Tell me something," she whispered. "Something you remember . . . like that."

"I . . . I can't think of anything."

"Anything. Who you like. What you like."

"I suppose my sister."

"What do you like about her?"

I shrugged and she could feel that. "I don't know. I barely see her now. I suppose we felt safe around each other."

"You mean you don't feel safe, not usually?"

"I don't know."

"Why don't you feel safe? Don't just shrug."

I looked up into the dark of the large empty room we were sleeping in.

"What are your parents like, Nathaniel?"

"They're all right. He works in the city."

"Perhaps you can ask me over to your house?"

"Okay."

"When?"

"I don't know. I don't think you will like them."

"So they're all right, but I won't like them?"

I laughed. "They're just not interesting," I said.

"Like me?"

"No. You're interesting."

"In what way?"

"I'm not sure."

She was silent.

I said, "I feel anything can happen with you."

"I'm a working girl. I got an accent. You probably don't want me meeting your parents."

"You don't understand, it's a strange household now. Really strange."

"Why?"

"There are always these people there. Strange people."

"So I'll fit in." More silence, waiting for me to answer her. "Will you come over to my flat? Meet my parents?"

"Yes."

"Yes?"

"Yes. I'd like that."

"That's surprising. You don't want me in your house, but you'll come to mine."

I said nothing. Then, "I love your voice."

"Fuck you." Her head moved away in the darkness.

Where were we that night? Which house? What part of London? It could have been anywhere. There was no one I liked as much to have beside me. And at the same moment there was a relief in us being possibly finished. Because even if I felt most at ease with this girl who had pulled me through, into, and out of those houses, with all the questioning that came so naturally to her, it was becoming too difficult to explain my double life. In a way I liked it that I knew nothing about her. I did not know her parents' names. I had never asked her what they did. I was curious only about her, even if Agnes Street was not her name but simply the location of the first house we went to in some borough I've now forgotten. She had once grudgingly told me her real name as we worked side by side in the restaurant. She did not like it, she'd said, and wanted a better one, especially after hearing mine. She'd mocked the poshness of "Nathaniel" at first, its pretentiousness, dragging it out even to four syllables. And then, after mocking my name in front of the others, she'd come across me silent during a lunch break and asked if she could "borrow" that piece of ham out of my sandwich. And I had not known what to say.

I never did with her. She was the talker, but I knew she longed to be the listener as well, in the way she wanted to embrace everything that was taking place around her. Just as she had insisted the greyhounds come into the house when I turned up that night in The Darter's car, so they had bounded in between her legs and later bent and focused their arrow-like faces towards the sound of our breathing when we were in each other's arms.

I did eventually have a dinner with her parents. I had to turn up at her restaurant and go back into the kitchens several times before she actually believed me. She must have felt I was just attempting politeness. We had not been alone since the night she had proposed it in the dark. They lived in a one-and-a-half-room council flat, so she moved her mattress into the living room at night. I watched her gentleness with her quiet parents, how she calmed their awkwardness around me. The wildness and sense of adventure I knew in Agnes from work and in those houses we met in did not exist here. Instead I became aware of her determination to escape her world, working eight hours a day, lying about her age so she could take the night shifts whenever possible.

She was inhaling the world around her. She wanted to understand every skill, everything people spoke about. With my silence I was probably a nightmare to her. She must have thought I was born with distance in me, secretive about what I feared, secretive about my family. Then one day she ran into me with The Darter and so I introduced him to her as my father.

The Darter was the only one of that cobbled-together group haunting Ruvigny Gardens whom Agnes was to meet. I needed to invent a situation where my mother travelled a great deal. I had become a liar not so much to confuse her as to remove the hurt she felt because I kept the inexplicable situation in my life from her—and perhaps from myself as well. But meeting The Darter was enough for Agnes to feel accepted. Now I had made my life clearer to her, if more confusing to myself.

The Darter, in this sudden new role as my father, took on a protective and avuncular air with Agnes. She, surprised by his manner, thought he was a "card." He invited her to a dog track one Saturday, and this finally provided her with an explanation as to how I had turned up that night in Mill Hill with four greyhounds. "The greatest night of my life, so far," she murmured to him. She loved arguing with The Darter. And I saw instantly what Olive Lawrence found enjoyable in his company. If he allowed himself a questionable remark, he would let Agnes grab him by the neck and attempt to strangle him. I was invited over for a further dinner at her shy parents', with my father, and he brought a bottle of foreign alcohol in an attempt to impress them. Hardly anyone did that in those days. Most people did not even own a corkscrew, so he took the bottle out onto the balcony and shattered the neck off on a railing. "Watch for glass," he announced cheerfully. He wondered if anyone at the table had ever eaten goat. "Nathaniel's mother loves it," he announced. He proposed changing the station on the radio from the Home Service to some livelier music so he could have a dance with Agnes's mother, who gave a terrified laugh and clung to her chair. I listened forensically to everything he said that evening, making sure he got the correct name of my school, my mother's name, and the rest of our prepared plot—for instance, that my mother was now up in the Hebrides for work reasons. The Darter enjoyed this verbose patriarchal role, though his preference was always to get others talking.

He got on with the parents but he loved Agnes, and so I came to love Agnes too. I started to recognize aspects of her through The Darter's eyes. He had that quick awareness about people. She walked with us after the meal down the stairs of the council flat building, and then to the car. "Of course! The Morris," she said, "which brought the dogs!" And if I felt any nervousness about the replacement of my real father with The

Darter, it subsided. After that Agnes and I would laugh over my father's excessive manners. So when I was with my sister and this supposed father floating up the River Lee in the borrowed barge, I almost began to see the three of us as a believable family unit.

One weekend The Moth had insisted on taking my sister somewhere, so I suggested Agnes replace her on the barge. The Darter hesitated but liked the idea of this pistol, as he called her, coming with us. She may have had a confused version of The Darter's profession but she was flabbergasted by where we took her. This was not an England she knew. We'd gone barely a hundred yards alongside Newton's Pool when she dove off the barge in her cotton dress. Then clambered from the water onto the bank, white as porcelain, covered in mud. "That's a too-caged greyhound," I heard him say behind me. I just watched. She beckoned us over and climbed back into the boat and stood there, the cold autumn clinging to her in the sunlight, pools of water at her feet. "Give me your shirt," she said. When we tied up at Newton's Pool we ate our lunch of sandwiches.

There's another map I learned by heart that I still have clear in my memory, which distinguishes what was river and what was canal or cut in those waterways north of the Thames. And where three locks existed and we had to pause for twenty minutes while river water was admitted into or released out of the dark chambers in which we hung, so we could rise or drop to another height, Agnes in awe as that old industrial machinery rolled and clambered around us. It was the unknown brave old world for her, this seventeen-year-old who usually was tethered to just what was allowed her by class and lack of money, a world she'd probably never leave, who had sadly recited that dream of the pearl. Those weekends were her first ventures into a rural world, and I knew she would always love The Darter for bringing her on what she assumed was his boat. She embraced me, still shivering in my shirt, for inviting her on this river journey. We moved under a panoply of passing trees, which simultaneously floated in the water below us. We entered the shadow of a narrow bridge, silent because The Darter insisted it was bad luck to talk or whistle or even sigh under any bridge. Such rules handed out by him—walking under ladders was not bad luck, but picking up a playing card on the street was tremendous luck—have followed me most of my life, and perhaps they have followed Agnes too.

Whenever The Darter read a newspaper or racing form he spread it on one thigh that was crossed over the other, and rested his head as if wearily on his hand. Always the same position. On one of those river afternoons I saw Agnes sketching him while he was lost in the intrigues of his Sunday paper. I got up and walked behind her, didn't stop, just glanced quickly down to see what she had done. It would be the only drawing I saw of hers apart from the one on butcher paper she had given me after that night storm. But it was not The Darter she was drawing, as I thought, but me. Just a youth looking towards something or someone. As if this was what I really was, perhaps would become, someone not intent on knowing himself but preoccupied with others. I recognized it even then as a truth. It was not a picture of me but about me. I was too shy to ask to look at it properly and I've no idea what happened to it. Perhaps she gave it to "my father," even if she did not believe her talent was anything special. She had worked at a day job from the age of fourteen, had never finished school, took an art course at a polytechnic on Wednesday nights that might offer a small window of escape. She would go to work the following morning energized by that other world. It was the one independent pleasure in her variously interlocked existence. During our evenings in borrowed buildings, she would wake suddenly from a deep sleep, see me watching her, and release a guilty and delicious smile. I suppose that was the moment I felt I belonged most to her.

That autumn our boat journeys must have been a glimpse of unattainable childhood for her—weekends with a boyfriend and his father. Agnes would chant, "Oh, I love your dad! You must love him too!" Then she would become curious again about my mother. The Darter, having never met her, was prone to excessive descriptions of her outfits as well as hairstyles. When it became clear he was modelling my mother on Olive Lawrence, it was easier for me to join in and insert more details beside his. With the help of such false information our life on the barge became even more domestic. In spite of its sparseness, the boat provided more furniture than the places where Agnes and I usually met. And there were now lock keepers she recognized and waved to as we passed. She brought a few pamphlets about the trees and about pond life, nameless to her until now. Then one about Waltham Abbey,

so she could rattle off information about what had been created there—guncotton in the 1860s, then bolt-action rifles,
carbines, submachine guns, flare pistols, mortar shells, all of
them made only miles north of the Thames at that monastery.
Agnes was a dry sponge for information, and after one or two
trips knew more about what had gone on at the abbey than the
lock keepers we passed. It was a monk, she told us, a monk! in
the thirteenth century who wrote about the formation of gunpowder, though being fearful of this discovery he had written
out the details in Latin.

There are times when I want to place those moments when
we were in the cuts and canals north of the Thames into other
hands, in order to understand what was happening to us. I had
lived a mostly harboured life. Now, cut loose by my parents, I
was consuming everything around me. Whatever our mother
was doing and wherever she was, I was strangely content. Even
though things were being kept from us.

I remember dancing with Agnes one night at a jazz club in
Bromley, The White Hart. It was a crowded dance floor, and
somewhere on the periphery I thought I caught sight of my
mother. I wheeled around but she was gone. All I hold from
that moment is the blur of a curious face, watching me.

"What is it? What is it?" Agnes asked.

"Nothing."

"Tell me."

"I thought I saw my mother."

"I thought she was away somewhere?"

"Yes, that's what I thought."

I stood very still, rigid on the heaving dance floor.

Is this how we discover the truth, evolve? By gathering together such unconfirmed fragments? Not only of my mother, but of Agnes, Rachel, Mr. Nkoma (and where is he now?). Will all of them who have remained incomplete and lost to me become clear and evident when I look back? Otherwise how do we survive that forty miles of bad terrain during adolescence that we crossed without any truthful awareness of ourselves? "The self is not the principal thing," was a half-wisdom Olive Lawrence murmured to me once.

I think now of those mysterious lorries that drove up to meet us in order to collect the unlabelled crates in silence, of the woman watching me dance with Agnes with, it seems in retrospect, such curiosity and pleasure. And the departure of Olive Lawrence, the entrance of Arthur McCash, the range of silences in The Moth . . . You return to that earlier time armed with the present, and no matter how dark that world was, you do not leave it unlit. You take your adult self with you. It is not to be a reliving, but a rewitnessing. Unless of course you wish, like my sister, to damn and enact revenge on the whole pack of them.

Schwer

It was almost Christmas and Rachel was in the back seat of the Morris with me. The Moth was taking us in The Darter's car to a small theatre called the Bark. We were supposed to meet him there. The Moth had parked in an alley alongside the theatre when a man got into the front seat beside him, put a hand behind his head and swung it forward, banging it against the steering wheel then against the door, pulled it back and did it again, even as someone else slid in next to Rachel and covered her face with a cloth, holding it there as she struggled, all the while watching me. *"Nathaniel Williams, right?"* It was the man on the bus when I was with Agnes, and again that night in the lift. Rachel's body collapsed into his lap. He reached over, grabbed my hair and put the same cloth over my face, saying, *"Nathaniel and Rachel, right?"* I already knew it must be chloroform and I didn't breathe, until I had to gasp it in. The *schwer,* I'd have thought if I had been conscious.

I woke in a large, barely lit room. I could hear singing. It felt miles away. I tried to mouth "the man on the bus" to myself so I would remember. Where was my sister? Then I must have slept again. A hand touched me in the darkness to pull me awake.

"Hello, Stitch."

I recognized my mother's voice. Then I heard her walk away. I lifted my head. I saw her dragging a chair across the floor. At a long table, at the other end of the room, I saw Arthur McCash sitting hunched over, blood on his white shirt. My mother sat down next to him.

"The blood," my mother said. "Whose is it?"

"Mine. Maybe Walter's too. When I picked him up. His head . . ."

"Not Rachel?"

"No."

"Are you certain?" she said.

"My blood, Rose." I was surprised he knew my mother's name. "Rachel's safe, somewhere in the theatre. I saw her carried inside. And we now have the boy."

She looked back and stared at me on the couch. I don't think she knew I was awake. She turned back to McCash and lowered her voice. "Because if she is not, I will publicly turn against all of you, none of you will be safe. This was your responsibility. This was the bargain. How did they get so close to my children?"

McCash pulled the sides of his jacket close together as if to keep himself secure. "We knew they were following Nathaniel. A group from Yugoslavia. Perhaps Italians. We're not sure yet."

Then they were talking about places I didn't know. She slipped her scarf off her neck and wrapped it like a bandage round his wrist.

"Where else?"

He pointed to his chest. "Mostly here," he said.

She moved closer. "All right. Oh, all right . . . all right." She kept saying those words as she opened up his shirt, tugging it free of the drying blood.

She reached for a vase on the table, threw the few flowers out and poured water from it onto his bare chest so she could see the cuts better. "Always knives," she murmured. "Felon often said they were going to come after us. Revenge. If not the survivors, the relatives, their children." She was swabbing the cuts on his stomach. I realized he must have got them protecting Rachel and me. "People don't forget. Not even children. Why should they. . . ." She sounded bitter.

McCash said nothing.

"What about Walter?"

"He might not make it. You need to take the boy and the girl away from here. There may be others."

"Yes . . . All right. All right . . ." She walked over to me, and bent down. She put her hand on my face, then lay beside me for a moment on the couch. "Hello."

"Hello. Where were you?"

"I'm back now."

"Such a curious dream . . ." I cannot remember now which one of us said that, which one of us murmured it into the arms of the other. I heard Arthur McCash stand up.

"I'll find Rachel." He passed us and disappeared. I heard later that he climbed every level of the narrow building, searching for my sister, hidden somewhere with The Darter. At first he couldn't find them. He went along the unlit hallways not sure if there were others still dangerous in the building. He entered rooms and whispered *"Wren,"* which was what my mother told him to say. If a door was sealed he broke it open and entered. He was bleeding again. He listened for breathing, said *"Wren"* again, as if a password, giving her time to believe him. *"Wren." "Wren."* Again and again, until *"Yes,"* she replied, not really sure, and so he found her crouched behind a painted stage landscape leaning against a wall, in The Darter's arms.

Sometime afterwards Rachel and I came down the carpeted stairs together. A small group was gathered in the lobby. Our mother, half a dozen men in plainclothes, who she said were there to protect us, McCash, The Darter. Two men in handcuffs lay on the ground, and separately a third, partially covered with a blanket, the face bloody, unrecognizable, gazing towards us. There was a gasp from Rachel. *"Who is that?"* A policeman bent down and pulled the blanket up over the face. Rachel began screaming. Then someone covered my sister's head and mine with coats so we were anonymous as we were led out onto the street. I could hear Rachel's muffled crying as we were bundled into separate vans, to be delivered to separate destinations.

Where were we going? Into another life.

PART TWO

INHERITANCE

In November of 1959, when I was twenty-eight, after some years of what had felt like wilderness, I bought a home for myself in a Suffolk village that could be reached by a few hours' train ride from London. It was a modest house with a walled garden. I purchased it without bartering over the cost with the owner, a Mrs. Malakite. I did not wish to argue with someone obviously distressed at having to sell the home she had lived in for most of her life. I also did not want to risk losing that particular property. It was a house I loved.

She did not remember me when she opened the door. "I am Nathaniel," I said, and reminded her of our appointment. We stood for a moment by the door, then walked into the par-lour. I said, "You have a walled garden," and she stopped in her tracks.

"How do you know that?"

She shook her head and walked on. She had been preparing to surprise me perhaps with the beauty of her garden when compared with the actual house. I had spoiled the revelation.

I told her quickly that I agreed to the proposed price. And because I knew there were plans for her to move soon into a retirement home, I arranged to come back and walk through the garden with her. She could show me the invisible details of it all then, give me some pointers about caring for the place.

I returned a few days later and once again I could see she barely remembered me. I brought a sketch pad and explained I wished her to help me locate where certain seeds of plants and vegetables were now buried. She liked the idea of that. As far as she was concerned, it might have been the first smart thing I had said. So together we created a map of the garden, copying it down from her memory, along with quick notes as to when certain plants would appear, and in which beds. I listed the vegetables that hemmed the greenhouse and skirted the brick wall. Her knowledge was detailed, clearly accurate. That was the segment in her memory from far in the past that she could still reach. It was also clear she had continued with the upkeep of the garden since the death of her husband, Mr. Malakite, two years earlier. Only the recent memories, with no one now to share them, had begun to evaporate.

We walked between the white-painted beehives and she produced from her apron pocket a wedge to raise the sodden ribs of wood so we could look into the lower level of the hive, the bees assaulted suddenly by sunlight. The old queen had been murdered, she told me casually. The hive would need a new one. I watched her stuff a piece of rag into the smoker and light it, and soon the queenless bees were quivering under the fumes she was puffing down on them. Then she sorted through the two levels of half-conscious bees. It was strange to consider their world being organized in such a godlike way by a woman who was remembering less and less of her own universe. Still it was clear watching and listening to her that details about the care of her garden and the three beehives and the heating of the angular greenhouse would be the last things forgotten.

"Where do the bees travel, when they are let out?"

"Oh . . ." She just gestured at the hills. "That sedge over there. Even as far as Halesworth, I wouldn't be surprised." She appeared sure about their tastes and familiar urges.

Her name was Linette and she was seventy-six. I knew that.

"You must feel you can always come back, Mrs. Malakite, to see the garden, your bees. . . ."

She turned from me without a word. Without even shaking her head she made it evident that it was a foolish thing to suggest, to return to where she'd lived all these years with her husband. There was much I could have said, but it would have insulted her more. And I had already been too sentimental.

"Are you from America?" she retaliated.

"I was there, once. But I grew up in London. For a while I lived near this village."

She was surprised by this and did not quite believe it.

"What do you do?"

"I work in the city. Three days a week."

"At what? Money, I suppose."

"No, it is sort of government work."

"Doing what?"

"Ah, that's the question. Various things . . ." I paused. I sounded ridiculous. I said, "I've always been comforted by the security of a walled garden, ever since my teens." I watched for any sign of interest from her, but all I could feel was that I was not making a good impression, she appeared to have lost all faith in me, this seemingly random fellow who had bought this place out from under her so casually. I tugged a sprig of rosemary off a bush, rubbed it between my fingers, inhaled it, and put it in my shirt pocket. I saw her watching my actions, as if trying to remember something. I held on to the diagram of the garden I'd drawn hastily that showed where she had planted leeks, snowdrops, asters, and phlox. Beyond the wall I could see the great spread of their mulberry tree.

The afternoon sunlight filled the walled garden, built to hold back tradewinds from the east coast. I had thought of this place so often. The warmth within its walls, its shaded light, the sense of safety I always found here. She kept watching me, as if I was a stranger in her garden, but in fact I could have composed her life. I knew a good deal about her years in this small Suffolk village with her husband. I could have entered and roamed within the story of their marriage as easily as I might have within the lives of others who had surrounded me in my youth, who were part of my self-portrait, composed from the way they had caught glimpses of me. Just as I now reflected Mrs. Malakite, standing in her cared-for garden during the last days of her ownership of it.

I used to wonder how affectionate and close the bond was between the Malakites. They were, after all, the only couple I saw regularly in my late teens, during those school breaks when I would stay with my mother. I had no other examples. Was theirs a relationship based on contentment? Did they irritate each other? I was never certain, for I was usually alone with Mr. Malakite, working in his fields or in what had once been victory gardens. He had his terrain, his certainties about soil, weather, and was somehow more at ease and varied when working alone. I used to hear him talking to my mother, and it was a different voice that spoke to her. He would actively propose she remove a hedge from the east side of her lawn, often laugh at her innocence about the natural world. Whereas with Mrs. Malakite he tended to leave the plans for an evening and the paths of conversations up to her.

Sam Malakite remained a mystery to me. No one really understands another's life or even death. I knew a veterinarian who had two parrots. The birds had lived together for years, even before she inherited them. Their feathers had a mixture of green and dark brown I found beautiful. I do not like parrots, but I liked the look of these two. Eventually one of them died. I sent a note of condolence to the veterinarian. And a week later, seeing her, I asked if the surviving bird was in a state of depression or at least at a loss. "Oh no," she said, "he's overjoyed!"

In any case, a couple of years after Mr. Malakite died, I bought and moved into their small timbered house protected by that walled garden. It had been a long time since I'd visited it regularly, but almost immediately a past that felt completely erased began returning. And there was a hunger towards it I never had when days had slipped past me at the speed of a blink. I was in The Darter's Morris and it was summer and the cloth roof of his car stretched up and folded back slowly. I was at a football match with Mr. Nkoma. I was in mid-river eating sandwiches with Sam Malakite. *"Listen,"* Sam Malakite says. *"A thrush."* And Agnes naked, to feel fully undressed, was pulling a green ribbon out of her hair.

That unforgotten thrush. That unforgettable ribbon.

*

After the attack in London, Rachel was enrolled quickly by my mother into a boarding school on the Welsh border, and I was spirited away for safety's sake to a school in America, where nothing felt familiar to me. I was distanced abruptly from the world I had belonged to, where The Darter and Agnes and the ever mysterious Moth had existed. In certain ways it felt a greater loss than when my mother had gone away. I'd lost my youth, I was unmoored. After a month I ran away from the school without any clear idea where I was going, since I knew almost no one there. I was found, then shuttled back urgently to another school, this time in the north of England, where I remained in a similar isolation. When our spring term ended, a large man picked me up at the school and drove me from Northumberland south for six hours to Suffolk, barely invading my distrustful silence. I was being brought to join my mother, who was living in White Paint, the house that had once been her parents', in the region called The Saints. It was in light-filled open country, about a mile from the nearest village, where, that summer, I would get a job with the large man who had picked me up at the school, whose name was Malakite.

It was a time when my mother and I were not close. The domestic ease we loved during those weeks before she abandoned my sister and me no longer existed. I could not erase my distrust, given her deceptive departure. It would be much later that I found out that once, or possibly twice, on returning to England to receive new orders, she had cleared her schedule to come and watch me dance, chaotic and Dionysian, at a Bromley jazz club with a girl she did not know, who leapt into and out of my arms.

The lost sequence in a life, they say, is the thing we always search out. But during my late teens when I would stay with my mother at White Paint, I discovered no clues. Until one day I came home early from work, walked into the kitchen, where she, in shirtsleeves, was scrubbing a pot in the sink. She must have assumed she was safely alone. She nearly always wore a blue cardigan. I thought it was used to hide her thinness. Now I saw a row of livid scars like those cut into the bark of a tree by some mechanical gardening tool—ending suddenly, as if innocently, in the rubber gloves she was wearing to protect her hands from dish soap. I was never to know how many other scars there were on her, but here were these slate-red ones down the soft flesh of her arm, evidence from that missing time. *It's nothing,* she'd muttered. *Just the street of the small daggers . . .*

She said nothing more about how she got those wounds. I did not know at that time that my mother, Rose Williams, after the attack on us had ended all contact with Intelligence. Although the fracas at the Bark Theatre had been quickly hushed up by authorities, there were hints of my mother's wartime work in the newspapers that gave her a brief but anonymous celebrity. The press had only got hold of her code name, Viola. Depending on their political persuasion, the newspapers referred to the unidentified woman as either an English heroine or a bad example of post-war government intrigue abroad. No connection was ever actually made to my mother. Her anonymity was secure enough that when she returned to White Paint, locals would still refer to the family home as belonging to her late father, who had worked in the Admiralty. The unknown Viola was soon forgotten.

A decade after my mother's death, I received an invitation to apply to the Foreign Office. My recruitment for such a post seemed initially strange. I participated in several interviews on my first day. One conversation was with an "intelligence collection body," another with an "intelligence assessment outfit"; both, I was informed, were separate bodies seated at the high table of British Intelligence. No one told me why I had been approached, and there was no one I knew among those who questioned me intricately but seemingly casually. My earlier spotted academic record did not cause them as much concern as I had expected. I assumed that nepotism and my bloodline must have been considered a reliable entrance into a profession that trusted lineage and the possibly inherited quality of secrecy. And they were impressed by my knowledge of lan-

guages. They never mentioned my mother during the interviews, and neither did I.

The job I was being offered was to review various files in
the archives covering the war and post-war years. Whatever
I unearthed during my research and whatever conclusions I
might draw were to remain confidential. I was to hand my
findings over only to my immediate superior, who would assess
them. Each superior had two rubber stamps on his desk. One
said *Improve*, the other *Redeemed*. If your work was "redeemed,"
it would progress to a higher level. Where, I had no idea—my
small landscape of work was only in the warren of archives on
the second floor of a nameless building close to Hyde Park.

It sounded like drudge work. But accepting a job that
included sifting through the details of the war might, I
thought, be a way of discovering what my mother had been
doing during the period she left us under the guardianship
of The Moth. We knew only the stories of her radio broadcasts from the Bird's Nest on the roof of the Grosvenor House
Hotel during the early stages of the war, or of a night drive to
the coast, when she was kept awake by chocolate and the cold
night air. We had known no more than that. Perhaps there was
now a chance of discovering that missing sequence in her life.
It was the possibility of an inheritance. In any case, this was
the government job I had enigmatically referred to that afternoon in Mrs. Malakite's garden while the bees moved uncer-
tainly in their hives and she had forgotten who I was.

I read through mounds of files brought up daily from the
archives. They contained mostly reports from men and women

who had operated on the periphery of war, about journeys that criss-crossed Europe and later the Middle East, as well as various post-war skirmishes—especially between 1945 and early 1947. I began to realize that an unauthorized and still violent war had continued after the armistice, a time when the rules and negotiations were still half lit and acts of war continued beyond public hearing. On the continent, guerrilla groups and Partisan fighters had emerged from hiding, refusing defeat. Fascist and German supporters were being hunted down by people who had suffered for five or more years. The retaliations and acts of revenge back and forth devastated small villages, leaving further grief in their wake. They were committed by as many sides as there were ethnic groups across the newly liberated map of Europe.

Along with a handful of others, I sifted through the files and dossiers that still remained, assessing what had been successfully achieved against what had perhaps gone wrong, in order to make recommendations as to what might need to be re-archived or now eradicated. This was referred to as The Silent Correction.

We were in fact the second wave of "correction." I discovered that during the closing stages of the war and with the arrival of peace, a determined, almost apocalyptic censorship had taken place. There had been, after all, myriad operations it was wiser the public never know about, and so the most compromising evidence was, as far as possible, swiftly destroyed—in both Allied and Axis Intelligence headquarters around the globe. A famous example had been the runaway fire in the Baker Street offices of the Special Operations Executive. Such deliberate conflagrations would be worldwide. When the British eventually departed Delhi, "burning officers," as they called themselves, took on the job of incinerating all compromising records, setting fire to them night and day in the central square of the Red Fort.

The British were not alone in this instinct to conceal certain truths of war. In Italy, the Nazis had destroyed the smokestacks of Trieste's Risiera di San Sabba, the rice mill they had turned into a concentration camp where thousands of Jews, Slovenes, Croats, and anti-Fascist political prisoners were tortured and killed. Similarly, no records were kept of the mass graves in the karst sinkholes in the hills above Trieste where Yugoslav Partisans disposed of the bodies of those who had opposed the Communist takeover, or of the thousands deported who perished in Yugoslav detention camps. There was a hasty, determined destruction of evidence by all sides. Anything questionable was burned or shredded under myriad hands. So revisionist histories could begin.

But fragments of truth remained among families or in villages that had been almost wiped off the map. Any Balkan village, as I overheard my mother once say to Arthur McCash, had cause to seek revenge against its neighbour—or whoever it was they believed had once been their enemy—the Partisans, the Fascists, or us, the Allies. Such were the repercussions of peace.

And so for us, a generation later in the 1950s, the job was to unearth whatever evidence might still remain of actions that history might consider untoward, and which could still be found in stray reports and unofficial papers. In this post-war world twelve years later, it felt to some of us, our heads bent over the files brought to us daily, that it was no longer possible to see who held a correct moral position. And a good many who worked in that government warren would in fact leave within a year.

The Saints

I bought the house from Mrs. Malakite, and on my first day as
its owner walked across the fields towards White Paint, where
my mother had been raised and which had now been sold to
strangers. I stood on a rise on the perimeter of what had once
been her land, with the slow meander of a river in the distance.
And I decided to write down what little I knew of her time
in this place, even if the house and the landscape that once
belonged to her family had never been the true map of her life.
The girl who had grown up beside a small Suffolk village was
in fact well travelled.

When you attempt a memoir, I am told, you need to be
in an orphan state. So what is missing in you, and the things
you have grown cautious and hesitant about, will come almost
casually towards you. "A memoir is the lost inheritance," you
realize, so that during this time you must learn how and where
to look. In the resulting self-portrait everything will rhyme,
because everything has been reflected. If a gesture was flung
away in the past, you now see it in the possession of another.
So I believed something in my mother must rhyme in me. She
in her small hall of mirrors and I in mine.

*

They were a country family who lived a modest and unassuming life in that recognizable era captured in the films made during the war. For some time that is how I imagined my grandparents and my mother, as they might have been represented in such films, although recently, watching the contained sexuality of those demure heroines, I was reminded of the statues that had travelled with the boy I once was, ascending and descending in the lift at the Criterion.

My grandfather, being born within a family of older sisters, was content to be surrounded by the company of women. Even when he eventually reached the rank of admiral, with no doubt draconian control of the men who obeyed his rigorous demands at sea, he relished his time in Suffolk and was at ease in the domestic habits of his wife and daughter. I wondered if this combination of a "domestic life" and a "life away" was what led my mother to first accept and then change the path of her life. For she herself would eventually insist on something more, so her married and then her professional life echoed the two worlds her father simultaneously inhabited.

Knowing he would spend most of his active life with the navy, my grandfather had intentionally bought a house in Suffolk that was not beside an "active river." So where my mother was taught to fish as a teenager was a wide but quiet stream. There was no rush to it. Water meadows sloped down towards it from the house. Now and then in the distance one heard a bell from one of the Norman churches, the same toll earlier generations had heard across those fields.

The region was made up of a cluster of small villages, a

few miles from one another. The roads between them were often unnamed, causing confusion to travellers, not helped by the fact that the villages were similarly named—St. John, St. Margaret, St. Cross. There were in fact two communities of Saints—the South Elmham Saints, made up of eight villages, and the Ilketshal Saints, which had half that number. A further problem was that the mileage on any signpost in the region was guesswork. A sign announced the journey between one Saint and another as two miles, so after three and a half miles a traveller would turn back assuming he had missed a turn, when in fact he needed to continue another half mile to reach the slyly hidden Saint. The miles felt long in The Saints. There was no assurance in the landscape. And for those growing up there, assurance felt similarly hidden. Since I spent some of my early years there, it might explain why as a boy in London I was obsessively drawing maps of our neighbourhood in order to feel secure. I thought that what I could not see or record would cease to exist, just as it often felt I'd misplaced my mother and father in one of those small villages flung down randomly onto the ground with too similar a name and with no reliable mileage towards it.

During the war, The Saints, being near to the coast, had taken on an even greater secretiveness. All signposts, however inaccurate, were removed in preparation for a possible German invasion. The region became signless overnight. There would in fact be no invasion, but American airmen assigned to the recently built RAF airfields were as a result constantly getting lost when they tried to get back from the pubs at night and were often found searching frantically for the correct aerodrome the next morning. Pilots crossing the Big Dog Ferry travelled unnamed lanes and found themselves crossing the Big Dog Ferry again going the other way, still attempting to stumble on their airfield. At Thetford the army created a life-sized model of a German town, which Allied troops were trained to surround and attack before their invasion of Germany. It was a strange contrast: English soldiers carefully memorizing the structure of a German town, while German troops were preparing to enter a bewildering Suffolk landscape where not one road sign existed. Coastal towns were secretly removed from maps. Military zones officially disappeared.

Much of the war work in which my mother and others participated was carried out, it is now clear, with a similar invisibility, the real motives camouflaged, the way childhood is. Thirty-two aerodromes, along with decoy airfields to confuse the enemy, were built almost overnight in Suffolk. Most of those flesh-and-blood airfields would never exist on a map, even if they appeared in several short-lived barroom songs. And eventually by war's end, the aerodromes disappeared, in much the way four thousand air force servicemen would leave the region as if nothing untoward had happened there. The Saints slipped back into everyday life.

As a teenager I would hear about those temporarily unmapped towns from Mr. Malakite as he drove me to and from work on what had once, long ago, been Roman roads. For on the periphery of the abandoned airfield at Metfield he was now growing vegetables, and it was on those old grass-covered runways that I once again was taught to drive, legally this time. Where the Malakites lived was called a "Thankful Village," for it had lost no men during the two wars; and it would be to that same village that I returned to live, a decade or so after my mother's death, in the small timbered house with its walled garden where I had always felt secure.

I used to wake early at White Paint and walk towards the village, knowing Sam Malakite would drive up alongside me, light a cigarette, and watch as I climbed in beside him. Then we'd be off to various town squares such as Butter Cross in Bungay, heap his produce onto the trestle tables, and work till noon. On the hottest days of summer we stopped at the Ellingham Mill where the river was shallow and stood in it, water up to our waists, eating Mrs. Malakite's sandwiches— tomato, cheese, onion, with honey from her own bees. A combination I've never tasted since. That his wife had made this lunch for us that morning several miles away felt parental.

He wore bottle-thick spectacles. His ox-like stature made him distinct. He had a long lowland "badger coat," made out of several skins, which smelled of bracken, sometimes of earthworms. And he and his wife were my watched example of marital stability. His wife no doubt felt I lingered around too much. She was organized, ardently neat, whereas he was the rabbit's wild brother, leaving what looked like the path of an undressing hurricane wherever he went. He dropped his shoes, badger coat, cigarette ash, a dish towel, plant journals, trowels, on the floor behind him, left washed-off mud from potatoes in the sink. Whatever he came upon would be eaten, wrestled with, read, tossed away, the discarded becoming invisible to him. Whatever his wife said about this incorrigible flaw did no good. I suspect, in fact, she took pleasure in suffering his nature. Though give him credit, Mr. Malakite's fields were immaculate. No plant left its bed and wandered off as a "volunteer." He scrubbed the radishes under the thin stream of a hose. He spread his wares neatly on the trestle table at the Saturday market.

It became the pattern of my spring and summers. I earned a modest wage and it meant I did not have to spend much time on one side of that seemingly uncrossable distance between me and my mother. There was a distrust on my part and a secretiveness on hers. So it was Sam Malakite who became the centre of my life. If we worked late I would have an evening meal with him. My life with The Moth, Olive Lawrence, the smoke-like Darter, my river-leaping Agnes, had been replaced by the easygoing and reliable Sam Malakite, oak strong as they used to say then.

During winter months, Mr. Malakite's fields slept. It was just a caretaking world for him then, with a cover crop of mustard with yellow flowers to build up organic material in the soil. Winters were quiet and still for him. By the time I returned the fields were already filling with vegetables and fruit. We began work early, had a noon lunch and a brief nap under his mulberry tree, then continued until seven or eight. We gathered green beans in five-gallon buckets and chard in a wheelbarrow. The plums in the walled garden behind the house would eventually be made into jam by Mrs. Malakite. The Stupice tomatoes that grew near the sea had an intense taste. I was back within the seasonal subculture of market gardeners and the endless discussions across the trestle tables about blights or the failure of spring rains. I would sit silently, listening to Mr. Malakite's gift of the gab with his customers. If we were alone he'd inquire about what I was reading, what I was studying at college. There was no mockery about my other world. He saw that whatever I was learning there came from some desire in me, though when I was with him I seldom thought about what I had been doing academically. I wished to be part of his universe. With him those indistinct maps from childhood now became reliable and exact.

I trusted each step I took with him. He knew the names of all the grasses he walked over. He'd be carrying two heavy buckets of chalk and clay towards a garden, but I knew he was also listening to a certain bird. A swallow knocked dead or unconscious from hitting a window silenced him for half a day. It remained with him, that bird's world, its fate. If I said something later that encroached on the event, I'd see a shadow in him. He would turn from our conversation and I'd have lost him, find myself suddenly alone, even if he was beside me, driving his truck. He always knew the layered grief of the world as well as its pleasures. He tugged off a sprig from every bush of rosemary he passed, smelled it, and pre-served it in his shirt pocket. Any river he came to distracted him. On hot days he removed his boots and clothes and swam through reeds, cigarette smoke still escaping from his mouth. He taught me where to find those rare parasol mushrooms like fawn-coloured umbrellas, with their pale gills underneath, that are to be found in open fields. "Only in open fields," Sam Malakite would say, holding up a glass of water as if making a toast. Years later when I heard he had died, I held up my glass and said, "Only in open fields." I was alone in a restaurant when I said this.

The shade of his one large mulberry tree. We used to work mostly in vigorous sunlight, so now it is the shade I think of, not the tree. Just its symmetrical dark existence, and its depth and silence, where he talked to me long and lazily about his early days, until it was time to go back to wheelbarrows and hoes. The breeze lifted itself over the shallow hill and entered what felt like our dark room, rustling against us. Could have stayed there forever, under that mulberry. The ants in the grass climbing their green towers.

In the Archives

I worked each day in a fractional corner of that nameless seven-storey building. There was only one man I knew there and he kept his distance. One day he entered a lift I had just stepped into, said, "Hello, Sherlock!" as if the name and greeting were enough of a code between us, and as if the exclamation point that his voice provided would be enough to satisfy the person surprisingly discovered in such a place. Tall, still bespectacled, the same sloping shoulders, as boyish as ever, Arthur McCash got off on the next floor, and I stepped out briefly to watch him wander away from me to some office or other. I knew, as very few probably did, that under his white shirt there were three or four deep scars on his stomach, a bevelled permanence on his white skin.

I was coming into London by train and staying during the week at a rented one-room flat near Guy's Hospital. There was less chaos in the city now, a sense of people reordering their lives. On weekends I returned to Suffolk. I was living in two worlds as well as two eras. This was the city where I half believed I might catch sight of a certain pale blue Morris belonging to The Darter. I recalled its military-looking crest on the bonnet, the amber-coloured indicator lights clicking up to signal a right- or left-hand turn, then withdrawing back into the structure of the door frame like the ears of a greyhound in aerodynamic flight. And how The Darter, as if a sensitive owl, would catch a false note in the timbre of the engine, a murmur in its heart, so that within minutes he'd be out and removing the valve cover on the 918 cc engine in order to brighten the points of the spark plugs with a strip of sandpaper. The Morris, I recalled, was his flawed joy, and any women he escorted in it needed to accept the fact that he showed it more love and concern than he would ever give them.

But I had no idea if The Darter still owned such a car, or how I might track him down. I'd attempted to visit him at The Pelican Stairs but he had moved away. The only person who had known The Darter well was The Forger of Letchworth, and I sought him out, but he too had disappeared. The truth was, I missed that remarkable table full of strangers who had altered Rachel and me more than our disappeared parents. Where was Agnes? There seemed no way of finding her. When I went to her parents' flat, they were no longer there. The restaurant in World's End did not remember her, the polytechnic had no address for her. So my eyes were constantly on the lookout for that familiar blue outline of a two-door Morris.

Months passed at my job. I began to realize that whatever papers might have contained material on my mother would never be revealed to me. Her activities were either already destroyed or deliberately withheld from me. A black hood seemed to have been placed over her war career and I would continue to remain in the dark.

To escape the confines of work I had begun walking the north bank of the Thames at night, sidling past old Anderson shelters where The Darter had once kept dogs. But there was no longer a bark or a scuffle within. I passed various docks, the St. Katharine's, the East India and the Royal Docks. The war long over, they were no longer padlocked so one night I entered, set the three-minute timer on a lock gate, borrowed a skiff, and caught the tide change.

The river was barely inhabited. It was two or three in the morning and I was alone. Just a tug now and then, towing rubbish out to the Isle of Dogs. I was conscious of the eddies caused by tunnels that ran underwater, so I had to row hard, barely staying in place, almost sucked towards Ratcliffe Cross or the Limehouse Pier. One night the boat I took had a motor, so I travelled as far as Bow Creek and into the two northern arms of that river, almost believing I would find my allies in those dark tributaries. I anchored the stolen boat so that on another night I might use it again to continue upstream into further cuts and canals. Then I walked back into the city, and by eight-thirty in the morning arrived at the office, refreshed.

I do not know what it was that altered me by my taking those journeys again up and down the river where we had once collected groups of dogs. I think it was becoming clear that it was not just my mother's past that had become buried and anonymous. I felt I too had disappeared. I had lost my youth. I walked through the familiar archive rooms with a new preoccupation. I'd spent the first months of my job knowing I was being watched as we gathered the detritus of a not yet fully censored war. I had never spoken of my mother.

When her name was briefly mentioned by a senior official I'd simply shrugged. I had not been trusted then, but now I was, and I knew the specific hours when I would be alone in the archives. I'd learned enough in my youth to be someone unreliable, good at loosening information from an official source, whether it was my school reports or greyhound papers I stole under the guidance of The Darter. His wallet contained slender tools that could be used for any entrance or exit, and I had watched him curiously, had once even seen him adeptly release a dog trap with a chicken bone. A minor anarchy was still in me. But till now I had had no access to the censored row of Double A files, concealed from innocents like me.

It was the veterinarian, the one who had inherited the two parrots, who taught me how to open locks on a filing cabinet. I had met her years earlier through The Darter and she was the only one I had managed to locate from that time. She befriended me on my return to London. I explained my problem and she recommended a powerful anaesthetic used on damaged hooves and bones that I could apply around a lock until a white condensation appeared. The freezing would slow down the lock's resistance to any trespass and allow me to carry out my next stage of attack. This was a Steinmann pin, which in a more legal world provided skeletal traction and protected the damaged bones of a racing greyhound. The smooth stainless-steel intramedullary pins, petite and efficient, were almost instantly successful, and the locks on the cabinets barely paused before they slipped open with their secrets. I began breaking into the locked files; and, in the usually deserted map room, where I ate my lunch alone, I pulled the borrowed papers out of my shirt and read them. An hour later I returned them to their padlocked homes. If my mother existed in this building, I would discover her.

I said nothing about my new knowledge, except to telephone Rachel to tell her of my discoveries. But she had no desire to reenter our youth. Rachel in her own way had abandoned us, did not wish to go back to what was for her a dangerous and unreliable time.

I had not been there when our mother was taken to see her after she had been found safe in The Darter's arms behind the large painting at the Bark Theatre. The after-effects of the chloroform were still in me. But apparently when my mother entered the room, Rachel would not leave The Darter. She clung to him and turned away from our mother. She had had a seizure during the kidnapping. I did not know the details. What happened that night was mostly kept from me. Perhaps they felt I would be upset, whereas their silence made it worse, more horrific. Rachel later would say nothing but *I hate my mother!* In any case, when The Darter had risen with her in his arms, and attempted to hand her over to my mother, my sister had begun to weep as if in close proximity to a demon.

She was not in her right mind, of course, then. She was exhausted. A seizure had been activated in her and she was probably never clear about the details of what had happened. I used to witness that often, when she'd look at me during the moments following a fit as if I were an actual devil. As if one of those love potions in *A Midsummer Night's Dream* had been applied, only what you first saw on waking was not a love object but a source of fear, the source of a pummelling you had been through minutes before.

But this could not have been true for Rachel in that moment. Because the person she saw first was The Darter holding her in his arms, placating her, doing whatever was the right thing in order to guide her to a state of safety, as he had in her bedroom once, when he told me that unlikely story of his epileptic dog.

And another thing. No matter how my sister responded to me just after a fit, whether with suspicion or anger, a few hours later she would be playing cards with me or helping me with my maths homework. This did not happen with our mother. Rachel's rough judgement of our mother would never abate. Rachel closed the door on her. She went instead to another boarding school that she disliked, in order to be away from her. "I hate my mother," she would continue to say fiercely. I had imagined that our mother's return would bring us back into her arms. But my sister's hurt was irreconcilable. And when she saw the body of The Moth in the Bark Theatre lobby, she turned and began screaming at our mother, and it feels as if she has never stopped. Our family, already splintered, was splintered again. From then on, Rachel felt safer with strangers. It had been strangers who saved her.

That was the night The Moth finally left us. He had promised me once, by the light of a gas fire in Ruvigny Gardens, that he would stay with me until my mother came back. And he had. Then he slipped away from all of us that night when my mother returned.

*

One day, I left the Archives early to attend one of Rachel's theatrical performances. We had not seen each other in a long time. I was aware of her avoiding me and I did not wish to invade her life. I knew she worked with a small puppet-theatre group, and heard she was living with someone, though she had never mentioned it to me. But now I had received a courteous if terse and noncommittal message from her, about a play she was involved with. She said I should not feel it was really necessary to be there, but the work was playing for three nights in an old barrel-maker's factory. I found her message heart-breaking in its cautiousness.

The audience took up only a third of the seats, so people tried ushering us forward at the last minute into the front rows. I myself always sit at the back, especially during any show where a relative or a magician is involved, so I remained where I was. We sat in darkness for a long time, then the play began.

When the performance was over I waited by the exit. Rachel did not appear so I worked my way back through various doors and temporary curtains. There were two stagehands smoking in a cleared space, speaking a language I didn't recognize. I mentioned my sister's name and they pointed to a door. Rachel was looking at herself in a small hand mirror, removing the white paste she had worn from her face. There was a baby in a small basket beside her.

"Hello, Wren." I moved forward and looked down at the baby, Rachel watching me. It was not her usual stare but a look balanced on two or more emotions, waiting for me to say something.

"A girl."

"No, a boy. His name is Walter."

Our eyes caught, held like that. It was safer to be without words just then. Omissions and silences had surrounded our growing up. As if what was still unrevealed could only be guessed at, in the way we had needed to interpret the mute contents of a trunk full of clothes. She and I had lost each other long ago in those confusions and silences. But now, beside this infant, we were within an intimacy, as when sweat covered her face after a seizure and I would hug her to me. When being wordless had been best.

"Walter," I said quietly.

"Yes, dear Walter," she said.

I asked her what it was like for her when we were under The Moth's spell, admitting I always felt unsure around him. She turned on me. "Spell? He cared about us. You had *no idea* what was happening. He was the one protecting us. He was the one taking me to the hospital, again and again. You managed to ignore what our parents had done to us."

She started to gather her things. "I have to go. I'm being picked up."

I asked her what the music had been at one moment in the play, when she was left alone on stage, embracing a large puppet. It had almost brought me to tears. It was not really important, but there was so much I wanted to ask my sister that I knew she would not respond to. Now she touched my shoulder as she answered.

"Schumann's *'Mein Herz ist schwer.'* You know it, Nathaniel. It's what we used to hear once or twice a week in our house, late at night, with the piano like a thread in the darkness. When you told me you imagined our mother's voice joining in. That was the *schwer*.

"We were damaged, Nathaniel. Recognize that." She pushed me gently to the door. "What happened to the girl you never told me about?"

I turned away. "I don't know."

"You can look. Your name is Nathaniel, not Stitch. I'm not Wren. Wren and Stitch were abandoned. Choose your own life. Even your friend The Darter told you that."

She was carrying her baby and used the child's small hand to give me a half wave. She had meant me to see her son, not to talk to me. I left the small room and found myself in darkness again. Only a thin line of light under the door I had just closed behind me.

Arthur McCash

What I came upon first was a cache of records of Rose's early activities as a radio operator during the war, beginning with her work as that supposed fire watcher on the roof of the Grosvenor House Hotel; then later at Chicksands Priory, where she intercepted enciphered German signals and sent them on to Bletchley Park for decoding as directed by the "deceivers in London." She had also made journeys to Dover to identify, among those giant aerials along the coast, the individual rhythms of specific German Morse operators—the art of being able to recognize the touch of a key being one noted example of her skills.

It was only in later files, buried deeper and more enigmatically, that it became clear she had also worked abroad after the war ended. Her name cropped up, for instance, in the investigation of the bombing at the King David Hotel in Jerusalem, as well as in fragments of other reports involving Italy, Yugoslavia, and elsewhere in the Balkans. One report noted that she had been based briefly with a small unit near Naples, two men and a woman sent in, the report bluntly stated, to "loosen the linch-pins" of a group still covertly operating. Some of her unit had been captured or killed. There was mention of a possible betrayal.

But most of the time I found only the names of cities stamped blurrily in her passports, along with fictional names she'd used, with the dates erased or crosshatched, so I gave up being certain where she had been exactly and when she had been there. I realized the wounds on her arm were the only real evidence I had.

I ran into Arthur McCash a second time. He had been abroad, and after a cautious conversation we went out for a meal. He never asked me what I was doing there, just as I did not ask him where he had been posted. I was adept by now in the social codes of the building and knew our conversational path at dinner that evening would need to avoid all significant mountains. I did at one point, feeling it was acceptable and on the innocent side of the information boundary, wonder out loud about The Moth's part in our lives. McCash waved the question away. We were in a restaurant a good distance from our office but he instantly looked around. "I cannot talk about this, Nathaniel."

Our days and nights at Ruvigny Gardens had taken place far from Whitehall territory, but McCash still felt he couldn't discuss a person I assumed had nothing to do with government secrets. Whereas it had everything to do with Rachel and me. We sat in silence for a while. I did not wish to give in or change the subject, annoyed that we were forced to be formal strangers to each other. Half taunting him, I asked if he remembered a beekeeper who often came to our house, a Mr. Florence. I needed, I said, to reach him. I now had bees in Suffolk and needed some advice. Did he have a contact for him?

Silence.

"He's just a beekeeper! I have a dead queen to replace. You're being ridiculous."

"Perhaps." McCash shrugged. "I should not even be having this meal, this repast, with you." He moved his fork closer to the plate and was silent while we were being served, then began talking again as he watched the waiter depart.

"There *is* something I do want to say to you, Nathaniel. . . . When your mother left the Service, she did so eliminating every trail behind her for one reason only. It was so that no one could come after you and Rachel again. And there were guardians around you, always. I essentially began arriving at Ruvigny Gardens a couple of times a week to keep an eye on you. I was the one who brought your mother—when she was briefly in England—to watch you dance at that club in Bromley so she might see you, from a distance at least. Also you must know the people she worked with, even after the war was supposedly over, people like Felon, Connolly, were crucial shields and spear-carriers for us."

Arthur McCash's gestures were what I would call "English Nervous." As he talked, I watched him move his water glass, a fork, an empty ashtray, and the butter dish several times. It told me how quickly his brain was firing and it was clear the movement of those obstacles helped slow him down.

I said nothing. I did not wish him to know what I had been

discovering on my own. He was a dutiful official and lived by the rules.

"She stayed away from the two of you because she was fearful you might be linked to her, they would use her to somehow strike at you. Turned out she was right. She was rarely in London, but she'd just been recalled."

"My father?" I said quietly.

There was barely a pause. He just made a dismissive gesture suggesting fate.

He paid the bill and at the door we shook hands. There was an emphasis in his goodbye as if it was permanent and we two would not meet again like this. Years ago at Victoria Station, he had approached me in a way almost too close for comfort and bought me a cup of tea in the cafeteria. I had not known then that he was my mother's colleague. Now he walked from me at a quick pace, as though relieved to get away. I still had no inkling about his life. We had circled each other for a long time. This man, content to be silent about his bravery the night he had saved us, when my mother returning into my life had touched my shoulder, and using my old nickname, said "Hello, Stitch." Then went quickly towards him, opening his bloodied white shirt, interrogating him about the blood.

Whose blood is it?

It's mine. Not Rachel's.

Under McCash's dazzling white shirts would always be the scars, reminders of the time he had protected me and my sister. But now I knew he had kept our mother informed about us, had been her secret camera at Ruvigny Gardens. Just as The Moth, as Rachel said, had cared for us more than I realized.

I thought back to a weekend when The Moth and I had stood at the edge of the Serpentine watching Rachel stride into the water towards something she wished to rescue, lifting her dress, her bare legs meeting her upside-down body. Was it a piece of paper? A bird with a broken wing? It doesn't matter. What was important was that when I glanced over at The Moth, I saw he was watching Rachel intensely, not just for what she herself was, but with a permanent concern for her. And all through that afternoon I recalled Walter—let us call him Walter now—had stared at anyone who came near us as if there might be some flaw of danger. There must have been days—all those times when I was not with them while busy with The Darter—when The Moth's eyes were focused on Rachel, in this protective way.

But now I knew that Arthur McCash had been a guardian too, coming by once or twice a week to keep an eye on us. But what I felt towards him as he walked away after our dinner was what I felt when I was fifteen. He was still that solitary presence, recently down from Oxford with his infamous limerick and with no sense of an authentic landscape behind him. Though if I had inquired about his school days, I am sure he could have described the colours on his school scarf or his boardinghouse, probably named after some English explorer. In fact, at times Ruvigny Gardens still feels to me like an amateur theatre company where a man named Arthur rushes on to perform his awkward conversations and when that is over walks off into—*what*? It was a role scripted for him, the minor character, and it led eventually to him being sprawled on a backstage sofa at the Bark Theatre with blood filling his white shirt and soaking the top of his trousers. A moment that had to remain classified, off stage.

But the tableau of that night keeps returning: my mother moving towards him, dragging a chair with her, the weak wattage of the one lamp in the room, and her beautiful neck and face bending down to kiss his cheek briefly.

"Can I help, Arthur?" I hear her say. "A doctor will come. . . ."

"I'm all right, Rose." She looks over her shoulder at me, unbuttons his shirt, pulls it loose from his trousers to discover how serious the knife slashes are, slides the cotton scarf off her neck to swab the welling blood. Reaches for the vase.

"He didn't stab me."

"Slashes. I see that. Where is Rachel now?"

"She's all right," he says. "She's with Norman Marshall."

"Who's that?"

"The Darter," I say across the room. And she turns to look at me again as if surprised there is something I know that she doesn't.

A WORKING MOTHER

I traced the trail of my mother's swift departure from Intelligence after her return, as she severed all connections then moved with no fanfare to Suffolk, while Rachel and I completed our last years at far-flung schools. So having had no mother during the time when she worked in Europe, we now had no mother during the period that followed, as she evolved back into being an anonymous civilian, erasing her false names.

I came across memos, from after she had left the Service, warning her that the name Viola had cropped up again in a recent document, and there was the possibility that those who had been searching for her had not given up. She responded by refusing the proposal of "bodies from London" to protect her, deciding instead to find someone outside her professional circle to watch over the safety, not of her, but of her son when he was with her. Therefore, unknown to me, she persuaded the local market gardener, Sam Malakite, to visit our house and offer me a job. No one from my mother's former universe was invited into our surroundings.

I had no suspicions that people were still searching for a Rose Williams, and I was unaware of the protection I was being given. It was only after her death that I discovered she always surrounded her children—even Rachel in her distant Welsh landscape—with various guardian owls. So Arthur McCash had been replaced by Sam Malakite, a market gardener who never carried a weapon, unless you considered his three-pronged hand shovel or his hedging tools.

I recall asking my mother once what had made her begin to like Mr. Malakite, for it was clear she was very fond of him. She was on her knees in the garden attending to nasturtiums and she leaned back, looking not at me but into the distance. "I must say, it was when he interrupted a conversation we were having to say, 'I think I smell cordite.' Perhaps it was the casual, unexpected word in the remark that pleased me so. Or energized me. It was a branch of knowledge I was familiar with."

But for me, that teenager, Sam Malakite represented only details from the world he lived in. I never imagined him as part of the world of arson or cordite. He was the most easygoing and stable person I'd encountered. For excitement on Wednesdays, on the way to work we picked up the four-page news sheet that was printed privately by the Reverend Mint, the pastor, who saw himself as the local Kilvert. The man did little for the community but give one sermon a week to a congregation of around twenty people. But there was his newspaper. His sermon and the newspaper forcibly dovetailed any local incidents into a moral parable. Someone having a fainting spell in the bakery, a telephone ringing constantly at the corner of Adamson Road, the stealing of a carton of wine gums from the confectionery, the misuse of the word "lay" on the radio—these worked their way into the sermon and then again into *The Mint Light*, with spiritual content hanging on for dear life.

In *The Mint Light*, an attack from Mars would have been ignored. This had even been its policy between 1939 and 1945, when it recorded mostly local complaints such as the presence of rabbits in the victory gardens. *Thursday, 12:01 a.m.,* a police officer felt "emotional" during a thunderstorm while making his last patrol of the night. *Sunday, 4:00 p.m.,* a female motorist was flagged down by a man carrying a ladder. By the time of the Sunday sermon, the borrowing of a ladder without permission or a schoolboy's shining of a torch at a neighbour's cat, "attempting to hypnotise it with a swaying and circular motion," had profound biblical overtones, the hypnotized cat easily linked to Saint Paul being blinded by rays on the way to Damascus. We bought *The Mint Light* and read sections aloud in ominous tones, nodding wisely and simultaneously rolling our eyes. Mr. Malakite believed his own death as the town's market gardener would be linked to the feeding of the five thousand. No one read *The Mint Light* more carefully than we did. Except, strangely, my mother. When Mr. Malakite drove me home on Wednesdays, she always invited him in for tea and fish-paste sandwiches, took *The Mint Light* from him, and withdrew on her own to a desk. She read it without any laughter, and I realize now that my mother was searching not for the absurd spiritual metaphors but to discover if there was any reference to a possible stranger in the vicinity. She tended to see no one but Mr. Malakite, or now and then the postman. She even insisted on having no pets. As a result there was a feral cat who lived outside and a rat who lived indoors.

My nomadic school life had made me tactful as well as self-sufficient, not fond of confrontations. I avoided the *schwer*. I retreated from arguments as if I had those epicanthic eyelids that birds and some fish have, that allow them to separate themselves silently, almost courteously, from present company. I shared with my mother a preference for privacy and solitude. A room without argument and a sparse table appealed to both of us.

Only in our habits of clothing was there a difference. My journeying from place to place had made me responsible for my neatness. Something like ironing my own clothes gave me a sense of control. Even for working in the fields with Mr. Malakite I washed and ironed what I wore. Whereas my mother would hang a blouse to dry on a nearby bush, then simply put it on. If there was scorn in her towards my fussiness she said nothing; perhaps she did not even notice it. But when we sat across a table from each other I was conscious of her lean, clear-eyed face above an unironed shirt that she felt was good enough for the evening.

She surrounded herself with silence, barely listened to the radio unless there was a dramatic adaptation of something like *Precious Bane* or *Lolly Willowes*, those classics she'd read as a teenager. Never the news. Never political commentary. She could have been in a world that existed twenty years earlier, when her parents lived at White Paint. This vacuum-like silence only emphasized the distance between the two of us. In one of the few no-holds-barred arguments with my mother, when

I complained about our abandonment, she responded too quickly, "Well, Olive was around you for a while. She kept me up-to-date."

"Wait a minute—Olive? You knew Olive Lawrence?"

She drew back, as if she'd revealed too much.

"The *eth-nog-ra-pher*? You knew her?"

"She was not just an ethnographer, Stitch!"

"What else was she?"

She said nothing.

"Who else? Who else did you know?"

"I kept in touch."

"Wonderful. You kept in touch. For your sake! I am so glad. You left us without a word. Both of you."

"I had work to do. I had responsibilities."

"Not to us! Rachel hates you so much she will not even talk to me. Because I'm here with you she hates me too."

"Yes, I have been damned, by my daughter."

I picked up the plate in front of me and flung it underhand viciously towards a wall as if that would finish our conversation. Instead the plate arced up, hit the edge of the cupboard, and broke, and a section of it leapt twisting towards her and cut into her forehead just above her eye. Then the noise of it falling to the floor. There was a pause, we were both still, blood coursed down the side of her face. I moved towards her but she held up her hand to keep me away, as if in scorn. She stood there impassive, stern, not even putting her hand up to her forehead to search out the wound. Just continued holding that palm out against me, to stop me from approaching, to stop me attempting to care for her, as if this was nothing.

There had been worse. It was the same kitchen where I'd witnessed the series of wounds on her arm.

"Where did you go? Just tell me *something*."

"Everything changed the night when I was with you and Rachel here at White Paint, when we listened to the bombers flying over us. I needed to be involved. To protect you. I thought it was for your safety."

"Who were you with? How did you know Olive?"

"You liked her, didn't you . . . ? Anyway, she was not only an ethnographer. I remember one time when she was with a group of meteorologists in gliders scattered over the English Channel. Scientists had been working all week recording wind speeds and air currents, and Olive was up there too, in the sky, forecasting the oncoming weather and the chance of rain to confirm or postpone the D-Day invasion. She was involved with other things too. But that's enough."

Her hand was still up, as if giving evidence, something she did not want to do. Then she turned round, bent down, and washed the blood off in the sink.

She began leaving books out for me, mostly novels she had read at college before marrying my father. "Oh, he was a great reader. . . . That's what probably brought us together . . . at first." There were a great many Balzac paperbacks in French around the house, and I knew these were her passion. She seemed no longer interested in whatever the intrigues were in the outside world. Only someone like Balzac's fictional character Rastignac interested her. I don't think I interested her. Though perhaps she felt she ought to influence me in some way. But I don't think she necessarily wanted my love.

Chess was her suggestion, a sort of metaphor, I suppose, for our intimate battle, and I shrugged in agreement. She turned out to be a surprisingly good teacher in the careful way she laid down the rules and movements of the game. She never proceeded to the next stage until she was sure I understood what I had just been taught. If I reacted with impatience, she began again—I couldn't fool her with a nod of understanding. It was incessantly boring. I wanted to be out in the fields. And at night I couldn't sleep because strategic pathways began suggesting themselves to me in the dark.

After my first lessons we started playing and she beat me mercilessly, then repositioned the fatal pieces to show how I could have escaped a threat. There were suddenly about fifty-seven ways to walk across an empty space, as if I were a cat with twitching ears entering an unknown lane. She spoke constantly as we played, either to distract me, or to say something crucial about focus, her role model being a famous chess victory of 1858 that was given the title "Opera" since it had actually been played in a private box overlooking a performance of Bellini's *Norma*. It was music my mother loved, and the American chess player, an opera enthusiast himself, had glanced now and then at the action on stage while playing against a French count and a German duke who continually and loudly discussed their moves against him. The point my mother was making was about distraction. Priests were being bribed and murdered on stage and central characters would eventually be burned on a pyre, and all the while the American chess and opera enthusiast remained focused on the strategic path he'd chosen, undeterred by the glorious music. It was my mother's example of peerless focus.

One night a thunderstorm perched at the top of our valley as we sat poised across from each other at a table in the greenhouse. There was a sodium lamp near us. My mother set up pawns and castles at their starting gates as the storm gradually rolled over us. The lightning and thunder made us feel defenceless within the thin glass shell. Outside, it could have been Bellini's opera; inside, there was the drugged air of plants, and two bars of electrical heat attempting to warm the room. We moved our pieces in the faint constant yellow of the sodium lamp. I was playing her well, in spite of the distractions. My mother in her blue cardigan smoked, barely looking at me. All that August there had been storms, and then in the morning clear, fresh daylight, as if a new century. Focus, she'd whisper as we sat down within the storm's gunfire and flare lights to another of our small contests of will. In a quarter second of lightning I saw her fall briefly into the wrong trench of the battle. I saw the obvious move I had been left, but then another that was wrong or that might be even better. I played it right away and she saw what I had done. The noise was all round us but now we both simply listened to it. A flood of lightning lit the greenhouse and I saw her face, her expression of—what? Surprise? A sort of joy?

So finally, a mother and a son.

*

If you grow up with uncertainty you deal with people only on a daily basis, to be even safer on an hourly basis. You do not concern yourself with what you must or should remember about them. You are on your own. So it took me a long time to rely on the past, and reconstruct how to interpret it. There was no consistency in how I recalled behaviour. I had spent most of my youth balancing, keeping afloat. Until, in my late teens, Rose Williams sat in a greenhouse and in the artificial heat of it played vicious competitive chess with her son, the only one of her two children who agreed to stay with her. Sometimes she wore a dressing gown that revealed her frail neck. Sometimes her blue cardigan. She'd lower her face into it so I could see just her distrusting eyes, tawny hair.

"Defence is attack." Said more than once. "The first thing a good military leader knows is the art of retreating. It's important how you get in and then how you get out undamaged. Hercules was a great warrior, but he died violently at home in a coat of poison, because of his earlier heroism. It's an old story. The safety of your two bishops, for instance, even if you sacrifice your queen. *No—don't!* Well, you played that, so this is what I do. An opponent will punish you for little mistakes. This will checkmate you in three moves." And before she moved her knight, she leaned forward and tousled my hair.

I could not remember the last time my mother had touched me. I was never sure whether she was going to teach me or brutalize me during those tournaments. At times she looked insecure, a woman from an earlier decade, mortal. It felt like a stage set. Something about those nights allowed me to focus on just her across our table in the semi-darkness—even if I knew she was the distraction. I saw how quick her hands were, how her eyes were interested only in what I was thinking. It seemed to both of us there was no one else in the world.

At the end of that game, before retiring, though I knew she would be up a few more hours on her own, she set up the chess board again. "This is the first game I memorized, Nathaniel. This is the game in the opera house I told you about." She stood over the board and played both hands, one hand white, one hand black. Once or twice she waited, to let me suggest a move. "No, this!" she'd say, not with irritation at my choice, but with wonder at the master's move. "You see, he went *here* with the bishop." She kept moving her hands faster and faster, until all of the blacks were overcome.

It had taken me a while to realize that I would in some way have to love my mother in order to understand who she now was and what she had really been. This was difficult. I noticed, for instance, that she did not like leaving me alone in the house. She avoided going out if I decided to remain indoors, as if she suspected me of wishing to rummage through whatever of hers was private. This was my mother! I mentioned this to her once and she was so embarrassed I pulled back and apologized before she needed to defend herself. I would later discover she was someone adept in the theatre of war, but I felt the response was not a performance. The only time she revealed something of herself was to show me a few pictures that her parents had kept in a brown envelope in their bedroom. There was the serious schoolgirl face of my seventeen-year-old

mother under our lime-tree bower, as well as photographs of
her with her strong-willed mother and a tall man, sometimes
with a parrot on his shoulder. He had a recognizable presence
and reappeared in a handful of later pictures with my mother,
slightly older, and her parents at the Casanova Revue Bar in
Vienna—I was able to read the name on the large ashtray on
the table, next to the dozen or so empty wineglasses. But otherwise there was nothing at White Paint that gave away anything about her adult life. If I were Telemachus I would find
no proof of her activities as that disappeared parent, no evidence of those journeys of hers on wine-dark seas.

Most of the time we puttered about, staying out of each
other's way. I was relieved to go off to work each morning,
even on Saturdays. Then one evening, after one of our light
suppers, I became conscious of my mother's restlessness, and
that she was clearly eager to get out of the house even with the
possibility of oncoming rain. Grey clouds had been above us
all day.

"Come. Will you walk with me?"

I didn't want to, and I could have pushed it, but I decided
to go along and was greeted with an actual smile. "I'll tell you
more about that game at the opera," she said. "Bring a coat. It
will rain. We don't want that to turn us back." She locked the
door and we headed west onto one of the hills.

How old was she around that time? Perhaps forty? I was
now eighteen. She had married young, the habit and fashion
of the time, though she had studied languages at university,
and once told me she had wished to take a law degree. But
gave that up and instead raised two children. She was in her

early thirties, so still youthful, when war started and she began working as a signals operative. Now she was striding beside me in her yellow slicker.

"Paul Morphy was his name. It was October 21, 1858. . . ."

"Okay. Paul Morphy," I said, as if ready for the second serve she was about to send over the net.

"Okay." She half laughed. "And I will only tell you this once. He was born in New Orleans, a prodigy. At twelve he beat a Hungarian grand master who was traveling across Louisiana. The parents wanted him to become a lawyer but he gave that up and followed the game. And the greatest match in his life was the one played in the Italian Opera House in Paris against the Duke of Brunswick and Count Isouard—who are remembered for only one reason, that they were beaten by this twenty-one-year-old." I was smiling to myself. All these titles! I still remembered Agnes naming one of the dogs who had eaten her dinner in Mill Hill the "Earl of Sandwich."

"But it was also the situation and location where the game was played that made them all famous, as if it were a scene in an Austro-Hungarian novel or an adventure like *Scaramouche*. The three players were sitting in the Duke of Brunswick's private box, practically above the stage. They could have leaned down and kissed the prima donna. And it was the opening night of Bellini's *Norma, or The Infanticide*.

"Morphy had never seen *Norma* and was eager to witness the performance for he simply loved music. He was sitting with his back to the stage, so he'd play quickly, then turn back to the footlights. Perhaps that's what made it a masterpiece, each move being a fast sketch in the sky, barely touching the reality of earth. His opponents would debate among themselves and make a tentative move. Morphy would turn, glance at the board, push forward a pawn or a knight, and return to the opera. His clock time during the whole game was probably less than a minute. It was inspired, it is still inspired, still considered one of the remarkable games. He was playing White.

"So the game begins with the Philidor Defence, a passive opening for Black. Morphy is not interested in taking black pieces in the early stages, preferring to mass his forces for a quick checkmate so he can get back to the opera. Meanwhile the theoretical discussions by his opponents grow louder and louder, irritating the audience and the lead singer, Madame Rosina Penco, who is playing the High Priestess Norma and keeps flinging her stare towards the Duke's box. Morphy brings out his queen and a bishop, working together to dominate the centre of the board, forcing Black into a tight defensive position."

My mother turned in the darkness and looked at me. "Are you following the game on the board?"

"I am following it," I said.

"Black is very soon in shambles. Now it is intermission. Everything has been occurring on stage—romantic love, jealousy, a wish to murder, notable arias. Norma has been abandoned and decides to kill her children. And all the while the audience has been watching the Duke of Brunswick's box!

"In Act Two the plot continues. The black pieces are idle, pinned to their king, the knights frozen by Morphy's bishops. Are you following?"

"Yes, yes."

"Morphy now brings a rook into the attack down the centre of the board. He makes a series of sensational sacrifices in order to squeeze Black into an increasingly hopeless position. And he follows with the stylish queen sacrifice I showed you the other night that will quickly lead to mate. By the time the climax of the opera occurs, when the Consul and Norma decide to die together in a funeral pyre, Morphy can give all his attention to the music, leaving his opponents in ruins."

"Wow," I say.

"Please don't say 'Wow.' You were only in America a few months."

"It's an expressive word."

"Beginning with that Philidor Defence, it was as if Morphy had invented a great philosophical profundity on his way to the opera. That happens, of course, when you are not looking at yourself too carefully. And it happened that night. It is almost a hundred years later, and that little move in the shadows, across the footlights from *Norma,* is still recognized as genius."

"What happened to him?"

"He retired from chess and became a lawyer, but was no good at it so he lived off the family money till he died, in his forties. Never played chess again, but he had his moment, with exceptional music."

We looked at each other, we were both soaked. I had been conscious of the rain at first, then forgotten it. We stood by the entrance to a copse and far below us was our lit white-painted house. I sensed that she was happier here than she would ever be in that secure warmth. Here, where we were no longer housebound, there was an energy and lightness in her I rarely saw. We walked under the cold darkness of the trees. She had no wish to turn back, and we were there for some time, barely talking, private. This is how she must have appeared to others she worked with, I thought, during her silent wars, in the midst of those unknown contests.

*

My mother has heard from Mr. Malakite that a stranger has moved into a house a few miles from White Paint and has been uncommunicative as to where he is from as well as what his profession is.

She hikes alongside Rumburgh Wood, passes the moat farms southwest of the village of St. James, until she is in visual distance of the man's house. It's early evening. She waits until all the lights go out, then another hour. Finally she returns home through the darkness. The next day she appears again a quarter of a mile away, and watches the similar lack of activity. Until the gaunt man emerges in the late afternoon. She follows him cautiously. He circles the perimeter of the old aerodrome. He is going nowhere, really, she can tell that, he's just on a ramble, but she stays with him until he returns home. Once more she waits in the same field, past the hour when nearly all of his lights are out. She makes her way closer to the house, changes her mind, and turns for home, again torchless in the dark.

She has a tentative chat the next day with the postman. "Do you talk with him when you deliver the mail?"

"Not really. He's a scarce one. Doesn't even come to the door."

"What kind of mail does he get? Does he get a lot?"

"Well, I'm not allowed to say."

"Really?" She almost laughs at him.

"Well. Books often. Once or twice a package from the Caribbean."

"What else?"

"Apart from books, I'm not sure."

"Does he have a dog?"

"No."

"Interesting."

"Do you?" he asks.

"No."

The conversation has not been of much use to her, and she ends the chat, which the postman by now seems eager to pursue. Later, with official help, she is able to discover what exactly is being delivered to the stranger, along with what he is mailing out. As well as the fact he comes from the Caribbean, where his grandparents were indentured servants at a sugar plantation in the British colony there. It turns out he is some sort of writer, apparently quite well known, even in other parts of the world.

She learns to pronounce and repeat the stranger's name to herself, as if it is a rare imported flower.

*

"*When he comes, he will be like an Englishman. . . .*"

Rose had written this in one of her spare journals I found after her death. As if even in the privacy of her home, even in a secret notebook, she needed to be careful with the revelation of a possibility. She may even have muttered it mantra-like to herself. *When he comes, he will be like an Englishman. . . .*

The past—my mother knew more than anyone—never remains in the past. So in the privacy of that notebook, in her home, in her own country, she knew she was still a target. She must have assumed that would be the disguise a person bent on vengeance would have to adopt in order to enter the depths of Suffolk and reach her without suspicion. The only clue to a motive would be that he would probably come from a zone of Europe where she had once worked, and where questionable decisions of war had been made. "*Who do you think is going to come for you someday?*" I would have asked her, if I had known. "*What did you do that was so terrible?*" And she would, I think, have said, "*My sins are various.*"

She admitted to me once that my shadowy father had been better than anyone at building levees and firewalls against the past.

"Where is he now?" I asked.

"Asia, perhaps?" The answer evasive. "He was a damaged man. We went our separate ways." She swept her hand horizontally, as if wiping a table clean. My father, who had not been seen by us since that long-ago evening when he boarded the Avro Tudor.

A changeling discovers his own bloodline. So I was never to know him as well as I knew The Darter or The Moth. It was as if the two of them were in a book I was reading in my father's absence and they would be the ones I learned from. I desired unstoppable adventures with them, or even a romance with a girl in a cafeteria who might fade from my life unless I acted, *insisted*. Because that was what fate was.

For a few days I tried breaking into other archives in the hope of discovering some presence of my father. But there was no evidence of him in any capacity, at home or abroad. Either there was no record of him there or his identity was more deeply classified. For this was a place where altitude took over, the higher echelons of the seven-storey building disappearing into a mist that had long ago cut its ties with the everyday world. A part of me wished to believe that here was where my father still existed, if anywhere. Not in some far reach of the empire, monitoring the Japanese military surrender, and going loco from heat, insects, the general complexity of post-war life in Asia. Perhaps all that was a blind fiction, like that promotion of his in the Far East, as opposed to what I wanted to imagine him doing, nearer to home—the evasive, smoke-like man, never referred to; not even, it seemed, existing in print.

For remembering how my father had a few times let me accompany him to his office in the city before his departure, showing me the large map where his various business dealings existed, the coastal harbours, and discreetly hidden island empires, I wondered if such offices had also served as intelligence centres during the war. Where *was* that office building in which my father explained how his company imported tea and rubber from the colonies, and where a lit map revealed a bird's-eye view of the economic and political terrain of his universe? It may have been this very place for all I knew, or some other location that had once housed similar covert activities. What role did my father really have in the office he took me to when I was a boy? Because in such establishments I have discovered that the height of the floor means power. And that building reminds me now of nothing so much as the Criterion, where some of us worked in the basement laundries and steam-filled kitchens, never allowed to enter the higher reaches of the building, instead winnowed like fish at the gates and ladders so no one got higher than banquet halls and then only by putting on the disguise of a servile uniform. Had I already been in one of those cloud-hidden office heights with my father in my youth?

Once, almost as a joke or a quiz, I wrote a list of possible fates of our father, and sent it to Rachel.

Strangled in Johor.

Strangled on board a ship on his way to the Sudan.

Permanently AWOL.

Permanently undercover, but active.

In retirement at a facility in Wimbledon, paranoia invading him, constantly irritated by sounds coming from a nearby animal hospital.

Still on the top floor of the Unilever building.

I never heard back from her.

So many unlabelled splinters in my memory. In my grand-parents' bedroom, I had been shown formal pictures of my mother as a student but there was not one of my father. Even after her death, when I scurried around White Paint to dis-cover whatever clues I could find of her life and death, I came across no photographic evidence of him. All I knew was that the political maps of his era were vast and coastal and I would never know if he was close to us or had disappeared into one of those distances forever, a person who, as the line went, would live in many places and die everywhere.

A Nightingale Floor

There was no coverage of my mother's death in the newspapers. The death of Rose Williams caused little public response in the larger world she had once belonged in. Her small obituary identified her only as the daughter of an admiral, and did not mention a location for her funeral. There was, unfortunately, mention of her death in *The Mint Light*.

Rachel was not at her funeral. I tried reaching her when I was given the news, but there was no reply to my telegram. Still, there were a surprising number of people from out of town who attended, people I assumed my mother had worked with in earlier days. This in spite of the secrecy of the location.

She was buried not in the village near to us, but some fifteen miles away in the parish of Benacre in the Waveney district. It was there her funeral took place. My mother was not religious, but she had loved the simple bearing of that church. Whoever had organized the service must have known that.

It was an afternoon funeral. The chosen time allowed those who had come from London to catch the nine a.m. train from Liverpool Street and return afterwards on the late-afternoon train back to the city. Who, I wondered, as I looked at the group gathered around the grave, had planned all this? Who had chosen the line for her gravestone, *"I have travel'd thro' Perils & Darkness not unlike a Champion."* When I asked the Malakites they claimed they did not know, though Mrs. Malakite thought it had all been done efficiently and tastefully. There were no journalists among the gathered, and those who came by car had the vehicles wait a few hundred yards from the graveyard's entrance so no attention was drawn towards them. I must have appeared distant in my grief for my mother. I had been given the news at college just the previous day and the anonymous mourners no doubt regarded the eighteen-year-old boy by the grave as parentless and adrift. One of them did, at the end, come over and wordlessly shake my hand as if this were adequate consolation, before continuing his slow thoughtful walk out of the graveyard.

I spoke to no one. Another gentleman approached me and said, "Your mother was a remarkable woman," and I did not even look up. In retrospect it was rude, but he had come to me as I was looking into the grave, at her narrow coffin in the fit of the earth. I was thinking the coffin maker and whoever had ordered it must have known how especially thin Rose Williams was. And known how she would have liked the black cherry-wood, known that the chosen words of the service would not have appalled her or been ironic to her, and might have even chosen the line by Blake for the gravestone. So I was looking at what was three or four feet below me and thinking of all that when I heard the man's quiet, almost shy voice speak. "Your mother was a remarkable woman." And by the time I came to an awareness of courtesy, the tall man whom I had not acknowledged but who had respected whatever privacy I was in had moved away and I saw him only from behind.

After a while the churchyard was empty save for me and the Malakites. The Londoners and the few village people who had come to pay their respects were gone. The Malakites were waiting for me. I had not seen them since the news of her death, had only spoken with Sam on the telephone. I approached and then he did this thing. He opened his large moist badger coat wide—his hands were in its pockets—and enclosed me within it, next to his warm body, next to his heart. He was someone who'd barely touched me in all the time I had known him. He seldom inquired how I was doing, though I knew he was curious about what I might become, as if I were still green in judgement. I stayed the night at their house, the window of the spare bedroom looking down onto their walled garden. And the next day he drove me to White Paint. I had wanted to walk but he said he needed to speak with me. That was when he told me how she died.

No one else in the village knew what had happened. He had not even told his wife. My mother had died in the early evening and Mr. Malakite found her about noon the next day. It was clear she had died instantly. He carried Rose Williams—he called her by her full name as if suddenly there was no intimacy between them anymore—into the living room. Then he dialled the telephone number that she once had given him, as he was supposed to do if and when anything, anything, happened to her. Even before he called me.

The voice at the other end of the line asked for his name and to identify where he was. It asked him to confirm once more that she was dead. He was told to wait. There was then a pause. The voice returned and said he should do nothing. Just leave the premises. That he was to be silent about what had happened and also about what he had just done. Sam Malakite reached into his pocket and passed me the original note she had given him two years earlier, with the number he was to call. It was informal but carefully written, without emotion, though I felt I could read in its clarity and exactness an unvoiced sentiment, even fear. He dropped me off at the rise that looked down towards our house. "You can walk from here," he said. Then I went towards my mother's home.

I entered her stillness. I put some food outside for the feral cat. And I banged a saucepan before entering the kitchen, as she used to, to ward off the infamous rat.

Someone had been there, of course. There was not a mark on the sofa where Mr. Malakite had laid her down. Anything that might have provided a clue had been taken away. I guessed there would be a prompt and efficient investigation of her death, and that if there was any retaliation by the government it was sure to be invisible. I would not be notified. And there would be nothing in the house they did not want found. Unless she had left something casually, for me to pick up and place beside some conversational grain of sand she might have once mentioned. "Mr. Malakite reminds me of a friend of mine. Though Mr. Malakite is more innocent," she had said. Only the word was not "innocent," it was "benign." Which was it? It was "benign," I think. Somehow it matters. There's a distinction.

For a while I did nothing. I circled the garden, and almost as if it was coincidence I could hear the call of a cuckoo moving round the house formally singing. When we were small our mother used to say, A cuckoo from the east means comfort, from the west luck, from the north sadness, from the south death. I searched for it, following the sound for a while, then entered the greenhouse, where she was supposed to have died. Whatever greenhouse panes had been shattered were now fixed. I kept recalling how I was seldom allowed to be alone in the house. And how she would always be eyeing me to see what I picked up or was interested in. Now that I was released from her watchful gaze, the rooms felt more potent. It grew dark outside. I pulled a few German paperbacks from the shelf to see if she had written her name in them, but she always had a printless foot. There was a book about Casanova in his later years, by a writer named Schnitzler. I took it upstairs with me and got into bed.

It must have been about eight in the evening when I did this, and I fell quickly into the strange compressed story of Casanova's attempt to return to Venice in middle age, all of its action taking place over a period of a few days and fitting within the small canvas of a novella. I focused on the unexpected and convincing compassion towards Casanova. It was in German, and I was lost to time. As the story ended with Casanova's sleep, I slept too, the bedside light on, the small book still in my hands.

I awoke in the bed I always slept in, turned off the bedside light, and found myself in the darkness of three in the morning, wide awake. I felt I needed to walk through the house with a different mind-set, the more European gaze of Schnitzler. Besides, it was now the hour when my mother was always awake.

I moved slowly through each room with the torch, opening cupboards, dresser drawers. I searched my bedroom first of all. It had been hers when a schoolgirl, though nothing of that time was evident on the walls. Then her parents' bedroom, frozen in their own era, left as it was since their death in the car accident. Then the third midsized room, which belonged to her, with its narrow bed, like her coffin. There was a Regency walnut desk inherited from her mother, where she often sat in the middle of the night, erasing as opposed to recording her past. It was where the barely used telephone in the house was. Mr. Malakite would have needed to come into this room to ring the number she had given him—perhaps in London, perhaps somewhere else.

In that walnut desk I did find, wrapped in one of my mother's crumpled shirts, a framed picture of Rachel I had never seen before. As I studied it, it became clear it must have been taken during the period when my mother was away from us, supposedly unaware of our activities. I wondered who had taken it. The Moth? How conscious of us had our mother been when we were unconscious of her? The stranger aspect of the picture was that Rachel appeared to be dressed more like an adult, with an adult's demeanour, than the teenager she was at the time. I had never seen her dressed like that.

By the end of my night search I had found nothing new, not even something forgotten on a top shelf of the cupboard in my bedroom. She had obviously scoured through it before suggesting I use it when I first came to stay during my holidays. All I had was the carefully framed and hidden picture of my sister, whom I realized I had not seen for over a year. It was about five in the morning now, and fully awake I decided to go downstairs. I walked down the stairs into a cold silence, and as I stepped on to the wooden floor at the foot of the stairs the nightingales began in the dark.

The suddenly loud squeaks would have woken anyone, as they had my mother a year earlier when I had come downstairs in the middle of the night. I'd simply been hungry then for some cheese and milk, and as I turned back captured within that chaotic noise, there was her figure already at the top of the stairs with something, I am not sure what, in her hand. When she saw me, she put it behind her back. Wherever I kept stepping for the next few moments—with her watching me, relieved but slightly scornful—the sounds kept revealing where I was in the semi-darkness. There was only one narrow edge of the floor a person could walk along to have silence. But now I was alone and simply walked down the hallway within the noise, until I entered her small carpeted living room with its fireplace, and the nightingale alarm stopped.

I sat down. My mind leapt strangely not to what my sister and I might have lost with Rose's death, but to her earlier departure from us, when it felt we had lost so much more. I thought of her pleasure in re-naming us. It had been my father who insisted on my being called Nathaniel, but that was too long a word for my mother. So I had been "Stitch" to her. Just as Rachel became "Wren." *Where on earth is The Wren?* Even with adult friends my mother enjoyed searching out better names than the ones they had been baptized with. She had plundered names from landscapes, called people by place-names of where they'd been born or even where she first met them. "There's Chiswick," she'd say about a woman she overheard on the radio, picking up a local accent. Such fragments of curiosity and information were always being shared with us when we were young. And she had taken all of that when she disappeared, waving goodbye. I thought of that erasing of herself, just as now, alone for the first time at White Paint, I realized I'd lost her living voice. All the quick-witted intelligence she owned when young, all the secret life she'd stepped into and kept from us, now lost.

She had reduced the house to a skeletal path. Her bedroom, the kitchen, the small living room that housed a fireplace, and the short passageway of books that led to the greenhouse. These were the locations of her life in the last years. A home once filled with country neighbours and grandchildren had been cut down to the bone, so during the two days I stayed after the funeral I saw more evidence of her parents than of her. I *did* come upon a few sheets of handwritten paper in a cupboard. One contained an odd meditation on her indoor rat as if it was a never-leaving guest she had in time become used to. There was a drawing to scale, probably by Mr. Malakite, of her garden. A constantly re-drawn map of the countries surrounding the Black Sea. But most of the cupboards were empty, as if someone had removed the essential evidence of her life.

I stood in front of her bookcase, modest for a person who lived alone in the country and who barely listened to the radio unless Mr. Malakite mentioned a storm warning. She must have been tired by then of other voices, save those she discovered in novels where a plot might swerve wildly and then somehow turn easily for home during the last two or three chapters. There were no ticking clocks in this stripped-down silent house. The telephone in her bedroom never rang. The only evident and therefore surprising source of noise was the nightingale floor. It comforted her, she told me, gave her safety. Otherwise, silence. During my holidays I could hear her give out a sigh or close a book in the next room.

How often did she return to the shelves of paperbacks, where she could be with Balzac's Rastignac and Félicie Cardot and Vautrin. *"Where is Vautrin now?"* she once inquired of me drowsily, coming out of a sleep, perhaps unaware whom she was speaking to. Arthur Conan Doyle claimed he never read Balzac, not knowing where to begin, that it was too difficult to locate the sources or first appearance of any of the central characters. But my mother knew all of *La Comédie Humaine*, and I began wondering in which of the books she might have found a version of her own unrecorded life. Whose career did she trace, scattered within those novels, until she could understand herself more clearly? She would have known that *Le Bal de Sceaux* is the one book in *La Comédie Humaine* in which Rastignac does not appear, but also that within it he is being constantly referred to. On a whim I pulled a copy of it from the shelf, flipped through, and inside, tucked between pages 122 and 123, found a hand-drawn map of what looked to me like a chalk hill, on six-by-eight quarto-sized paper. With no place-names on it. A fragment that probably meant nothing.

I went back upstairs again and opened that old brown envelope of photographs, still in my grandparents' room. But there were fewer of them now. There weren't the more playful, innocent ones she had shown me during an earlier summer. I saw again my mother's serious young face under the lime bower that led from the kitchen—but later photographs, the ones I had loved best, were no longer there. So perhaps they had not been innocent. The ones of Rose with her parents and the tall man familiar from the other photographs—one, especially, of them all, in the foreign decor of the Casanova Revue Bar in Vienna, with my mother in her late teens sitting in a haze of cigarette smoke in the midst of this adult entourage, an ardent violinist bending towards her. And even a few other pictures, as if in time lapse, taken maybe an hour later, all of them in the back of a taxi, crushed together and laughing.

"That was my father's friend. He was our neighbour, his family were thatchers," Rose had told me when she showed me the photographs that were no longer there. I had pointed to the extra man and asked who he was. "He was the boy who fell from the roof."

"What was his name?"

"I don't remember."

But now, of course, I knew who he was.

He'd been the one at my mother's funeral, with the shy, quiet voice, who stood beside her grave and attempted to speak to me. He was older, but I recognized him from those scattered photos, where he had the same height and presence.

I had once or twice seen him in the hallways of our building, a legend in the office, waiting to take one of the restricted blue lifts to a high, unknown floor, up to a landscape only imagined by most of us working there.

My last night at White Paint, two nights after the funeral, I went to my mother's room, got into her narrow sheetless bed and lay there in the dark, the way she must have done, looking up at the ceiling. "Tell me about him," I said.

"Who?"

"The person you lied to me about. The man whose name you said you couldn't remember. The man who spoke to me at your funeral."

THE BOY ON THE ROOF

He would look down from that sloped straw roof whenever one of Rose's family emerged from the house to collect eggs or get into the car. The sixteen-year-old Marsh Felon had entered my mother's childhood as a teenager because the roof of White Paint needed re-thatching. He and his father and his two brothers had roosted up there through the early summer, sometimes sunstroked, sometimes buffeted by great winds, the clan of them working with efficiency, always in conversation with never a doubt among them, myth-like in unison. Marsh was the youngest, a listener. During the winter he cut and stacked reeds, solitary in the nearby marshes, so they would be dry by spring when his brothers pierced and weaved them into the long-stem straw on the roof with pliant willow branches that they bent like hairpins.

The sudden gale had lifted Marsh and flung him off the roof, and he fell grabbing at branches of the lime bower, attempting to slow his fall before he landed twenty feet down on the paving stones. The others came down out of the loud wind and carried him horizontally into the back kitchen. Rose's mother made up the daybed. He needed to remain immobile and not be moved. So Marsh Felon would become a resident for a while in this back kitchen of strangers.

The L-shaped room was lit only by natural light. There was a woodstove, a map of the region of The Saints depicting every footpath and river crossing. It would become his world for the weeks his brothers continued working on the roof. He heard them as they left at sunset and he woke to their loud persistent conversations as they climbed their ladders the next morning. After the first few minutes their talk was not quite audible, he heard only the laughter and yells of irritation. Two hours later he became aware of the family moving in the house, their conversations hushed. The world felt close yet distant to him. It was the way he felt even when working on the roof, sensing the great active world far away was passing him by.

The eight-year-old girl brought him breakfast and left quickly. She was often his only visitor. She would just stand in the doorway. He could see the further reaches of the house behind her. Her name was Rose. His own family had been motherless and womanless for years. Once she brought him a book from the family library. He consumed it, and asked for another.

"What's this?" She had noticed a few sketches on the last, blank page of a book she had given him to read.

"Oh, sorry. . . ." Marsh felt mortified. He'd forgotten his sketch.

"Don't mind. What is it?"

"A fly."

"Odd fly. Where'd you see it?"

"No, I make them, flies for fishing. I can make you one."

"How? From what?"

"Maybe a blue-winged olive nymph . . . I'll need thread. Waterproof paint."

"I can get that." She almost left.

"No, there's more. . . ." He asked her for paper, something to write on. "I'll make a small list."

She watched.

"What's *this* say? You got awful handwriting. Just tell me."

"All right. Small goose feathers. Red copper wire, not much thicker than human hair. They use it on small transformers—"

"Slow down."

"—or dynamos. Perhaps you could bring me a needle? Also some silver foil to let it shine."

The list continued. Cork, pieces of ash. Some of what he asked for he had never used before. Could she bring him a small notebook? He was only imagining possibilities, as if he were in an unvisited library. She asked for details of the thread, the size of the hooks. She noted even then that unlike his handwriting the sketches were meticulous. They seemed made by a different person. The youth felt this was his first conversation in years. The next day he heard the motorcar leaving the driveway, the girl with her mother.

Most of the day he sat by the sunlit window, his fingers constructing the fly, echoing his drawing but for the colours. Or stood awkwardly in front of their map and searched it for what he already knew and what he had not known before—the clear line of oaks along the straight Roman road, the long curve of the river. At night he slid from the bed into the darkness and tried to move his ungainly body. It was important he couldn't see himself. If the hip gave way, he fell against a wall or the bed. He moved as long as he could, then got back into the bed, covered in sweat. All this was unknown to his family or the girl's family.

During their last week of work the brothers slipped themselves into their rope halters and leaned over the roof, using the blade of the long-flew knife or the long eaves knife to trim the gable ends. Looking up through the window, the boy could see just the iron blades sweep back and forth, the remnants of straw falling like barley.

Then the family carried him, once more horizontal, back onto their cart and disappeared. The silence that had been lost filled the house again. Now and then in the following months the girl and her parents would hear of the Felons working on a house in a distant village, as if crows had found a new copse to nest in. But the youngest son, Marsh, whenever he was allowed free time, attempted to overcome his limp. He'd wake in the dark and walk past houses they had once thatched, or go down into the river valleys as night began dissolving, already with birdsong. It was the hour with that tense new light that Marsh Felon now began searching for in books whenever the writer strayed from a plot to attempt a description of that special hour, perhaps remembered from the author's youth too. The boy began reading every evening. It allowed him a deafness while his brothers talked. Even if he knew the thatcher's craft, he was separating himself from them.

Plenitude. What does that mean, exactly? A surfeit of things? Replenishment? A complete state? A wished-for thing? The person named Marsh Felon wished to study and inhale the world around him. When Rose's family rediscovered him two years later, a young man, they barely recognized him at first. He was still watchful, but he had become another, already serious, curious about the workings of the wider world. Her parents gathered him in as they had once done during the injured solitude of his youth. Aware of his intelligence, they were to support him through his university years. He had essentially left his own family.

*

Felon nested himself against brick cornices, then climbed up the college tower in the dark, more than a hundred and fifty feet above the unseen landscape of the quadrangle. Three nights a week he tested himself along the rain-slicked tiles until the hour or two before light when buildings and lawns began to display themselves. He had never considered the public tests of rowing or rugby; just his scarred fingers and quick movements revealed his strength. In a secondhand bookstore he had found an anarchic work, *The Roof-Climber's Guide to Trinity*, and assumed at first its obsessions were a fiction, a childhood adventure, so he had begun to climb as if to search out its truthfulness, or perhaps a meticulous raven's nest in a belfry. He saw no one else there on those nights, until one evening he came across two names scratched with a nail, beside the year 1912. He strolled the cloister roofs, ascended rough walls. He felt ghost-like even to himself.

He started seeing other nocturnals. It turned out to be a climbing tradition based on that privately printed book Marsh had discovered by Winthrop Young, a rock climber before his Cambridge days, who, missing such adventures, turned what he called the "sparsely populated and largely anonymous buildings" into his college Alps. *The Roof-Climber's Guide to Trinity*, with maze-like illustrations and meticulous descriptions of the best climbing routes, had during the two previous decades inspired generations of "stegophilists" who ascended drainpipes along the "Beehive Route" and slithered across the insecurity of tiles cresting the Babbage Lecture Theatre. So there would be other climbers, yards away, alongside Felon. He stilled when he saw them, slid past with no acknowledgement. Just once, in a windstorm, his hand reached out and gripped a coat as a body fell past him, and he pulled the person into his arms, the shocked face staring through the buffeting wind at him, an unrecognized first-year student. Felon left him there on a safe ledge and climbed higher.

In December, descending a chapel tower, Felon passed a woman who touched his arm, refusing to let him pass without a greeting. "Hello. I'm Ruth Howard. Mathematics—Girton College." "Marsh Felon," he found himself saying. "Languages." She continued, "You must be the one who caught my brother. You're the secretive. I've noticed you up here before." He could barely see her face. "What else are you studying?" he said. His voice felt loud to him in the dark. "Mostly the Balkans, it's still a mess." She paused, while looking out at nothing. "You know, I'm sure you do . . . there are a few roof sections no one can achieve alone. Would you like to team up?" He made a tentative but negative gesture of his head. She lowered herself and was gone.

The following summer in London he kept in shape by scaling city buildings at night, including the recently built expansions to Selfridges. Someone had charted the emergency exits while the building had been going up, so he was there in rainstorms as well as clear weather. "Marsh Felon," the woman's voice said as if she had just recognized him, though he was in fact hanging on to a slowly loosening gutter with one hand.

"Wait a minute." "All right. It's Ruth Howard, by the way." "I know. I saw you a few nights ago on the east wall, above Duke Street." "Let's go for a drink," she said.

At the Stork she told him about other good climbs she knew of in the city—a few Catholic churches, and Adelaide House along the river, were, she said, the most enjoyable. She told him more about Winthrop Young, as his *Roof-Climber's Guide* was almost a New Testament to her. "He wasn't just a climber, he won the Chancellor's Medal for English Verse and he joined the Friends' Ambulance Unit as a conscientious objector in the Great War. My parents lived near him and knew him. He's a hero to me."

"Are you a conscientious objector?" he asked.

"No."

"Why?"

"It's complicated."

"Were you ever a student at Trinity?" he asked her later.

"Not really. I was looking for the right type of people."

"Who did you find?"

"Someone I followed and picked up on the slopes of Selfridges. He bought me a drink."

Felon found himself blushing.

"Because I caught your brother?"

"Because you told no one about it."

"Am I the type, then?"

"I'm not sure, yet. Let you know, when I know. How did you fall?"

"I never fall."

"You have a slight limp."

"It was the boy in me that fell."

"Even worse. Means it's more permanent. The fear. You come from Suffolk. . . ."

He nodded. Felon had given up guessing how and what she knew about him.

"When you fell, why did you fall?"

"We were thatchers."

"Quaint."

He said nothing.

"I mean it's romantic."

"I broke my hip."

"Quaint," she said again, making a joke out of herself. Then, "We need someone there on the east coast, by the way. Near where you used to live . . ."

"In what way?"

He was prepared for her to say almost anything.

"To keep an eye on certain people. We've finished one war, but there's probably another coming."

He studied maps she had given him of the east coast, all the small paths between its coastal towns, from Covehithe to Dunwich. And then the more detailed maps of farms belonging to people on her list. They had done nothing wrong, were only suspect. "We need to keep an eye on them in case of an invasion," she'd said. "Their sympathies lie with Germany. You could slip in, leave no trace, a hit-and-run, as Lawrence calls it. And that tool . . . what is it called?"

"A long-flew knife."

"Yes. Good name."

He never saw the woman named Ruth Howard again, though he came across her name many years later in a confidential government report about the continuing, unforgiving turbulence in Europe, on a note attached to someone's angry scrawl: *We find ourselves in a "collage" in which nothing has moved into the past and no wounds have healed with time, in which everything is present, open and bitter, in which everything coexists contiguously. . . .*

It was a fierce note.

Still, Ruth Howard had been his introduction to secret wars. She'd taught him the "lost-roof technique" on the heights of Trinity, a phrase, she said, borrowed from Japanese art, where a high perspective, as from a belfry or cloister roof, allows you to see over walls into usually hidden distances, as if into other lives and countries, to discover what might be occurring there, a lateral awareness allowed by height.

And Ruth Howard was correct, he was a secretive. Few would know how or where Felon participated in the various conflicts that would smoulder through the next decades.

Wildfowling

Marsh drove up to White Paint in the dark, and he and the dog watched Rose walk towards the dimmed light of the car and climb into the back seat. Felon reversed, then aimed the car towards the coast. He drove for almost an hour. She was asleep against the liver-coloured dog. Now and then he looked at them. His dog. The fourteen-year-old girl.

At the estuary he let the animal out and set up the camouflage blind. He carried the guns in their hard oilcloth cases from the boot of the car back to where the dog stood, already poised as if stretching towards something out there over the muddy waterless estuary. It was that same unrecorded hour, almost nonexistent, that Marsh Felon was always fond of, with the tide beginning to come in, inch-deep at first. He could hear it in the dark. The only capsule of light anywhere was in the shell of the car where the girl was asleep, her door left open so the amber could be a marker, a compass point. He waited about an hour for the tide to enter and fill the estuary, then went back and held Rose's shoulder till she wakened. She stretched, pushing her arms against the felt of the roof, then sat for a moment looking out into the dark. Where were they? Where was Felon's dog?

He led her through the thick grass to the shoreline, the passing of time still being signalled by the growing depth of water. As light came up it was a foot deep, the landscape almost recognizable. Suddenly everything was awake, the birds were moving out from their nests, the gun dog, formal on the edge of the now two-foot-deep estuary, was moving backwards as the water rose, swirling fast. It would be dangerous to a stranger who was not a strong swimmer; he would be pulled away, even by this shallow tide, whereas earlier he could have walked waist-deep across the hundred-yard stretch of the Blyth estuary to that small temporary island.

Felon fired and the empty cartridge bucked free of the shotgun. The bird's silent fall down into the water. The dog swam out, tussled with it a moment, circled and swam back with the fowl. She noticed how the dog had grabbed it by its feet so he could breathe as he swam. Birds flew over him in chaotic sixes and Felon fired again. Clearer light now. He picked up the other shotgun, explained how to break it open and double-load it. He didn't show her, he explained it, speaking quietly, watching her face's response for what she was actually taking in. He always liked and trusted how she listened, even when younger, her head lifted, watching his mouth. Dogs did that. She fired into the sky at nothing. He made her keep doing that to get used to the sound and recoil.

Sometimes they drove to the Blyth estuary, sometimes to the Alde. After that first night journey, whenever Felon took her wildfowling along the tidal coasts, she climbed into the front seat and stayed awake, even if they barely spoke. She'd peer into the last darkness, the grey trees rushing at them, passing alongside as if uncaught. She was already thinking ahead, rehearsing how heavy the gun would be in her hands, the cold grip of it, the sweep of it up to the accurate height and moment, the recoil and echo of noise along the silence of the estuary. So she could become accustomed to all that while the three of them journeyed towards it in the dark car. The dog leaned between the seats and placed his warm muzzle on her right shoulder, and she leaned over and pressed her own head against his.

*

Rose's taut body and face barely changed over the years, kept a leanness. There was vigilance in her. Marsh Felon could never tell where it came from, for the landscape she grew up in was placid, a self-sufficient place without urgency. Her father, the Admiral, reflected that placidness. He appeared unconcerned with what took place around him, but this was not the complete portrait of him. Marsh was aware that the father, just as he did, had a busier, more official life in the city. The two men accompanied each other on Sunday walks, with Marsh, always the amateur naturalist, speaking of the mystery of chalk hills, where "whole faunas come and go, while the layers of the chalk are built from the efforts of infinitesimal creatures working in almost limitless time." Suffolk, for Rose's father, was such a slow, gradual universe, a plateau of rest. He knew the real and urgent world was the sea.

Between the father and Felon's easy friendship was the girl. Neither of the men seemed tyrannical or dangerous to her. Her father might appear a stuffed shirt when asked about political parties, but he let the family dog, Petunia, clamber onto the sofa and then into his arms. His wife and daughter watched such responses well aware they did not exist for him at sea, where even a scuffed lanyard would be a punishable matter. And he was sentimental about music, would hush them when a specific melody came over the airwaves. When he was not there, his daughter missed that calm maleness that she could sidle next to for warmth when her mother's rules were restrictive. Which perhaps was why Rose, in his absence, sought out Marsh Felon, listening to him openmouthed about the insistent habits of hedgehogs, about a cow eating the afterbirth of its calf in order to renew its strength. She wanted the complex rules of adults and nature. Even in her youth Felon would always talk to her as an adult.

When Marsh Felon returned to Suffolk after long periods of time abroad, she would come to know him again. But she was no longer the young girl he had taught to fish or go wildfowling. She was married, with a daughter, my sister Rachel.

Felon watches Rose with the daughter tucked under her arm. She places Rachel on the grass and picks up the fishing rod, his gift. He knows her first response will be to test its weight, balance it on her fingers, then smile. He has been away too long. All he wants is to again catch that smile. She rubs her open palm against the grain of the impregnated rod, then picks up the infant and walks over to embrace Felon, the child awkwardly between them.

But he watches her now in an alternative way; she is no longer a learning youth, and it disappoints him. Whereas she, having driven up to her parents' home in Suffolk and seeing him again, does not imagine him as anything other than that ally from childhood. The sense of a difference between them is not in Rose, even if she is in the midst of constant breastfeeding, waking at three or four in the darkness. If she is thinking of anything somewhere in the back of her mind, it is not Felon her neighbour from the past, for whom she still has affection, but the career she had been moving towards that her marriage has now expelled from her life. She has a child, is already pregnant with another, so a career as linguist appears lost. She is to remain a young mother. She feels less gymnastic. She even thinks of mentioning this to Felon on their walk, when she is free of the child for an hour.

It turns out that Felon is mostly in London, where she also lives with her husband in nearby Tulse Hill, but they do not run into each other. In London they have separate lives. Felon works at the BBC, along with other projects he says little about. And although he is known as the loveable naturalist on his radio show, behind that portrait he is known by some as a ladies' man—"the boulevardier," her father keeps calling him.

So this afternoon on her parents' lawn at White Paint is the first time she has seen him in years. Where has he been, she wonders. Still, it's now her birthday, and he has surprised her by arriving at her mother's lunch for her with this gift of a fishing rod. And as they meet they promise to save each other an hour's walk alone. "I have the blue-winged olive nymph you once made," she says. It feels like a confession.

But she has become a stranger for him, that taut frame altered and tethered permanently to the child. She is less private, less vigilant, he does not know what it is, exactly, but he feels she has given up what she was, in some way. There was a pouncing manner in her he liked, which is no longer there. And then as she sweeps a cedar branch out of her way he recognizes the faint line of bones at her neck that brings his affection back to what he thought was no longer there.

So he proposes an idea of work to this brightest of women to whom he had once taught all manner of things: that list of the oldest rocks in the county in order of age; the best wood for an arrow, for a fishing rod—the wood she has just recognized by its smell as she held his gift to her face, when he saw the thrill of her smile. Ash. He wants her in his world. He knows nothing about her adult life, that she was, for instance, hesitant and shy longer than was perhaps usual, till she stepped towards what she desired with a determination from which none could prise her away—a habit she will always have, that pattern of hesitancy at first and then complete involvement—just as later on, in the coming years, nothing will draw her away from Felon, no logic of her husband, not even the responsibility of her two children.

Is it Felon who chooses her, or is this something Rose always wished for? Do we eventually become what we are originally meant to be? It may not have been a path built by Marsh Felon at all. Perhaps such a life was what she always wanted, the journey she knew she would at some time leap towards.

He buys and slowly rebuilds an abandoned cottage that makes him a distant neighbour to White Paint. But the small cottage stays mostly uninhabited, and when there he is always alone. His role as host of *The Naturalist's Hour* on BBC Radio, which is heard on Saturday afternoons, displays perhaps his truest nature in those public soliloquies on newts, river currents, the seven possible names for a riverbank, the grayling flies made by Roger Woolley, the varying wingspans of the dragonfly. It is much the way he conversed with Rose whenever they crossed fields or riverbeds. Marsh Felon as a boy housed lizards in his fingers, swept up crickets with his palm and released them into the air. Childhood had been intimate and benign. That was him as he may originally have wished to be, the amateur lover of the natural world he entered whenever he could.

But he is by now "a secretive," with an unnamed position in a government office, and journeying into unstable zones of Europe, so there will be unknown stages in his story. Some theorize that what gives Felon skill in intelligence work derives from his knowledge of animal behaviour—one person recalled Felon making him sit on the bank of a river while explaining warcraft as he fished. "In these local rivers it's the art of coaxing—everything is a waiting game." And another time, as he cautiously dismantled an old wasps' nest, remarking, "You need to know not just how to enter a battle zone but how to get out of it. Wars don't end. They never remain in the past. 'Seville to wound, Córdoba to die in.' That's the important lesson."

Sometimes when he returns to The Saints he catches sight of his family gathering reeds from the marshes, the way he had done as a boy. Two generations back their grandfather had planted reeds along the river marshes, and now his heirs harvest it. There is still no pause within their conversations, but their loud words are now unshared with him and he will not hear of their disappointments in a marriage or their pleasure in a new child. He had been closest to his mother—being hard of hearing had been her defence against their endless talk, and when Marsh read a book it was similar to that comfort of deafness. Now the brothers keep their distance from him, weaving together their own communal stories, for instance about an anonymous thatcher on the coast who took the name of "Long-Flew Knife," prepared, it was said, to kill German sympathizers in the event of an invasion. It was a country myth that spread in whispers. There had been a killing with such a blade, seemingly random, some said part of a local row. From the height of a one-storey roof his brothers looked towards the coast and spoke of it, the name of a thatcher's tool suddenly known in every village.

No, Marsh lost them long ago, even before he left The Saints.

But how did he become what he became, this rural boy curious about the distant world? How did he work his way into a war-skilled gentry? He had been a youth who at twelve could sail a lure and land it faultlessly on a river surface, then swing it across the current to drift towards the presence of a trout; at sixteen he would change his unreadable handwriting to clearly record the design and tying of flies. He needed to be exact about this passion—cutting, sewing the camouflage of dry flies. It filled the silence of his days when he could make a grayling fly blindfolded, even with a high fever, even in high winds. By his mid-twenties he had memorized the topography of the Balkan States, and had an expert knowledge of old maps where distant battles had been fought, now and then journeying to some of those innocent fields and valleys. He learned as much from those who barred the door to him as from those who let him in, gained a slow informal knowledge of women who were to him more like hesitant foxes he once had held briefly and endearingly in his arms as a boy. And by the time a war grew again in Europe, he had become a "Gatherer" and "Sender Out" of young men and women, luring them into silent political service—because of what? perhaps some small anarchy he glimpsed in them, an independence they needed to fulfill—and releasing them into the underworld of the new war. A group that eventually included (unknown to her parents) Rose Williams, the daughter of his neighbours in Suffolk, my mother.

Night of the Bombers

On weekends Rose drives up to Suffolk to visit her children who are living with her mother, safe from the Blitz that is terrorizing London. During one visit, on her second night there, they hear the bombers flying in from the North Sea. A long night. They have all established themselves in the living room of the darkened house, the children sleeping on the sofa, her mother, tired, kept awake by the noise of the planes, sitting by a fire. The house, the earth around it, does not stop shuddering, and Rose imagines all the small animals, voles, worms, even night owls and lighter birds in the air, caught in the avalanche of noise coming from the sky—even fish in the rivers under the turbulence of water because of the never-ending planes from Germany coursing low through the night. She realizes she is thinking the way Felon thinks. *"I need to teach you how to protect yourself,"* he said once. He'd been watching her cast. *"The way a fish—if he sees your line land—will work out where it comes from. He learns to protect himself."* But Felon is not there this particular night of the bombers while she and her mother and children are alone in the darkness of White Paint, with only the face of the radio lit, which speaks quietly about parts of the city—

Marylebone, sections of the Embankment—that are already in ruins. A bomb has landed near Broadcasting House. There are unimaginable casualties. Her mother doesn't know where her father is. It is only the children, Rachel and Nathaniel, her mother and she, who are supposedly safe in this noisy countryside, waiting for the BBC to tell them something, anything. Her mother nods off, then is startled awake by more planes. They were speaking earlier about where Felon might be, and her father. Both somewhere in London. But Rose knows what her mother wants to talk about. As the planes quieten, she hears her say, "Where is your husband?"

She says nothing. The planes recede into the darkness, heading west.

"Rose? I was asking—"

"I don't know, for god's sake. He's overseas, somewhere."

"Asia, is it?"

"Asia is a career, they say."

"You should never have married so young. You could have done anything after university. You fell in love with a uniform."

"As you did. And I thought he was brilliant. I didn't know then what he had been through."

"The brilliant are often destructive."

"Even Felon?"

"No, not Marsh."

"*He's* brilliant."

"But he is also Marsh. He wasn't born into this world. He's the accident, with, it seems, a hundred careers—thatcher, naturalist, an authority on battle sites, and whatever else he is now. . . ."

There is again a weight of silence from her mother. Rose eventually stands up and goes to her, and in the firelight she sees her peacefully asleep. Everyone has their own marriages, she thinks. After the recurring bouts of thunder from the planes her children are asleep on the sofa, defenceless. Her mother's pale fine hands are on the armrests of her chair. Northeast of them is Lowestoft, southeast is Southwold. All along the coast, the army has buried mines on the beaches to protect against a land invasion. They have commandeered homes, stables, and outbuildings. At night everyone disappears, and five-hundred-pound bombs and high-explosive incendiaries whistle down on the sparsely populated houses and streets, so it seems as light as day. Families sleep in cellars, moving their furniture in with them. Most of the children have been evacuated away from the coast. The German planes returning to Europe will jettison their remaining bombs as they head back. So the only evidence of inhabitants comes after the sirens cease and they gather on the Front Parade to gaze at the sky and watch the planes departing.

Rachel struggles awake just before dawn. Rose takes her by the hand and they walk out into the stilled fields, down to the river. Whatever route the bombers took they have not come back this way. The water is flat, undamaged. They hold on to each other and walk along the bank in the dark, then sit, waiting for light. It is as if everything is hiding. *The important thing is I need to teach you to protect those you love.* She still has some of Marsh's long-ago words in her. The morning gets warmer and she removes her sweater. Nothing moves in the shell-shocked water. Her bladder is full but she keeps it that way as part of a prayer. If she does not crouch down, if she does not piss, they will all be safe, in London as well as here. She wants somehow to participate, to control what is happening around her. In this time of unsafety.

"A fish camouflaged in shadow is no longer a fish, just a corner of land-scape, as if it has another language, the way we need to be unknown some-times. For instance, you know me as this person, but you don't know me as another person. Do you understand?"

"No. Not quite." And Felon explained it to her again, glad she did not just say "Yes" to him.

An hour later Rose walks with Rachel towards the faint outline of the house. She is trying to imagine Felon's other lives. At times it feels he is more innocently himself only when he has a creature in his arms or a parrot on his shoulder. His parrot, he has told her, repeats everything it hears, so he can say nothing of importance in its vicinity.

She realizes it is this unknown and unspoken world she wants to participate in.

Quiver

When people in the Service who knew him spoke casually of Felon in public places, any reference to an animal would do. And the range of creatures chosen to depict him often led to comic extremes. The New World porcupine, a diamondback snake, the madrigal weasel—whatever came to mind at that moment was not important, being there only for camouflage. It was this range of creatures assigned to Felon that suggested how unknowable he was.

So he could be photographed in Vienna having dinner at the Casanova Revue Bar with a beautiful teenager and her parents, and, after sending his companions off in a taxi to their hotel, be elsewhere two hours later, with a courier or a stranger. And if a few years later he was seen at that same Vienna bar with Rose, the same beautiful young woman no longer a teenager, he was there not for the seemingly obvious reason but for another purpose, as she was. They would slip from one language to another, depending on who was beside them, or who was noticed over the other's shoulder. They behaved as uncle and niece without irony. It was believable, even to themselves. For he needed to release her often on her own into another role—undressing down to her nakedness into one disguise or another. She might be in a European city working with him, then return on leave to her two children. And after a time she would be with him again in another city where Allied and enemy agents stumbled across each other. But for him, their roles of uncle and niece were a decoy, not only for their work, which freed him to be with her, but to continue his growing obsession.

His job as a Gatherer meant finding talent in either the semi-criminal world or among specialists—such as a well-known zoologist who had spent most of his life in labs weighing the organs of fish, and could thus be relied on to precisely construct a two-ounce bomb in order to destroy a small obstacle. It was only with Rose, eating across from him at some roadside inn, or driving beside him from London towards Suffolk on the dark roads, her pale hands blond under the speedometer as she lit a cigarette for him, it was only with her that the purpose of his work slid from him. He desired her. All those inches of her. Her mouth, her ear, the blue eyes, the quiver at her thigh, her skirt lifted and bunched: was it to satisfy him? His hand wishing to be there. Everything left his mind but that tremor.

The one thing he did not allow himself was to consider how he must appear to her. Normally he'd have assumed he could seduce a woman with his wisdom, character, whatever it was that might have drawn her to him in the first place. But not simply as a man. He felt old. Only his thoughtful eyes could swallow her without hesitation or consent.

And she? My mother? What did she feel? And was it he or she who had persuaded the other into this adventure? I still don't know. I like to believe they entered this tremulous universe as teacher and student. For this was not just physical love and desire: it encompassed the neighbouring skills and possibilities of their surrounding work. The knowledge of how to retreat if contact with the other was broken. Where to hide a weapon in a train carriage so the other would know where it was. Which bone to break in the hand or the face to make a person irrational in response. All of that. Alongside his wish for a moment when she might awaken as if there were Morse between them in the darkness. Or the place she perhaps wished to be kissed. How she would turn onto her stomach. The whole dictionary of love, war, work, education, growing up, growing older.

"There's a walled city near Ravenna," Felon whispered, as if its location needed to remain secret. "And inside the city, within its narrow streets, is a small nineteenth-century theatre, an intimate jewel, that looks as if the rules of its construction were based only on the principles of miniatures. Someday we can visit it." He said this more than once, but they never went there. There were other mysteries he knew of: escape routes out of Naples or from Sofia, the surrounding plains that three armies had camped in with a thousand tents before the second Siege of Vienna in 1683—there was a map he'd seen, made from memory, long after the siege. He explained how mapmakers were once hired, even by great artists such as Bruegel, to help choreograph their crowd scenes. And there were the remarkable libraries to see, such as the Bibliothèque Mazarine in Paris. "One day we can stand within it." He tossed out the offer. It was a further mythical destination, she thought.

What did she contain in comparison to all that experience? It was like the embrace of a giant, she felt raised a league or a fathom into the air in order to witness such knowledge. Even though married, even though a linguist skilled in argument, she felt she had no vista of importance, that she was no more than a girl threading a needle by candlelight.

She had been surprised to discover Felon was secretive and complex almost out of a gentlemanly or shy courtesy. He was better at response, while she was cleverer at intellect, which was why she was eventually put in charge of harvesting data on enemy manoeuvres—as she'd once done on a small scale from a hotel roof, aided by that singular man known to me and my sister as The Moth; and in the fourth year of the war herself began broadcasting over the airwaves into Europe. She who once listened to everything Felon said was no longer the pupil. She became more actively involved, parachuted into the Low Countries after another radio operator was killed, journeying to Sofia, Ankara, and other, smaller outposts that cordoned off the Mediterranean, or wherever uprisings occurred. Her radio signature, Viola, became known widely on the airwaves. My mother had found her way into the larger world, somewhat the way that young thatcher had done.

The Astral Plough

Long before I came to work at the Archives, just after my mother's funeral, I had pulled that paperback from one of her shelves and discovered in it the hand-drawn map on eight-by-six-inch paper of what looked like a chalk hill with low-gradient contour lines. For some reason I had kept this drawing that had no place-names. Years later, when I worked in the Archives, I discovered that whatever needed to be written down or typed up had to be done so on both sides of that same quarto-sized paper stock, single spaced. Every person in the service had to abide by this rule, from the interrogator "Buster" Milmo to a temporary secretary taking shorthand. It was a practice observed in almost every intelligence office, from Wormwood Scrubs—parts of which had once been used as an intelligence headquarters, and where as a boy I assumed my mother was entering to serve a prison term—to Bletchley Park. No other paper stock was allowed. I realized I had a map connected with Intelligence, which had been kept by my mother.

Our building housed a central map room where giant charts floated loosely in midair, so that they could be pulled down on a roller and gathered like landscapes into your arms. I would go there every day to eat a solitary lunch, sitting on the floor, the banners barely moving above me in that nearly windless room. For some reason I was at ease there. Perhaps it was the memory of those distant lunches with Mr. Nkoma and the others, as we waited to receive his casually illicit stories. I went there with the drawing after having it copied onto a transparency and began projecting the slide onto various maps. It took two full days before I found its exact match, on a map whose altitude lines fitted neatly against my original drawing. What I now had, by linking the chalk hill drawing to its reality on a large, specifically named map, was a precise location. Which was where I now knew my mother had once briefly been based with a small unit sent in, as the report had stated, to loosen the linch-pins of a post-war guerrilla group. Where one of them was killed and two of them were captured.

The hand-drawn map suggested intimacy, and I was curious to discover whose intimacy it was, since the drawing, at one time useful, had been saved in a favourite Balzac paperback. My mother had thrown nearly everything else away from that period when they were all doing god knows what, destroying the linch-pins. In our warren we had often come upon cases where the survivors of political violence had taken up the burden of vengeance, sometimes into the next generations. *"How old were they?"* I half remember my mother asking Arthur McCash the night of our kidnapping.

"People behave disgracefully sometimes," my mother had once said to me, when I and three boys in the Fifth Form were temporarily suspended from school for stealing books from Foyles bookshop on Charing Cross Road. Now, these many years later, reading fragments of what clearly were silent political killings committed in other countries, I was appalled not only by my mother's activities, but that she had put my theft in a similar category. She'd been shocked at the stealing of books. "People behave disgracefully!" A mockery of herself perhaps along with her judgement of me.

"*What did you do that was so terrible?*"

"*My sins are various.*"

*

One afternoon a man knocked on my cubicle wall. "You speak Italian, don't you? Your file says so." I nodded. "Come with me. The bilingual in Italian is ill today."

I followed him up a flight of stairs to a section occupied by those fluent in languages, aware that whatever the job was his status was higher than mine.

We entered a windowless room and he handed me a heavy set of earphones. "Who is it?" I asked.

"Doesn't matter, just translate." He switched on the machine.

I listened to the Italian voice, at first forgetting to translate, until he waved his arms. It was a recording of an interrogation, a woman doing the questioning. The audio wasn't good—it seemed to have been done in something cave-like, full of echoes. Also, the man being questioned was not Italian and wasn't being helpful. The recording kept being turned off then switched on again, so there were gaps of time. The interrogation was clearly at an early stage. I had read and heard enough of these now to know they would knock the ground out from under the man later on. For now he was protecting himself by seeming uninterested. His answers wandered. He went on about cricket, complained about some inaccuracies in *Wisden*. They got him off the topic by asking him bluntly about a massacre of civilians near Trieste and about the English involvement with Tito's Partisans.

I leaned forward, stopped the machine, and turned to the man beside me. "Who is this? It would help to have a context."

"You don't need that—just tell me what the Englishman is saying. He works with us, we need to know if anything important was revealed."

"When is . . . ?"

"Early forty-six. The war is officially over, but . . ."

"Where is it happening?"

"It's a recording we captured after the war, from one of the remnants of Mussolini's puppet government—Mussolini already strung up but some of his followers still around. It was found in an area outside Naples."

He signalled me to put on the headphones and started the tape again.

Gradually, after several time jumps in the tape, the Englishman began talking—but about women he'd met here and there, details about the bars they went to, what kind of clothes they wore. And if they had spent the night together. He was easy with the information, offering data that was obviously unimportant: the hour a train got into London, et cetera, et cetera. I turned the machine off.

"What's wrong?" my colleague asked.

"It's useless information," I said. "He's just talking about his affairs. If he's a political prisoner he hasn't revealed anything political. Only what he specifically likes about women. He doesn't seem to like crudeness."

"Who does. He's being clever. He's one of our best. This is stuff that interests only a wife or husband." He turned the tape back on.

Then the Englishman was talking about a parrot that had been found in the Far East, which had lived for decades with a tribe that was now extinct, its whole vocabulary lost. But a zoo had the parrot and it turned out the creature still knew the language. So the man and a linguist were attempting to re-create the language from that one bird. The man was obviously tiring but kept talking, almost as if this way he could delay specific questions. He had been useless to the interrogators so far. The woman was clearly looking for someone, identifications, place-names they could link to a map, a town, a killing, the failure of an expected victory. But then he spoke about one woman's "air of solitude," and in another pointless aside, about a pattern of birthmarks on her upper arm and neck. And suddenly I realized this was something I had seen as a child. And had slept against.

And so it was that during my translation of a recorded interrogation that included descriptions of possibly invented women, and parrot lore—all put forward by the captured man as useless information—I heard described the pattern of birthmarks on my mother's neck.

I returned to my office. But the interrogation stayed with me. I half believed I had heard the man's voice before. I even thought for a while it might belong to my father. Who else would have known those distinguishing marks—the unusual cluster of moles whose pattern, the man had joked, resembled a star formation called the Astral Plough.

*

Each Friday, I boarded the six o'clock train at Liverpool Street Station, and relaxed, just stared at the ribbon of landscape passing me. It was the hour of distilling everything I had gathered during the week. Facts, dates, my official and unofficial research fell away and were replaced by the gradual story, half dreamed, of my mother and Marsh Felon. How they had eventually walked towards each other without their families, their brief moment as lovers and then their retreat, but still holding on to their unusual faithfulness to each other. I had barely a clue as to their cautious desire, of travels to and from dark airfields and harbours. All I had, in reality, was no more than a half-finished verse of an old ballad rather than evidence. But I was a son, parentless, with what was not known to a parentless son, and I could only step into fragments of the story.

*

It was the night driving home from Suffolk after her parents' funeral. The speedometer light on her dress covering her knees. *Damn.*

They had left in darkness. All afternoon she had watched him courteous at the grave, and at the reception listened as he spoke shyly and tenderly about her parents. Country neighbours she had known since childhood came up to her to give condolences and ask after the children who were at home in London—she had not wanted them at the funeral. She had to explain again and again that her husband was still overseas. "A safe return then, Rose." And she would incline her head.

Later she witnessed Felon struggling to move a full and overlapping punchbowl off a rickety table onto a more solid one, the guests' laughter loud beside him. For some reason she'd never felt so relaxed. When everyone had gone, about eight in the evening, she and Felon left for London. She did not want to stay in the empty house. They drove immediately into fog.

They crept along for a few miles, stopping warily at every junction, and paused at a railway crossing for almost five minutes because she thought she heard the howl of a train. If there was a train it remained howling in the distance, as cautious as they were.

"Marsh?"

"What?"

"Do you want me to take over?" The dress had moved as she turned to him.

"Three hours to London. We could stop."

She flicked on a small light.

"I can drive. Ilketshall. Where's that on the map?"

"Somewhere in this fog, I guess."

"Okay," she said.

"Okay what?"

"Let's stop. I don't want to drive in this, after the way they died."

"I know."

"We can go back to White Paint."

"I'll show you my house. You've not seen it in a while."

"Oh." She shook her head, but was curious.

He turned the car—it took three attempts on the narrow fog-blind road—then drove to the cottage he had rebuilt long ago.

"Come."

It was cold inside. "Bracing," she would have said if it was morning, but it was pitch-black, not a clue of light. He had no electricity, just a stove he cooked on, and that kept the place warm. He began burning wood in it. He dragged a mattress in from an unseen room; it was too far, he said, from the heat. All this he had done within five minutes of entering. She'd not said a word, was just watching Felon to see how far he would go, this always careful man, always careful with her. She was disbelieving about what was happening. There was already too much closeness in the room. She was used to being with Felon in open country.

"I'm a married woman, Marsh."

"You are nothing like a married woman."

"And of course you know married women. . . ."

"Yes. But he is in no way a part of your life."

"It's been a long time since that."

"You can sleep here by the fire. I don't have to."

A long silence. Her mind tumbling.

"I think you might need to now."

"Then I want to be able to see you."

He went over to the fire, opened the flue, and it brightened their room.

She lifted her head and watched him directly. "You too, then."

"No, I am not interesting."

She saw herself lit only by the stove's flickering light, with the long sleeves of the dress she'd worn at the funeral. It felt strange. Something had slid under her reason. And also that this was a night of fog, with the world around them invisible, anonymous.

She woke enveloped. His open palm under her neck.

"Where am I?"

"This is where you are."

"Yes. It seems 'this is where I are.' Unexpected."

She slept, and woke again.

"What is it about funerals?" she asked, her head against his body. It would be cold, she knew, beyond the fire's reach.

"I loved them," he said. "Just like you."

"I don't think that's it. I mean, to sleep with their daughter. And after their funeral?"

"You believe they are rolling in their graves?"

"Yes! Besides, now what? I know about your women. My father called you a boulevardier."

"Your father was a gossip."

"I think, after tonight, I am going to stay away from you. You're too important to me."

Even in this distilled, cautious version of Felon and Rose there is a confusion and even uncertainty about what may have happened, what may have been said; nothing quite fits within the rhyme of their story. Who was it, or what, exactly, would break off the relationship that began that night by an iron stove?

She had not been a lover as she had been this night for a long time. What would it be like for him, she wondered, to leave her after this? Would it be like one of his historical anecdotes, where a small army departed a Carolingian border town with courtesy and silence, or would everything around them clatter with repercussions? She would need to leave him before that happened, leave a pawn blocking the river bridge, so neither she nor he could cross it anymore, to make clear it was an ending after this sudden and remarkable glimpse of the other. It needed to still be her life.

She turned to face Felon. She rarely called him Marsh. It was almost always Felon. But she loved the name Marsh. It sounded as if he went on and on and was difficult to cross, to fully understand, that she would get her feet wet, that burrs and mud would attach themselves to her. I think it was then, after their night by the stove, that she decided to return safely to who she still was, and remain separate from him, as if suffering was always a part of desire. She couldn't let her guard down with him. She would wait, however, a bit longer for full light, when the joyous lover he had been would once again become unknown to her, a mystery. At dawn she heard a cricket. It was September. She would remember September.

*

There is a moment during Felon's questioning by the Italian woman when the interrogators swivel away the bright light that is blinding him, and it flares briefly past her face and he, always so damn quick to pick up what occurs around him, sees her clearly. He has, as someone said, "those strangely inattentive eyes that miss nothing." And he notices the smallpox marks on her skin and judges her instantly as no beauty.

Do they intentionally make him aware of the woman questioning him? Can they tell that he is a sensualist, that he can be teased into a petite flirtation? And the brief revelation of the woman—what does that do to him? What is his response? Does it moderate his flirtation? Is he gentler, or more confident? And if they know that much about him, enough to place a woman on the other side of the arc light, hidden in the dark, is that movement of the light accidental or intentional? "Historical studies inevitably omit the place of the accidental in life," we are told.

But Felon in fact is always open to casual accident, a sudden dragonfly or the unexpected revelation of character, and he will play off it, wrongly or rightly. He is inclusive, just as he is broad-shouldered, boisterous in the company of strangers, all this an escape from his secretiveness. He has an openness that grows from having once been a discovering youth. His will is curious more than ruthless. So he needed a tactical executioner beside him, and he found that ability in Rose. He knows he is not the one they are after, but her—the unseen but regularly heard Viola—the woman intercepting their elusive signals over the airwaves, the voice reporting their movements, betraying their whereabouts.

Still, Felon is also a double-sided mirror. Thousands hear him as the genial broadcaster on *The Naturalist's Hour*, mulling over the weight of an eagle or discussing the origin of the term "bolted lettuce," as if he were a neighbour speaking over a shoulder-high fence, unaware of others overhearing him in faraway Derbyshire. Yet to all of them he is unseen as well as familiar. There has been no photograph of him in the *Radio Times*, only a pencil sketch of a man striding in the middle distance, far enough away to be unidentifiable. Now and then he may invite a specialist on voles or a tackle-and-fly designer into the basement studio of the BBC, and during such times try to be the humble listener. But his audience prefers it when he speaks for himself. They are accustomed to his roving mind, as when he unearths the John Clare line where "fieldfares chatter in the whistling thorn," or recites a poem by Thomas Hardy about the devastation to small animals on the seventy or so fields where the Battle of Waterloo was fought.

> The mole's tunnelled chambers are crushed by wheels,
> The lark's eggs scattered, their owners fled;
> And the hedgehog's household the sapper unseals.
>
> The snail draws in at the terrible tread,
> But in vain; he is crushed by the felloe-rim.
> The worm asks what can be overhead,

And wriggles deep from a scene so grim,
And guesses him safe. . . .

It is his favourite poem. He reads the passage slowly and gently, as if in animal time.

*

The woman behind the glare of the arc light constantly alters the line of questioning to catch him unawares. He has chosen to confess to nothing but unfaithfulness and betrayal, perhaps thinking he might blind her with irritation. He has joked his way through the conversation with her on the other side of the lights, but I wondered: had they put a subtle woman in his path to ask him simple questions—allowing him to believe he is misdirecting her with personal details. But were his fictions revealing to her? She seeks a physical description of the woman they hold responsible. Sometimes her questions are obvious and they both laugh, he at her trickery, her laugh more thoughtful. Most of the time, even though exhausted, he recognizes the hidden intent in the question.

"Viola," he repeats, as if bemused when she first brings up the name. And because Viola is a fictitious name he helps compose a fictional portrait for the interrogators.

"Viola is modest," he says.

"Where is she from?"

"From farming country, I believe."

"Where?"

"Not sure." He needs to recapture ground, having perhaps given away too much. "South London?"

"But you said 'farming country.' Essex? Wessex?"

"Oh, you know Hardy. . . . Who else do you read?" he asks.

"We know her signature style on the airwaves. But the one time we intercepted her voice we thought she had a coastal accent we cannot quite place."

"South London, I believe," he reiterates.

"No, we know it is not that. We have specialists. When did you take on that accent you have?"

"What on earth do you mean?"

"Have you always had that way of speaking? A self-made man? Is the difference between you and Viola then to do with class? Because she does not sound like you, does she?"

"Look, I hardly know the woman at all."

"Beautiful?"

He laughs. "I suppose so. A few moles on her neck."

"How much younger than you, do you think?"

"I don't know her age."

"Do you know Denmark Hill? An Oliver Strachey? Long-Flew Knife?"

He is quiet. Surprised.

"Do you know how many of our people were killed by the Communist Partisans—your new allies—in the *foibe* massacres near Trieste? How many hundreds died there—buried in the sinkholes . . . do you think?"

He says nothing.

"Or in my uncle's village?"

It is hot and he is glad when they turn all the lights off for a while. The woman continues speaking in the dark.

"So you don't know what happened there, in that village? My uncle's village. Population four hundred. Now ninety. Nearly all of them killed in one night. A child witnessed it, she was awake, and when she spoke of it a day later the Partisans took her out and killed her too."

"I wouldn't know."

"The woman who calls herself Viola was the radio link between your people and the Partisans. She told them where to go that night. And other locations—Rajina Suma and Gakova. She provided them with information, the mileage from the sea, the blocked exits, how to enter."

"Whoever she is," he says, "she would have just been passing on instructions. She would not have known what was going to happen. She may not even know what happened."

"Perhaps, but hers is the only name we have. Not a general or an officer, just her code name, Viola. No other name."

"What happened in those villages?" Felon asks in the dark, though he knows the answer.

The large arc light is turned on.

"You know what we call it now? 'Bloody autumn.' When you threw your support behind the Partisans to crush the Germans, we were all—Croats, Serbs, Hungarians, Italians—categorized by you as Fascists, and German sympathizers. Ordinary people were now criminals of war. Some of us had been your allies, now we were the enemy. A shift of wind in London, some political whisper, so everything changed. Our villages were turned into ground. There's no evidence of them now. People were lined up in front of common graves, bound with wire so they couldn't run. Old feuds now an excuse for murder. Other villages also erased. In Sivac. In Adorjan. The Partisans always circling closer to Trieste, until they could drive us into the city, where there would be more annihilation. Italians, Slovenes, Yugoslavs. All of them. All of us."

Felon asks, "What was the name of that first village? Your uncle's village?"

"It no longer has a name."

*

Rose and the soldier were moving fast over the rough terrain, wet from the constant river crossings, hurrying to reach the location before it got dark, uncertain where exactly it was. Just a few more valleys, she thought, and she told the soldier that. Everything was in flux. They could not carry a shortwave radio, only the hastily made identity papers they had been given. The man beside her had a gun. They were searching for a hill, a hut at its base, and they eventually saw the structure an hour later.

Their arrival surprised the ones who were there. When Rose and the soldier entered the hut, shivering, their clothes wet, she saw Felon, looking immaculate, fully dry. He was wordless for a moment, then annoyed. "What are you doing . . . ?"

She waved the question away as if to postpone it. She saw another man and a woman, and they stepped towards her, she knew them. There was a kit bag at Felon's feet and he gestured with almost comic aloofness, as if providing clothing was his only role in being there. "Use whatever you want, I suppose," he said. "Get dry." And he walked out. They divided the clothes between the two of them. A heavy shirt was taken by the soldier. She took a pair of pyjamas and what she knew was Felon's Harris Tweed jacket. She had often seen him wear it in London.

"What the hell are you doing?" he asked again when she came outside.

"They've taken control of the airwaves, so there's radio silence. You could not be reached. So I came myself. They've been tracking our communiqués. They know where you are. I've been sent to tell you you have to get out."

"This is not safe for you here, Rose."

"None of you are safe. That's the point. They have your names, they know where you're headed. They've got Connolly and Jacobs. They also claim to know who Viola is." She referred to herself in the third person, as if someone might be listening.

"We'll stay the night," he said.

"Why? Because you have a girl here?"

He laughed. "No. Because we also just arrived."

They ate close to the fire. The talk among them was careful, each uncertain how much the others knew. Each of them had always created a border between themselves and others so that a destination or purpose would not be exposed if any one of them was caught. No one else here knew she was Viola. Or that the man she was travelling with was her bodyguard. Her soldier was shy, as she'd discovered in her attempts at conversation on their sudden two-day journey, even when she asked him where he had grown up. He had no idea what her mission was. Just that she was a woman he had to safeguard.

When she and Felon stepped outside again to talk after the meal, the soldier came too and she asked him to move away so she and Felon could speak privately. He walked off and lit a cigarette in the distance, and she watched the faint pulse of it over Felon's shoulder whenever he inhaled. They could hear the others laughing inside.

"Why?" Felon said it with a tired sigh of judgement. It was almost not a question. "It didn't have to be you."

"You would not have listened to anyone else. And you know too much—everyone's at risk if you're caught. We're without rules of war now. You'd be interrogated as a spy, then you'd disappear. We're not much better than terrorists these days." She said it bitterly.

Felon said nothing, trying to find a weapon, some utensil, to get back into the argument. She reached out and put her hand on him and they stood very still in the dark. A faint light from the fire inside the hut flickered on his shoulders. Everything seemed peaceful, still, as when, during a long-ago evening in Suffolk, a barn owl, white, with a huge head, had floated silently to the earth near them, picked up a small animal—a rodent? or a shrew?—as if a piece of litter on the lawn, and glided up into a dark tree without breaking the arc of movement. "If you come upon their nests," he'd told her then, "you'll find they eat everything. The head of a rabbit, the remnants of a bat, a meadowlark. They're powerful. Their wingspan—you just saw it—what is it—almost four feet? Yet if you ever get to hold one . . . there is no weight at all behind the strength."

"How did you get to hold one?"

"One of my brothers found a barn owl, it had been electrocuted. He passed it over to me. It was large with its beautiful range of feathers, as if scalloped. Yet it weighed nothing at all. When he put it in my hands, my hands lifted, because there wasn't the resistance I was expecting. . . . Are you warm enough, Rose? Shall we go in?" When he spoke to her now suddenly in the present, she had to remember where she was, outside a hut, somewhere near Naples.

Inside, the fire was nearly out. She rolled herself into a blanket and lay there. She could hear the others adapting themselves to comfortable positions. She had mentioned to Felon that she was confused about the location, and he'd quickly sketched a map on a loose sheet of paper to clarify where they were. So her mind was racing over the drawn landscape stretching away from this hut till it reached their two possible escape routes, one of them a harbour where she had to contact a person named Carmen if things went wrong. She could smell the steam from their wet clothes by the fire, and Felon's jacket was rough against her body. There was whispering. The previous year, working with him, she suspected he was involved with Hardwick, the other woman in the hut. Now she could make out muffled talk and movement in the corner of the room where he had bedded down. She forced her mind back to the landscape and imagined the journey ahead with her bodyguard. When she woke it was first light.

Rising early was another remnant of her education with Felon, from the times they used to go wildfowling, or hiking along a river to fish. She sat up and looked towards the darker end of the hut and saw Felon watching her, his companion asleep next to him. She rolled out of the blanket, gathered her dry clothes, and went outside to dress in private. A minute later the bodyguard discreetly followed her.

Felon was up and the rest were awake when she came back in. She went over and gave him back his jacket. She had felt the heaviness of it against her all night. During their quick breakfast he was courteous with her, as if she, not he, were the authority in the group. It had begun earlier, when his eyes watched her from across the hut, while she imagined him in the shadow of his involvement with the other woman.

It would be a few days later that Felon was captured and interrogated, just as she had warned him.

*

"You are a married man, are you not?"

"Yes," he lies.

"I think you're good with women. Was she your lover?"

"Met her just once."

"Was she married? Children?"

"I really don't know."

"What was it made her attractive? Her youth?"

"I wouldn't know." He shrugs. "Perhaps her gait?"

"What is 'gait'?"

"A way of walking, the way one walks. You know people by their gait."

"You like 'gait' in women?"

"Yes. Yes, I do. That's really all I remember about her."

"There must have been something else . . . her hair?"

"Red." He is pleased with his quick fiction, though perhaps he has been too quick.

"When you said 'mole' a while ago, I thought you meant like the animals!"

"Ha!"

"Yes, you confused me. What is it, exactly?"

"Oh, you know, they . . . they are like birthmarks, on skin."

"Ah! One or two birthmarks?"

"I didn't count them," he says quietly.

"I don't believe the red hair," she says.

By now Rose would be in Naples, Felon thinks. Safe.

"Also I think she is very attractive." The woman laughs. "Otherwise you wouldn't avoid admitting it."

They let him go then, rather to his surprise. It is not him they are after, and by then they have located and identified Viola. With his help.

The Street of Small Daggers

She wakes, her face against the word ACQUEDOTTO, a burning pain in her arm, her mind scrambling to know where she is, the hour. Instead she remembers another time, hearing a cicada. It had been six in the evening then and she'd woken to find herself lying on grass, almost the same position she is in now, her cheek against her upper arm. She'd been fully aware of her senses then. All that was wrong with her that time was tiredness. She had walked many miles into the town to meet Felon and having to wait a few hours found a small park beside a footpath and slept, then woke suddenly to hear the mournful cicada. But at first, similarly, she had been unaware of what she was doing there. She had been waiting that time for him in a small park.

Confusing her now is the word *acquedotto,* meaning a path for water, a drain. She raises her head off the drain cover. She needs clarity, to know why she is here like this, needs to think. She sees the range of still-wet cuts on her arm. If there is something voicing itself mournfully now, it is in her. She holds up her wrist, wipes blood off her broken watch, a star of glass, it says it is five or six, early in the morning. She looks at the sky. She begins to remember slowly. She needs to reach a safe house. There is a woman named Carmen she must make contact with, in case she needs help. Rose stands, raises a fold of the dark skirt, holds it in her teeth, and rips the lower third off with her good hand so she can bandage her arm tightly against the pain. Then crouches, breathing heavily. Now downhill to the harbour to find Carmen, wherever she is, and get to a boat. There are always miracles here, they say about Naples.

She leaves the street of the small daggers and recovers the map in her head. Posillipo is the name for the rich part of the city, meaning "break from sorrow." A Greek word, still used in Italy. And she needs to get to the Spaccanapoli, the street that splits the city in two. She moves downhill repeating the names—Spaccanapoli and Posillipo. The racket of seagulls is loud, meaning water. Find Carmen, then the harbour. There's light in the sky now. But what is most alive is her left arm, where the pain is, the bandage already heavy with blood. She remembers now the small knives they used on her. They had discovered her and the soldier after the group separated to take different routes out of the country. How? Who gave something away? As she had entered the outskirts of the city they identified her, killed the soldier. He was just a boy. In some building they began cutting open her arm with each question. After an hour they stopped, left her. She must have somehow got away, crawled onto the street. They would be looking for her. Were they finished with her? Now she is walking downhill, thinking, her senses returning. "A break from sorrow." "A rest from grief." What is *tombiro*? She turns a corner and realizes she has stumbled awkwardly into a brightly lit square.

This was the light in the sky all the time. Not the dawn. But families and other groups surrounding a bar, eating and drinking in the night air, a ten-year-old girl singing in their midst. It is a familiar song, one she sang to her son years before in another language. The scene in front of her could be any evening hour, but it is not early morning. Her watch must have stopped earlier when they interrogated her, the watch said five or six but it meant late afternoon, not the hour before dawn. It must still be before midnight. But the seagulls? Were they attracted only to the light in this crowded square?

She leans against a table, a stranger, watching them talk and laugh, while the girl on a woman's lap sings. It feels medieval, the kind of canvas of a master Felon loved to describe, pointing out its hidden structures, how a crowd radiates out and fills the canvas from something as small as a loaf of bread, which gives it all an anchor. That is how the world interacts, he would say. Here, for her, the loaf of bread is the small girl singing with private joy. It is how she herself feels having come into this loud gathering by following the Spaccanapoli towards where she is supposed to find Carmen. She could take one step forward and be more exposed, but instead she pulls out a chair and sits, resting her wounded arm on the table, the continuous mural around her. She has not lived such a life, of families and community, for a very long time. She has accepted a world of secretiveness, where there is a different power, where there is no generosity.

A woman behind her places her hands gently on her shoulders. "There are always miracles here," the woman says to her.

*

Some months later Felon walks with Rose, as he had once promised they would, into the Bibliothèque Mazarine. They have lunched at La Coupole long into the afternoon, watching each other swallow oysters, drink champagne from slender flutes, until they finish their meal with a crêpe they share. When she reaches out for a fork, he sees the scar above her wrist.

"A toast," she says. "Our war is over."

Felon doesn't raise his glass. "And the next war? You will go back to England, and I shall stay here. Wars are never over. 'Seville to wound. Córdoba to die in.' Remember?"

In a taxi, dizzy, she will lean against him. Where are they going? They swerve onto the Boulevard Raspail, then the Quai de Conti. She is full of uncertain senses, tethered still to this man, guided by him. The past hours have slid into each other unaccountably. She has woken alone across her bed so wide she believed she was drifting on a raft, just as at La Coupole this afternoon the hundred or so empty tables spread in front of her like an abandoned city.

He puts his hand on her shoulder as they walk into the brown building—the great library of Mazarin, who, he announces, was "the default ruler of France after Richelieu's demise." Only Felon, she believes, would use the word "demise" so unconsciously, this man with barely an education before the age of sixteen. The word from a secondary vocabulary he memorized, just as he re-trained his own handwriting away from the coarse script she'd seen in his childhood notebooks beside those precisely sketched molluscs and lizards he would draw from the natural world. A self-made man. An arriviste. Therefore not trusted as authentic by some in the trade, not even himself.

Entering the Bibliothèque, Rose realizes she is, well, vaguely drunk. Her mind drifts from the sentences he is speaking. Three flutes of champagne in the early afternoon anchored by the weight of nine oysters. And now they have somehow entered the fifteenth century, with a thousand or so remnants confiscated from monasteries or surrendered by overthrown aristocracies, even incunabula from the infancy of printing. All of it gathered and protected here after once being damned and therefore hidden for generations. "This is the great afterlife," Felon tells her.

On an upper floor he watches her silhouette move against the luminous windows of the building as if she were being passed by a lit train. Then she is standing in front of a great map of France with its thousand churches, just as he once imagined she would, so this feels like it is a replica of an earlier desire in him. Those maps always oppressive with faith, as if the only purpose in life was to journey from one church altar to another rather than cross the meticulous blue of a river to reach a distant friend. He prefers older maps that are cityless, marked only by contour lines so they can even now be used for accurate reconnaissance.

Felon stands beside a gathering of marble scholars and philosophers, turning quickly as if he might catch a look or a thought in them. He loves the permanent judgement on the faces of statues, their clear weakness or deviousness. In Naples he stood before a brutal emperor, and he remembers still how the eyes in that evasive stone face never met his, no matter how much he moved from side to side in order to catch his attention. There are times he feels he has become that man. Rose prods him with her fingers and he turns to her. They walk beside a row of antique desks, each lit with its own amber light. One reveals the hurried handwriting of a saint, another that of one executed in his youth. A chair holds Montaigne's folded jacket.

Rose inhales everything. It feels like the continuation of their meal, the taste of oyster suddenly alongside the smell of desk varnish and ancient paper porous in the air. She has barely spoken since arriving here. And when he points out a detail, she does not respond, eager to discover only what this means for herself. She has adored this man all her life but feels the clash of herself against this ancient place. *This is the great afterlife.* Just as she perhaps is his. Did he always see her this way? She's drunk with this small perception.

She ignores a light rain as she walks the city alone, having slipped his leash. When she loses her way, she does not ask for directions, intent on uncertainty, laughing as she passes the same fountain twice. She wants accident, freedom. She has been brought into this city for a seduction. She can imagine everything, how it will occur. His clearly visible ribs that she will lean her head against. Her hand on the fur of his belly, rising with the twitch of it. Her mouth open with praise and kindness as he turns, enters her. She crosses a bridge. It is four in the morning when she comes back to her room.

She wakes at first light and walks into his adjoining room. Felon is asleep in the more modest bed he has chosen. He insisted when they arrived that she take the grander room. He is on his back, eyes shut, hands at his sides, as if praying or tied to a mast. She draws back the high, heavy curtains so the room fills with wintry light and furniture, but he does not wake. She watches him, conscious of him now in some other world, perhaps as the uncertain boy he was in his teens. She has never met Felon as an uncertain person: it is the remade man she knows. He has shown her over the years the great vistas she desired; but she thinks now that perhaps the truth of what is before you is clear only to those who lack certainty.

She moves through the brocaded room of the hotel. She has not taken her eyes off him, as if they are in the middle of a mimed conversation they have never had. There has been this long twinned story between them, and she is no longer sure how to remain still allied to him. A Paris hotel. She will remember the name always, or perhaps she will need to forget it. In the bathroom she washes her face to clear her thoughts. She sits on the edge of the bathtub. If she has imagined his courtship of her, she has also imagined hers.

She returns to his room, watching for any small movement in him, in case this is false sleep. Pauses, realizes that if she leaves now she will never be sure. Slips off her shoes and moves forward. Lowers herself onto the bed and stretches out beside him. My ally, she thinks. She remembers small particles of their history she will never be able to let go of, some forgotten whisper of confidence, some grip of his hand, a recognition across a room, him dancing with an animal in a field, how he learned to speak clearly and slowly on *The Naturalist's Hour* so his near-deaf mother could understand him during those Saturday afternoons, how he knotted and bit the fine nylon when he completed that blue-winged olive nymph. When she was eight. When he was sixteen. That was only the first layer. There were more private depths. Him lighting a stove in a cold, dark cottage. The almost silent notes of a cricket. Then, later, him in a hut in Europe, standing up, leaving Hardwick asleep on the hut floor. All the scars on her arm he has not seen. She rolls onto her side to look at his face. Then she will leave. This is where you are, she thinks.

*

So much left unburied at the end of a war. My mother returned to the house built in an earlier century, which still signalled its presence over the fields. This had never been a hidden place. You could make out its whiteness almost a mile away as you listened to the rustle of pines surrounding you. But the house itself was always silent, a fold in the valley protecting it. A place of solitude, with water meadows sloping to the river, and where if you stepped outside on a Sunday you might still hear the bell from a Norman church miles away.

Rose's most insignificant confession to me during our last days together may have been the most revealing. It was about this house she had inherited. She ought to have chosen a different landscape, she said. Her wish for disinheritance or exile had been proclaimed years earlier when she separated herself from her parents, hiding from them what she was doing during the war, and becoming unknown even to her children. Now her return to White Paint was, I assumed, what she wanted. But it was an old house. She knew each slight incline of hall, every stiff window casing, the noise of winds during different seasons. She could have walked blindfolded through its rooms into the garden and stopped with assurance an inch from a lilac. She knew where the moon hung each month, as well as which window to view it from. It was her biography since birth, her biology. I think it drove her mad.

She accepted it not just as safety or assurance, but as fate, even that loud noise from the wooden floor, and the realization of this shook me. It was built in the 1830s. She would open a door and find herself in her grandmother's life. She could witness the generations of women in their labours with a husband's visit now and then, and child after child, cry after cry, wood fire after wood fire, the bannister smoothed from a hundred years of touch. Years later I would come across a similar awareness in the work of a French writer. "I thought about it some nights till it almost hurt . . . saw myself preceded by all those women, in the same bedrooms, the same twilight." She had witnessed her mother in such a role when her father was at sea, or in London returning only on weekends. This was the inheritance she had come back to, the prior life she had run from. She was once more back in a small repeating universe that included few outsiders—a family of thatchers working on the roof, the postman, or Mr. Malakite arriving with sketches for the greenhouse he was building.

I asked my mother—it was probably the most personal question I asked her—"Do you see yourself in me at all?"

"No."

"Or do you think I might be like you?"

"That is of course a different question."

"I'm not sure. Perhaps it's the same."

"No, it isn't. I suspect there might be a similarity and connection. I'm distrustful, not open. That may be true of you. Now."

She had gone way beyond what I was considering. I was thinking of something such as courtesy or table manners. Though her present solitary life had not made her courteous.

She had little interest in what others were up to, as long as they left her alone. As for table manners, she'd shaved the consumption of meals down to an aerodynamic minimum: one plate, one glass, with the table wiped clean ten seconds after the roughly six-minute meal was over. Her daily path through the house was so ingrained a habit she was unaware of it unless it was interrupted. A conversation with Sam Malakite. Or a long walk into the hills while I was working with him. She felt protected by what she believed was her total insignificance and anonymity to those in the village, while within the house there was the nightingale floor—that landmine of noises which would signal any intruder entering her territory. Her nightingale in the sycamore.

But that eventual stranger she expected never stepped indoors.

"Anyway, why?" She now insisted on continuing our small conversation. "What were you thinking could have been the same between the two of us?"

"Nothing," I said smiling. "I thought perhaps table manners, or some other recognizable habit?"

She was surprised. "Well, my parents always said, as everyone's parents probably did, 'Someday you may be eating with the king, so watch your manners.'"

Why had my mother chosen to alight on just those two thin branches she saw as questionable skills or weaknesses in herself? "Distrustful" and "not open." I understand now how she might have needed to learn those qualities in order to protect herself in her work, as well as in her marriage to a destructive and disappearing man. So she broke out from her chrysalis and slipped away to work with Marsh Felon, who had broadcast those seeds of temptation when she was young. His was the faultless campaign of a Gatherer. He had waited, drawing her into the Service in much the same way he himself had been drawn in, almost innocently. Because what she wanted, I suspect, was a world she could fully participate in, even if it meant not being fully and safely loved. "Oh, I don't want to be just worshipped!" as Olive Lawrence had announced once to Rachel and me.

We never know more than the surface of any relationship after a certain stage, just as those layers of chalk, built from the efforts of infinitesimal creatures, work in almost limitless time. It is easier to understand the mercurial, unreliable relationship that existed between Rose and Marsh Felon. As for the story of my mother and her husband, that ghost in her story, I have only the image of him sitting in that uncomfortable iron chair in our garden, lying about why he was leaving us.

I had wanted to ask her if she saw my father in me at all, or if she thought I might be like him.

*

It was to be my last summer with Sam Malakite. We were laughing and he leaned back on his heels and watched me. "Well, you have changed. You barely spoke the first season you worked with me."

"I was shy," I said.

"No, you were quiet," he said, being more aware and conscious of what I had been than I was. "You have a quiet heart."

Now and then, in an uninterested way, my mother asked how my work with Mr. Malakite was going, was it at all difficult?

"Well, there is no *schwer*," I replied, and caught a rueful smile on her face.

"Walter," she murmured.

So it was something he must often have said, even to her. I took a breath.

"What happened to Walter?"

A quietness, then, "What did you say you two called him?" She threw the book she was reading onto the table.

"The Moth."

She'd lost the wry smile I had witnessed seconds earlier.

"Was there even a cat?" I asked.

Her eyes startled. "Yes, Walter told me about your talk. Why did you not remember the cat?"

"I bury things. What exactly happened to Walter?"

"He died protecting you both that night, at the Bark. The way he protected you when you were small, that time you ran away, after your father killed your cat."

"Why were we not told he was protecting us?"

"Your sister realized. It is why she will never forgive me his death. I suppose he was the true father to her. And he loved her."

"Do you mean he was in love with her?"

"No. He was just a man without children, who loved children. He wanted you safe."

"I didn't feel safe. Did you know that?"

She shook her head. "I think Rachel felt safe with him. I know you felt safe with him as a small boy. . . ."

I stood up. "But why were we not told he was protecting us?"

"Roman history, Nathaniel. You need to read it. It is full of emperors who cannot tell even their children what catastrophe is about to occur, so they might defend themselves. Sometimes there is a necessity for silence."

"I grew up with your silence. . . . You know I leave soon, and I won't see you until Christmas. This could be our last talk for a while."

"I know, dear Nathaniel."

It was September when I began college. Goodbye, goodbye. There was no embrace. I knew that every day she would at some point climb into the hills and reaching a crest look back at her house tucked safely into its fold of earth. Half a mile away would be the Thankful Village. She'd be at a great height, as Felon had taught her. A tall, lean woman coasting the hills. Almost certain of her defences.

*

When he comes, he will be like an Englishman, she had written. But
the person who came for Rose Williams was a young woman,
somebody's heir. This is, I now tell myself, how it happened.
Our mother never went into the village, but the villagers knew
where Rose Williams lived, and the woman had come straight
to White Paint, dressed as a cross-country runner, no props or
disguises. Even that might have been obvious to my mother,
but it was a dark October evening and it was too late when she
made out the woman's pale oval face through the condensation of the greenhouse window. She was standing there, still.
Then broke the pane with her right elbow. She's left-handed,
my mother must have thought to herself.

"You are Viola?"

"My name is Rose, dear," she said.

"Viola? Are you Viola?"

"Yes."

It must have felt no worse than all the possibilities of death
she had imagined, even dreamt about. Quick and fatal. As if
it was finally an ending of feuds, of a war. Perhaps allowing
a redeeming. That is what I think now. The greenhouse was
humid and with the broken pane there was a breeze. The young
woman fired again to make sure. And then she was running like
a harrier over the fields as if she were my mother's soul leaving her body, the way my mother herself had fled this house at
the age of eighteen to go to university in order to study languages and meet my father during her second year, give up the
idea of law school, have two children, and then flee us as well.

A WALLED GARDEN

A year ago I came across a book by Olive Lawrence in our local store, and that afternoon while I set up a humming twine to scare the scavenger birds in the garden, I kept waiting for evening so I could read it without interruption. Apparently it was the basis of a forthcoming television documentary, and so the next day I went out and bought a television set. Such an object has never been part of my life, and when it arrived it was a surreal guest in the Malakites' small living room. It was as if I had suddenly decided to buy a boat or a seersucker suit.

I watched the programme, unable at first to compare the Olive Lawrence I saw on the box to the one I'd known as a teenager. To be truthful I no longer remembered what she looked like. She had been mostly a presence for me. I remembered how she moved, as well as the no-nonsense clothes she wore, even when arriving for a night out with The Darter. As for her face, the one I saw speaking to me now had the same enthusiasm, and this quickly became the face I attached to my earlier memories of her. Now she was clambering up a rockface in Jordan, now rappelling down while still addressing the camera. Once again I was being offered specific wisdoms about water tables, the varieties of hail across the European landmass, how leaf-cutter ants could destroy whole forests—all this data about the complex balance of nature was being handed with clarifying ease to us in that same small female palm of hers. I had been right. She could have knitted together my life wisely, not avoiding the complexity of distant rivalries or losses that were unknown to me, in much the way she was able to recognize a tempest preparing itself, or the way she had recognized Rachel's epilepsy by some gesture or quiet evasion in her. I had benefited from the clarity of female opinion in this person who had no close connection to me. In the brief time I knew her, I believed Olive Lawrence was on my side. I stood there and was perceived.

I read her book, watched the documentary in which she hiked across ravaged olive orchards in Palestine, stepped on and off Mongolian trains, bent over and diagrammed the figure-eight path of the lunar sky on a dusty street using walnuts and an orange. She was unchanged, still constantly new. A long time after my mother told me of Olive's war work, I'd read the terse official reports of how scientists recorded wind speeds, preparing for D-Day, and how she and others had risen into a dark sky infested with other gliders that shuddered in the air brittle as glass, in order to listen to how porous the wind was and search for rainless light, so they could postpone or confirm the invasion. The weather journals she had shown me and my sister, full of medieval woodcuts depicting varieties of hail, or sketches of Saussure's cyanometer, which distinguished the various blues in the sky, were never just theoretical to her. She and others must have felt like magicians at that moment, conjuring up what generations of science had taught them.

*

Olive was the first to reappear out from that half-buried era when we all had met at Ruvigny Gardens. As for The Darter, I still had no clue as to where he lived. It was years since I had seen him, and I could not even remember his real name. He and The Moth and the others existed now only in that ravine of childhood. While my adult life had been spent mostly in a government building, attempting to trace the career my mother had taken.

Now and then there would be days in the Archives when I'd come across information from distant events that overlapped with my mother's activities. I would in this way glimpse details of another operation or place. And so one afternoon, following a tangent to her activities, I came upon references to the transportation of nitroglycerine during the war. How it was transported secretly across the city of London and, because it was dangerous freight, how this needed to be done at night, with the public unaware. This had continued even during the Blitz, when there was just warlight, the river dark save for one dimmed orange light on bridges to mark the working arch for water traffic, a quiet signal in the midst of the bombing, and the barges ablaze, and shrapnel frapping across the water, while on the blacked-out roads the secret lorries crossed the city three or four times a night. It was a thirty-mile journey from Waltham Abbey, where the Great Nitrator produced nitroglycerine, to an unnamed underground location in the heart of the city, which turned out to be on Lower Thames Street.

Sometimes a floor gives way and a tunnel below leads to an old destination. Barely pausing I made my way to the large room of hanging maps. I pulled down various charts, searching out possible routes the nitro trucks might have taken. I knew, almost before my hand traced their path, the indelible names: Sewardstone Street, Cobbins Brook Bridge, a jog west from the graveyard, then south, until it reached Lower Thames Street. The night route I used to take with The Darter, when I was a youth, after the war was over.

My long-forgotten Darter, that smuggler, a minor criminal, had possibly been a hero of sorts, for the activity was danger-ous work. What he'd done after the war was just a consequence of the peace. That familiar false modesty of the English, which included absurd secrecy or the cliché of an innocent boffin, was somewhat like those carefully painted formal dioramas that hid the truth and closed the door on their private selves. It had concealed in some ways the most remarkable theatrical performance of any European nation. Along with undercover agents, who included great-aunts, semi-competent novelists, a society couturier who'd been a spy in Europe, the designers and builders of false bridges on the Thames that were meant to confuse German bombers who attempted to follow the river into the heart of London, chemists who became specialists on poisons, village crofters on the east coast who were given lists of German sympathizers to be killed if and when the invasion came, and ornithologists and beekeepers from Kew, as well as permanent bachelors well versed in the Levant and a handful of languages—one of whom turned out to be Arthur McCash, who continued in the Service most of his life. All of them abiding by the secrecy of their roles, even when the war was over, and receiving only, years later, a quiet sentence in an obituary that mentioned they had "served with distinction in the Foreign Office."

It was nearly always a wet, pitch-black universe when The Darter drove the cumbersome nitroglycerine lorries, passing gardens with their Anderson shelters, his left hand at the gears, shifting them in the dark, aiming the missile-like vehicle towards a warehouse in London. It was two in the morning, there was the map in his head, so he could travel at ridiculous speeds through the night.

I spent the afternoon with these discovered dossiers. Learning about the make of the lorries, the weight of the nitro transported on each journey, how during the night certain streets had muted blue lights to discreetly illuminate a sudden turn. For most of his life The Darter's careers had been camouflaged, unknown to others. The illegal boxing rings in Pimlico, the dog tracks, the smuggling. But in his wartime career he had been watched and fully known. He needed to sign in, have his face confirmed against a photograph, then sign out at Lower Thames Street. His every night journey recorded. For the first and only time in his life, he was "in the books." He who had been so proud of not appearing in that encyclopaedic manual listing dog-track criminals. Three journeys a night from the

Gunpowder Mills, back and forth, when most of the East End of the city was asleep and unaware of the existence and danger of what was happening on night roads. But always recorded. So now, these years later, in that room of hanging maps, I was able to find the marked-up routes, aware how similar the journeys were to those we had taken those nights from the East End, from somewhere near Limehouse Basin to the centre of the City.

I stood in the empty map room, the banners swaying as if touched by a sudden breeze. I knew somewhere there would be a file on all the drivers. I remembered him still only as The Pimlico Darter, but along with a passport-sized photograph would be his real name. In an adjacent room I pulled open cabinet drawers, looking at index cards of black-and-white photographs of gaunt men still in their youth. Until there was the name I had not remembered, beside a face I did. Norman Marshall. My Darter. "Norman!" I now recalled The Moth yelling in our crowded living room in Ruvigny Gardens. It was a fifteen-year-old picture of him with, somehow obsessively beside it, his updated address.

Here was The Darter.

There would be a lit cigarette in his left hand resting on the wheel as he swerved those corners, his right elbow on the open window frame so his arm was wet from the harsh rain that was keeping him alert. There was no company to talk to on those nights, and he was no doubt singing that old song to stay awake, about a dame, who was known as the flame.

*

Our heroes do not usually, after a certain age, teach or guide us anymore. They choose instead to protect the last territory where they find themselves. Adventurous thought is replaced with almost invisible needs. Those who once mocked the traditions they fought against with laughter now provide only the laughter, not the mockery. Was this what I came to believe about The Darter the last time I saw him? After I had become an adult? I am still not sure. I now had an address for where he was, and went to see him.

But during that final meeting, I could not tell if he was simply uninterested in me, or whether there was a hurt or an anger towards me. I had after all upped and left his world suddenly years ago. And now here I was, no longer that boy. And while I remembered my adventures with him during that confused and vivid dream of my youth, The Darter would not speak of the past as I wished him to do. I had wanted to catch up on all of them, but he kept steering me back to the present. What was I doing now? Where did I live? Was I . . . ? So all that I could really do was interpret the visit by recognizing the conversational barriers he set up. Just as I noticed that he seemed obsessively careful of where things existed and needed to remain in his kitchen, so if I picked up something—for instance a glass, a coaster—he recalled where it had to be returned to.

He had not been expecting me to arrive at his door that day, at that hour, in fact had not been expecting me at all. So the order in his flat was clearly an everyday habit, whereas my memory of The Darter, which I admit may have become exaggerated over the years, was of a man around whom things got lost or fell to pieces. But here was a welcome mat on which you needed to brush the soles of your shoes before entering, a neatly folded tea towel, and down the hall two doors that I saw him carefully close as we walked back to the kitchen to put on the kettle.

I was living a solitary life, so I recognize solitary, as well as the small dimensions of order that come with that. The Darter was not solitary. He had a family now: a wife named Sophie, he said, and a daughter. This surprised me. I tried to guess which of his paramours had ensnared him or had been ensnared by him. Surely not the argumentative Russian. In any case, that afternoon he was alone in the flat and I did not meet Sophie.

The fact that he was married and had a child was as far back as he would go in speaking of the past. He refused to talk about the war and brushed off my laughing questions about the dog trade. He said he remembered little of that time. I asked if he had seen the programme Olive Lawrence had done for the BBC. "No," he said quietly. "I missed it."

I did not want to believe him. I hoped he was just continuing to be evasive. I could forgive that, that he had not forgotten but had shut her out of his life as well, rather than that he could not be bothered to turn on a television. Or perhaps I was the only one left who remembered those times, those lives. And so he kept placing obstacles on the road back to our past, that wouldn't allow me to reach it, though he could see that was why I had come. He seemed nervous too—I wondered at first if he assumed I was judging whether he had done well or had made a disappointing choice in life.

I watched him pour tea into each of our cups.

"I heard from someone that Agnes had a difficult time. I tried to find her but couldn't."

"I think we all went our own way," he said. "I moved to the Midlands for a while. I could be a new face there, if you know what I mean. Someone without a past."

"I remember those nights with you on the barge, with the dogs. Most of all."

"Do you? Is that what you remember most?"

"Yes."

He raised his cup in a silent ironic toast. He would not return to those years. "So how long are you here? What do you do with yourself?"

It felt to me that both questions, side by side, showed a lack of interest. So I told him without too much detail where I was living, what I did. I invented something for Rachel. Why did I lie? It may have just been the way he asked me. As if all the questions were insignificant. He appeared to want nothing from me. "Do you still import things?" I asked. He waved the remark away. "Oh, I go up to Birmingham once a week. I'm older, not travelling much now. And Sophie works in London." He stopped there.

His hand smoothed the tablecloth and I got up eventually after too much silence from the man whose company I had at one time grown to love, after first disliking him and then fearing him. I thought I had experienced every aspect of him, the roughness, then the generosity. So it was difficult now to see him so static, to have every sentence of mine swept cleverly away to a dead end.

"I should go."

"All right, Nathaniel."

I asked if I could use his bathroom for a moment and went down the narrow hall.

I looked at my face in his mirror, no longer the boy who had travelled with him on those midnight roads, whose sister he had once helped save from an attack. I turned around in that small space as if the room had an unbroken seal, was the only place that might reveal something more of my wild, unreliable hero from the past, my teacher. I tried to imagine what kind of woman he had married. I picked up the three toothbrushes on the edge of the sink and balanced them on my palm. I touched and smelled his shaving soap on the shelf. I saw three folded towels. Sophie, whoever she was, had brought order to his life.

All this was surprising to me. All this was sad. He'd been an adventurer, and now I stood there, claustrophobic within his life. How calm and content he had appeared, pouring the tea, stroking the tablecloth. He who was always taking bites out of other people's sandwiches while rushing to some questionable meeting, excitedly picking up someone's dropped playing card on a street or waterfront, tossing the peel from a banana over his shoulder into the back seat of the Morris, where Rachel and I sat with the dogs.

I went out into the narrow hall and looked for a while at a framed piece of cloth embroidered with words. I don't know how long I stood there looking at it, reading it, and rereading it. I put my fingers on it, then pulled myself away and very slowly walked to the kitchen. As if this was certain to be the last time I was here.

At the front door of The Darter's flat, about to leave, I turned to say, "Thanks for the tea. . . ." I was still not sure what to call him. I had never called him by his real name. The Darter nodded with a precise smile, enough of a smile so as not to appear rude or angry with me for invading his privacy, then closed the door on me.

I was miles away, caught up in the noise of the train back to Suffolk, before I allowed myself to gather our lives through the prism of that afternoon visit. There had been no attempt to forgive or punish me. It was worse. He did not wish me in any way to understand what I had done, with my quick and unwarned disappearance those years ago.

What led me to understand what had taken place in his flat was remembering what a great liar The Darter was. How, when surprised by a policeman or security guard at a warehouse or museum, he would improvise an unplanned lie that was so intricate and even so ridiculous that he would be laughing at it himself. People did not usually lie and find it funny at the same time, that was his disguise. "Never plan a lie," he told me during one of those night journeys. "Invent as you go along. It's more believable." The famous counterpunch. And the way he always breasted his cards. The Darter had poured the tea so calmly, while his mind and heart must have been on fire. He barely looked at me as he spoke. He watched only the thin stream of ochre-coloured tea.

There was always care in Agnes for those around her. This is what I remembered most about her. She could be loud, argumentative. Tender with her parents. She clutched at all aspects of the world, but there was care. She had drawn the little portrait of us at our meal, then double-folded the butcher paper, so it was contained in what looked like a frame, and put it in my pocket. That is how she would hand over a gift, even something as worthless, as priceless, as that, saying, *"Here, Nathaniel, for you."* And I, who was still a naïve, coarse fifteen-year-old, had received it and kept it in silence.

We are foolish as teenagers. We say wrong things, do not know how to be modest, or less shy. We judge easily. But the only hope given us, although only in retrospect, is that we change. We learn, we evolve. What I am now was formed by whatever happened to me then, not by what I have achieved, but by how I got here. But who did I hurt to get here? Who guided me to something better? Or accepted the few small things I was competent at? Who taught me to laugh as I lied? And who was it made me hesitate about what I had come to believe about The Moth? Who made me move from just an interest in "characters" to what they would do to others? But above all, most of all, how much damage did I do?

There had been a closed door ahead of me as I stepped from The Darter's bathroom. Beside it, on the wall, was a framed piece of cloth with an embroidered blue sentence.

> *I used often to lie awake*
> *through the whole night,*
> *and wish for a large pearl.*

Below it, stitched with thread of a different colour, was a birthdate, with the month and the year. Thirteen years ago. There was no reason why The Darter should have known that a piece of embroidered cloth would give it away. "Sophie," his wife, had made it for herself and the child. It was something she used to say to herself before she fell asleep. I remember. She probably would not even recall she had said the line to me once, or if she still remembered that night when we talked to each other in the darkness of that borrowed house. Even I had forgotten it until now. Besides, she would never have assumed I would reappear one afternoon, in her home, and see that wish of hers so evident on the wall.

And now a landslide, from a simple stitched sentence. I did not know what to do. Hers had been the story I never followed. How could I travel back through time to Agnes of Battersea, to Agnes of Limeburner's Yard, where she'd lost that cocktail dress. To Agnes and Pearl of Mill Hill.

If a wound is great you cannot turn it into something that is spoken, it can barely be written. I know where they live now, on a treeless street. I need to be there at night and yell her name out so she can hear it, her eyes opening silently from sleep, and sit up in the darkness.

What is it? He will say to her.

I heard . . .

What?

I don't know.

Go to sleep.
I suppose so. No. There it is again.
I keep calling and wait for her response.

I had not been told anything, but like my sister with her theatrical inventions, or Olive Lawrence, I know how to fill in a story from a grain of sand or a fragment of discovered truth. In retrospect the grains of sand had always been there: the fact that no one had spoken to me of Agnes when I assumed they might have, the now understandable cold-blooded silence of The Darter in his flat towards me. And the folded towels—she had after all been a waitress, a washer and cleaner like me in various kitchens, and lived in a small council flat, where neatness was a necessity. The Darter must have been amazed by such rules and beliefs in a pregnant seventeen-year-old girl who would go on to cordon off the bad habits of his life so efficiently.

I imagine the two of them—with what? Envy? Relief? Guilt that I had not known what I was responsible for till now? I thought how they must have judged me. Or was I the unspoken subject in much the way The Darter had responded to Olive Lawrence's television programme, as well as her book that he had never picked up. A dismissal of us all . . . he didn't have time now, he needed to travel to the Midlands once a week, there was a child to raise, the times were sparse and hard.

A few weeks after Agnes discovered she was pregnant, and with no one else she felt able to speak to about it, she had taken one bus, then another, and got off near The Pelican

Stairs, where The Darter lived. She had not seen me for over a month and assumed that was where I was. It was dinnertime. There was no answer at the door, so she sat on the steps while the street darkened around her. When he did return home she was asleep. He touched her awake, she didn't know where she was, then recognized my father. So that upstairs, when she told him her situation, not knowing where I was or where I had gone to, The Darter had needed to confess another truth, as to who he really was, and the way he really knew me, and where I might have gone or been taken.

They sat there all night in his narrow flat, beside a gas fire; it was like a confessional. And during and after the several repeated and circular conversations to calm her disbelief, did he tell her what he did, what his profession was?

A short while ago I saw an old film revived in a cinema where the central character, an innocent man, is wrongly convicted and his life ruined. He escapes from a chain gang but will be forever on the run. In the last scene of the film he meets the woman he loved in his earlier life but can be with her only briefly, knowing he is in danger of being caught. As he steps back, away from her into the darkness, she cries out, *"How do you live?"* And our hero, played by Paul Muni, says, *"I steal."* And with that last sentence the movie ends, and the film darkens, closing on his face. When I saw that film, I thought of Agnes and The Darter, and wondered when and how she had discovered the illegality of what he did. How she had dealt with this knowledge of her husband's insecure criminality in their life together, in order that they could survive. Everything I remembered about Agnes I still loved. She had pulled me out from my youthful privacy by making me so fully aware of her. But she also was the most truthful person I knew. She and I had broken into houses, stolen food from the restaurants we worked in, but we were harmless. She argued at dishonesty or unfairness. She was truthful. You did not damage others. What a wondrous code to already have at that age.

So I thought of Agnes and this man she had liked so much, the one she believed was my father. When and how did she discover what he did? There are so many questions I want answered by some version of the truth.

"How do you live?"

"I steal."

Or did he keep that from her a little longer, until another meeting on another night in that narrow Pelican Stairs flat? One solution, one resolution at a time. First this. And then that. And only afterwards would he say what he was willing to do, and it was no longer one of those moments in a love song he hummed to himself about how everything occurred spontaneously through quick cause and effect, so that one fell in love while down by the shore an orchestra was playing. No longer the simplicity of coincidence, happenstance. There was, I knew, a great affection between them. They had that to go forward with, alongside their different ages and suddenly different roles. There was no one else, in any case.

He had assumed he would always be independent and gateless. He felt he knew the intricacies of women. He may have even told me earlier that his numerous suspect professions were to affirm his independence and lack of innocence to others. So now, as he simultaneously attempted to calm her, to make her understand the less innocent, less truthful world, he needed in some way to bring her out from her focused self-defeating self. Were there many conversations before he suggested marriage? He knew she needed to be aware of what he really did, before she could make a decision. It must have shocked her—not because he might be taking advantage of her but because of something more surprising. He was offering a safe path out of the closing world she was in.

She moved with him into a small flat. There was no money for anything larger. No, I suspect they did not think of me. Or judge me or dismiss me. That is my sentiment from a distance. They were in a busy life, where each farthing mattered, where every tube of toothpaste was bought at a specific price. What was happening to them was the real story, while I still existed only in the maze of my mother's life.

They were married in a church. Agnes/Sophie wished for a church. A clutch of associates were there, along with her parents and her estate-agent brother—one girl from work, a couple of "lifters" he used on jobs, The Forger of Letchworth who was his best man, as well as the merchant who owned the barge. Agnes had insisted on him. The parents, then, and six or seven others.

She needed to find another job. Her co-workers at the res-taurant were unaware she was expecting a child. She bought newspapers and looked through the classifieds. Through a contact of The Darter's from that earlier time, she found work at Waltham Abbey, which was reemerging now during the post-war years as a research centre. It was where she'd once been happy. She knew its history, had read all those pamphlets on our borrowed barge as we moved silently beneath loud birdcalls or rose slowly within the locks of those canals dug during the previous century to connect the abbey's source of weapons to the arsenals along the Thames at Woolwich and Purfleet. Her bus took her past Holloway Prison, along Seven Sisters Road, and let her off at the grounds of the abbey. She was back in that same rural landscape where she had once been with The Darter and me. Her life had become circular.

She worked at one of the long tables in the airless, cavern-like rooms in East Wing A, two hundred women focusing only on what was in front of them, never pausing. No one spoke; they sat on stools too far away from one another for conversation. Apart from the noise made by the movement of their hands, there was silence. What was this like for Agnes, so used to laughter and argument while she worked? She missed the chaos of those kitchens, unable to talk, get up and look from a window, tethered instead to the speed of an unhesitating conveyor belt. They changed locations on alternate days. One day in the East Wing, the next day the West, always wearing protective goggles, measuring the ounces of explosive on a scale, spooning it into the containers that slid by. Grains of it were caught under her fingernails, disappeared into her pockets, into her hair. It was worse in the West Wing, where they worked with the yellow crystals of tetryl, packing it into a pill form. The stickiness from the explosive crystals remained on their hands and turned them yellow. Those who worked with tetryl were known as "the canaries."

Lunch hours allowed conversation but the cafeteria was another enclosed space. She took her packed lunch and walked south to the woods she remembered, ate her sandwich by the riverbank. She lay on her back, exposing her belly to the sunlight, she and the baby alone in this universe. She listened for a bird or the movement from a bush stirred by wind, some alarm of life. She walked back to the West Wing, yellow hands in her pockets.

She did not know what really took place in the strangely shaped structures she passed, where steps disappeared underground into climatic chambers built to test new weapons in desert heat or arctic conditions. There was barely evidence of human activity. On a hill in the distance was the Great Nitrator, in which nitroglycerine had been made for over two centuries. Beside it, underground, were its immense wash pools.

Accessing the old files in the Archives had given me knowledge of the half-buried buildings that Agnes would have walked beside when pregnant with Pearl. I knew now what all those buildings and landmarks at Waltham Abbey had been used for. Knew that even the seemingly innocent forest pool into which Agnes at the age of seventeen had leapt, was where underwater cameras had been set up to measure the power and effect of explosives that would later bomb the Ruhr Valley dams in Germany. That forty-foot-deep pool, where Barnes Wallis and A. R. Collins tested their bouncing bomb, was where she had surfaced, shivering and breathless, then climbed onto the deck of the mussel boat and shared a rolled cigarette with The Darter.

At six in the evening she walks out from the gates of Waltham Abbey and catches a bus back to the city. She leans her head against the window, her eyes gazing over the Tottenham Marshes, her face darkening as the bus passes under the bridge at St. Ann's Road.

Norman Marshall is there in the flat when she returns—her pregnant body exhausted as she passes him without letting him touch her.

"I feel filthy. Let me wash first."

She hunches over the sink and pours water from a bowl onto her head to remove the gunpowder grains from her hair, then frantically scrubs her hands and arms up to the elbows. The gum-like filling used to pack cartridges into boxes and the tetryl have attached themselves to her like tree resin. Again and again Agnes washes her arms and as much of the skin on her body as she can reach.

Nowadays I eat at the hour the greyhound does.

And in the evening, when he feels ready for sleep, he will drift silently to the table where I work, and lower his tired head onto my hand in order to stop me. I know this is for comfort, needing something warm and human for security, a faith in another. He comes to me even with all my separateness and uncertainties. But I too wait for this. As if he might wish to tell me about his haphazard life, a past I do not know. All the unrevealed needfulness that must be in him.

So I have the dog beside me, who needs my hand. I am in my walled garden that is in every way still the Malakites' garden, with now and then a surprise of blossoms I was not told about. This is their longer life. When Handel had his breakdown, he was, according to my opera-loving mother, "the ideal man" in that state, honourable, loving the world he could no longer be a part of, even if the world was a place of continual war.

I have been reading recently an essay by one of my Suffolk neighbours on the *Lathyrus maritimus*, the sea pea, and how war helped the plant survive. Mines had been placed along our beaches to protect the country from invasion, and this resulted in an abundance of rough green carpets of sea peas with fat and sturdy leaves, thanks to the lack of human traffic. Thus the resurrection of the almost extinct sea pea, "a happy vegetable of peace." I am attracted to these surprising liaisons, such sutras of cause and effect. As I had once linked a farce, *Trouble in Paradise*, with the secret transportation of nitroglycerine into the city of London during the war, or seen a girl I knew loosen a ribbon from her hair in order to dive into a forest pool where bouncing bombs had once been conceived and tested. We lived through a time when events that appeared far-flung were neighbours. Just as I still wonder whether Olive Lawrence, who later taught me and my sister to walk fearlessly into a night forest, ever felt her handful of days and nights along the coast of the English Channel was the highlight of her life. Few knew of her work during that period; she did not mention it in her book or on the television documentary I watched as an adult. There were so many like her, who were content in the modesty of their wartime skills. *She was not just an ethnographer, Stitch!* my mother had spat out scornfully, more willing to tell me of Olive than of what she herself had done.

Viola? Are you Viola? I used to whisper to myself, slowly discovering who my mother was on the second floor of that building I worked in.

We order our lives with barely held stories. As if we have been lost in a confusing landscape, gathering what was invisible and unspoken—Rachel, the Wren, and I, a Stitch—sewing it all together in order to survive, incomplete, ignored like the sea pea on those mined beaches during the war.

The greyhound is next to me. He lowers his heavy bony head onto my hand. As if I were still that fifteen-year-old boy. But where is the sister who offered only that indirect farewell to me with a puppet-like wave, using the small hand of her child? Or the young girl I might one day catch sight of, picking up a playing card on the street, and rush after to ask, *Pearl? Are you Pearl? Did your father and mother teach you to do that? For luck?*

Before Sam Malakite gathered me up from White Paint on my last day there, I washed some of Rose's clothes and dried them outside on the grass; a few I stretched over bushes. Whatever she had been wearing when she was killed had been taken away. I brought out an ironing board and ironed a checkered shirt she was fond of, its collar, the cuffs she always rolled up. The shirt had never witnessed this heat or pressure before. Then the rest of the shirts. I laid a thin cloth over the blue cardigan she wore that disguised her thinness, and pressed the iron onto it lightly, at half heat. I took the cardigan and the shirts to her room and hung them in the cupboard and came downstairs. I walked loudly along the nightingale floor, closed the doors, and left.

ACKNOWLEDGEMENTS

While *Warlight* is a work of fiction, certain historical facts and locations have been used within its fictional framework.

In terms of texts and sources I would like to acknowledge research drawn from a number of excellent books: *The Secret Listeners* by Sinclair McKay, *The West End Front* by Matthew Sweet, *Defend the Realm* by Christopher Andrew, and *Empire of Secrets* by Calder Walton, *Dangerous Energy* by Wayne D. Cocroft, *The Roof-Climber's Guide to Trinity* by Geoffrey Winthrop Young, *London's Lost Rivers* by Paul Talling, Jules Pretty's *This Luminous Coast, The Waterways of the Royal Gunpowder Mills* by Richard Thomas, and *Men of the Tideway* by Dick Fagan. Information on the Blitz was drawn from newspaper articles of the time as well as from the archives at the University of South Carolina, and from *The People's War* by Angus Calder and *Austerity Britain* by David Kynaston. Research on unrest in Europe in the aftermath of World War II came from various sources, including Susanne C. Knittel's *The Historical Uncanny: Disability, Ethnicity, and the Politics of Holocaust Memory,* Gaia Baracetti's "*Foibe*: Nationalism, Revenge and Ideology in Venezia Giulia and Istria, 1943–5" that was published in the *Journal of Contemporary History,* and David Stafford's *Endgame, 1945: The Missing Final Chapter of World War II.* I would like specifically to acknowledge the writer Henry Hemming for his generous, authoritative suggestions regarding intelligence work during the war.

I would like to thank Claudio Magris whose essay, "*Itaca e oltre,*" on the turmoil of post-war Europe is briefly quoted. I have drawn from "A Piece of Chalk," an essay by T. H. Huxley, as well as Robert Gathorne-Hardy's essay on the sea pea—"*Capriccio: Lathyrus Maritimus.*" The lines on the pearl are by Richard Porson (1759–1808). I have included a couplet from A. E. Housman's "From the wash . . . ," two stanzas from Thomas Hardy's *The Dynasts,* a line from García Lorca's poem "Sevilla," as well as an idea and a line from Marguerite Duras's *Practicalities*. Thanks also to James Salter's *Burning the Days* for two remarks, John Berger in his commemorating of Orlando Letelier, C. D. Wright, and Paul Krassner's remark about relatives. I have drawn from letters sent by Dorothy Loftus about wartime Southwold in 1940, used courtesy of Simon Loftus, as well as from an article by Helen Didd on the preparations for D-Day that appeared in *The Guardian.* I also drew from a *New York Times* "The Rural Life" article by Verlyn Klinkenborg called "The Roar of the Night," which quotes Robert Thaxter Edes on crickets. Numerous sources on greyhound racing included archival articles from the *Greyhound Star, A Bit of a Flutter* by Mark Clapson, and Norman Baker's "Going to the Dogs—Hostility to Greyhound Racing in Britain," published in the *Journal of Sport History.* A few lyrics that appear briefly are by Cole Porter and Ira Gershwin, while two lines by Howard Dietz were moved to a slightly earlier period without permission. A remark by Robert Bresson made during a filmed interview is the epigraph to this book.

Many thanks to Simon Beaufoy, who introduced me to Gordon and Evelyn McCann and Jay Fitzsimmons while I was researching canals and tides and life on barges, as well as other river information; they were invaluable guides. Also Vicky Holmes for making available river archives during the war at The Museum of London Docklands, West India Quay. Thanks also to the London Metropolitan Archives, and to those who worked at Waltham Abbey and the Gunpowder Mills when I was there in April 2013, especially Michael Seymour and Ian MacFarlane.

*

I want to thank everyone who helped and welcomed me whenever I was in Suffolk during my research—especially Liz Calder and Louis Baum, Irene Loftus, John and Genevieve Christie, and the remarkable Caroline and Gathorne Gathorne-Hardy. Special thanks to Simon Loftus, who spent many days guiding me through The Saints and its complex and intricate history as well as sharing his encyclopaedic knowledge of the region.

Thanks to Susie Schlesinger and her tin house, guarded during the years of this writing by Bellamy, the fabled ox; Skip Dickinson, who many years ago took me to a greyhound museum in Abilene; and Mike Elcock for his long-ago letter about a "couturier"; to David Thomson, Jason Logan, David Young, Griffin Ondaatje, Lesley Barber, Zbyszek Solecki (whose father may have bought a dog from The Darter), Duncan Kenworthy, Peter Martinelli, Michael Morris, and Coles and Manning for a borrowed idea. Thanks also to *The Point Reyes Light*, and to Jet Fuel.

I'm grateful to Jess Lacher for her research, and Esta Spalding for her perceptive suggestions to do with the structuring of this book. Also to my friends Ellen Levine and Steven Barclay and Tulin Valeri, who have supported me in so many ways during the years.

Thank you to Katherine Hourigan and Lydia Buechler, who

ACKNOWLEDGEMENTS

guided this book so carefully and graciously through production at Knopf, as well as to Carol Carson, Anna Jardine, Pei Loi Koay, Lorraine Hyland, and Leslie Levine. Also to David Milner in England, and Martha Kanya-Forstner at McClelland & Stewart in Toronto; as well as Kimberlee Hesas, Scott Richardson, and Jared Bland. Many thanks to Robin Robertson, my editor at Cape. As well as Sonny Mehta at Knopf.

My heartfelt thanks to Louise Dennys, my editor in Canada, who has worked with me on this book since first seeing it in manuscript two years ago, and has been its invaluable supporter at every stage.

I would like to thank and acknowledge the community of friends and writers in Toronto that I have been close to all these years.

Above all, my thanks and love to Linda from the red river shore.